Holiday Headlock

HOLIDAY HEADLOCK

a romantic comedy
by Terry Armstrong

Paperback ISBN: 978-1-7365720-9-2

Hardcover ISBN: 978-1-7365720-5-4

Digital ISBN: 978-1-7365720-6-1

Cover illustrations: Rick Muccio and Christopher Fowler

Cover and interior design: SHR Book Design

Grandma was a huge fan of professional wrestling and introduced me to it, with her and Grandpa taking me to countless wrestling shows throughout my childhood. Grandma used to often remind me, "Blackjack Mulligan patted you on the head before you could even walk." I could never thank her and my grandpa for all they did for me and my family, including instilling a life-long love of "rasslin," as Grandma would say.

Terry's grandma with professional wrestler Preston Steele

Chapter 1

For twenty years, I have been in the glare of arena lights. Tonight, I was under another spotlight: the set of *The Foxx Denn*, my live interview show. Set to go live between a women's championship bout and the main event, a battle royal featuring sixteen superstars from the night's show, the energy was palpable.

I gripped my microphone tightly and scanned the sea of 20,000 fans. Their screams were deafening. My black leather jacket gleamed under the lights, the custom fox graphic catching every beam. My heart raced.

I knew my mission. I had to make Brent "Wrecking Ball" Haynie shine. Brent was a rookie, with just one year on the main roster. He was built like a tank. Sculpted muscles, towering presence, a mix between Dave Bautista and Pumping Iron era Arnold Schwarzenegger. This was all part of a build up to Wrecking Ball quickly entering the main event scene.

Unlike me and many wrestlers like me who trained in closed down gyms and oversized garages, Brent was made in a corporate training facility. I had to convince the crowd he belonged in the title spotlight. They needed to believe he was a force, whether they cheered for him or hated his opponent.

And speaking of opponents, Vito Garramone, pronounced with an over-the-top Italian accent "Gar-a-MOAN-A" was the meanest heel in the business. He had been around forever. His jet-black fedora and goatee were as dark as his reputation.

The cameras rolled, and I stepped up to the mic. My pace was a smooth, deliberate, classic Sorkin walk and talk style. "Brent Haynie," I said, my voice cutting through the noise. "A rookie? Maybe. But what he's about to show you…" I paused, letting the words hang. "…is something the world has never seen."

The crowd buzzed. The tension built.

The set was a throwback, all Christmas lights and wreaths. It was like we were filming a Hallmark movie, but there was nothing warm and fuzzy about what was coming next. I glanced at Brent. He was ready. Crafting his underdog story? It was tough. He was a wrecking machine. But I could make them believe. Every sarcastic smirk from Vito, every jab, would chip away at their doubt. It was the perfect friction.

The atmosphere was almost cinematic when Vito's theme—a sultry, Dean Martin-ish tune reminiscent of "That's Amore"—began to swell. Vito made his entrance with his signature flair: sporting his iconic Italian-flag jacket, a slightly crumpled black fedora that shadowed his piercing eyes, and a goatee that seemed deliberately sculpted and carried a menacing scowl.

Vito leaned in, "Brent doesn't scare Vito. And when the dust settles, you'll all know who is truly ready to take on the world." I turned away from Vito, knowing Brent's moment was coming. It was up to me to make everyone see it.

Earlier in the day, Brent, Robbie Hiland—AKA *Rockin' Robbie*—and I held a heartfelt meet and greet in a small, brightly lit room at the local children's hospital. Kids in recovery filled the space with wide eyes and tentative smiles.

A little boy piped up excitedly, "I'm getting discharged today!" His parents held his small hands tightly.

After a moment of thought, I pulled the man and woman aside and asked, "Do you think Seth has enough energy to come to tonight's show?"

The mother exchanged a hopeful look with his father. Then she said, "Yes! He's fully recovered!" Yet their voices revealed mixed joy and worry about sold-out tickets and high ticket broker prices.

I said, "How about free tickets? All I ask is a little favor." I pictured Brent bringing Seth on during The Foxx Denn interview segment. The idea was simple: let a rising babyface share his story and ignite the crowd. Their eyes lit up in gratitude.

Before Seth could speak, his mom whispered, "You know, Fabulous Freddy Foxx isn't just Seth's favorite wrestler—he's my husband's too!"

I chuckled. I saw his dad shift in a mix of excitement and slight discomfort.

"My boy may soon step into the arena with his hero," the woman added softly.

I smiled and said, "Seth's one lucky boy. You all are amazing parents."

His dad grasped my hand with a firm shake. "Thanks, Freddy. Folks think it's odd we watch wrestling with Seth," he admitted.

I grinned and replied, "Are you kidding? That's just good parenting!"

As we talked, the room buzzed with joyful energy. I felt a pang of reflection amid the cheerful chaos. Here I was in my thirties, surrounded by families, yet wondering if I had sacrificed too much for the business and not having a family of my own.

Brent shared with the crowd his recent visit to the children's hospital, including the classic hometown shout-out: "Right here in Tacoma, Washington." This was designed to stir the crowd—

affectionately known as "Cheap Heat"—and pay homage to legends like wrestler Mick Foley who perfected the bit. He then said to the crowd, "Help me welcome a young man we met at the hospital today. Come on out, Seth."

The air sizzled with anticipation. Every moment buzzed with promise, dialogue, and vibrant action, setting the stage for an unforgettable night.

As the segment continued, the cheers grew louder for Brent who was emerging as the vibrant emblem of a "new generation" of wrestlers. His growing charm mixed with his eagerness to help the little boy painted him as a true defender of the underdog.

In a scene that could have been scripted by a seasoned director, Vito removed his shimmering championship belt and, in an almost ritualistic gesture, walked over to where Seth sat on a modest chair set on the interview stage. Brent's eyes locked onto Vito with an expression that silently warned, "Don't you dare harm that little boy."

Vito extended the belt towards Seth in a booming voice that mixed his best Italian-English accent—"YOU-LIKE-A-THE-BELT?"—and the kid's initial faint tremble turned into unbridled excitement as he clutched it, his face lighting up like a Christmas tree. The atmosphere crackled as fans roared their approval.

Vito snatched the microphone from my grip and knelt down to Seth's level. With an almost paternal sternness, Vito said, "I am GLAD-A-YOU-LIKE. I have a yittle Christmas surprise for you." He paused dramatically, everyone thinking, is he going to give young Seth the belt to keep? Vito unfurled a cloth from his jacket's inner pocket and handed it to Seth with a the forceful command, "SHINE-UP-A-THE-BELT real nice for me."

The crowd erupted into boos and chants of "Wrecking Ball" turning into electrified chants of "Seth, Seth, Seth" as Wrecking Ball came to the aid of young Seth. The segment flowed perfectly from there with Vito and Wrecking Ball exchanging creative banter while squaring off against one another.

As Vito strode off to close out the Foxx Denn segment of the show, Wrecking Ball, now donning a Santa hat, hoisted Seth onto his shoulders as the crowd's cheers rose in a crescendo. I slipped backstage past the infamous Gorilla Position—a cramped area near the curtain named in honor of wrestling legend Gorilla Monsoon, where wrestlers historically gathered before making their entrance.

In that space, I glanced over to see Don Kennedy, the CEO of the World Continental Wrestling League, whose handshake was as firm and aggressive as his reputation. Dressed in a vintage suit that might have been charming in another era, Don greeted me with a clipped, "Fine work, Freddy. You always find a way to take the crowd exactly where we need them."

His eyes, calculating but congenial, hinted at business always lurking behind every personal exchange. "After you wrap up in the locker room, come see me," he added, his tone laced with the promise of future negotiations.

Before I could register his words, however, Robbie—my lifelong friend stepped over to me with a serious look and whispered: "Paige has your sister on the phone, Aaron. She says she wants you to call her back as soon as you can."

I exchanged a quick glance with Kennedy and said, "Give me half an hour and I'll be back to talk with you." It was clear that Kennedy's praises were a prelude to discussing my contract, which expired that coming Sunday. After twelve long years, while I'd earned more money than I had ever dared imagine, we wrestlers had bled success into Kennedy's bottom line too, and his praise now felt like it was as much about commerce as it was about character.

Don Kennedy's marketing genius was legendary. He had turned *Fabulous Freddy Foxx*, the name and character I had painstakingly cultivated on the independent circuit, into a lucrative brand empire. From *The Foxx Denn* interview show to my finishing move, a DDT I branded *the Foxx Trot*, and even a line of *Foxx*-branded merchandise, every bit of it had filled his coffers. Kennedy even put together a team of valets to accompany me to the ring, calling them the *Foxxy Ladies*, a concept that did not age well.

I took great pride in how I would cheekily "bribe" referees with *Foxx Bucks*—play money bearing my proud, defiant face, which Kennedy also monetized by selling them to wrestling fans as collectible memorabilia. Yet despite these successes, my share of the licensed product revenue was disappointingly small. With my time in the ring seemingly waning and my role behind the microphone on the rise, I feared the new contract would reduce my salary and share of merchandise sales. Kennedy had always been an expert at squeezing talent for every last dime.

I finally returned to the locker room where Robbie and Paige were waiting. Unlike our usual upbeat interactions, their faces were etched with concern. Paige Rivera, known in the ring as Page Turner, the wrestling librarian with her signature move "Book Ends," looked unusually somber as she invited me to sit down.

In a voice that trembled with urgency, she broke the news. "Aaron, your sister called. Your mom was hospitalized today. She's been having some serious cognitive issues, and today it got worse. They're running tests and evaluating her, but your sister said it's bad enough that you might want to go home to see her."

I sank into a battered chair, stunned into silence. My mother had always been the steady rock in an all too often turbulent world. She worked tirelessly in a series of part-time jobs during my childhood when my father was plagued by one failed business venture after another. Her quiet fortitude had sustained us through many financial struggles. When I left for college myself, Mom worked towards becoming a nurse, and she was wonderful at it. I had never imagined that the woman who had seemed invincible would come under the shadow of illness. If my sister was urging my return, it could only mean that things were much worse than I had thought.

Robbie and Page immediately offered to come with me, but I insisted that I had to set off right away. With the wrestling schedule relentless between Thanksgiving and year's end, Don Kennedy certainly wouldn't want to lose them for any length of time when I was out.

I dialed my sister Jenny and, through anxious static on the phone, learned that Mom was resting in a local hospital. The doctors were considering transferring her to a specialized memory care facility for a proper evaluation. It was the day before Thanksgiving Eve, and the thought of flying from Tacoma, Washington to Deer Creek Falls, Ohio, with all its logistical hurdles loomed large.

I'd soon need to confront Don Kennedy about my contract, too.

Kennedy's mobile office was set up like a pop-up command center in the arena, strategically placed so he could monitor the pulse of every show, from the energy in the locker rooms to the flurry of merchandise sales. A semi self-made titan who had inherited and then revolutionized the company from his uncle's modest beginnings, Don had an air about him that was part high-class carnival barker and part shrewd businessman.

Today, he appeared a bit taller than me in his ill-fitting, outdated suit and his receding hairline and bad combover. The picture of a man always trying too hard.

I stepped into his office, and without preamble he fixed me with a steely look and said, "Sit down a minute, Freddy." He never used my real name, Aaron. I was unsure if this was due to my being Fabulous Freddy Foxx now for so many years or that my boss just didn't take the time to learn my real name.

With a measured cadence he continued, "I've made you a lot of money in this business. You know, loyalty counts for something. I know Los Angeles might be throwing money your way, but you remember who gave you your big break, don't you?" His voice was firm, laced with the unspoken rivalry between the big three pro wrestling organizations: New York, Los Angeles, and Miami. It has been become commonplace in our business to use the name of the city the federation was headquartered when talking about them. Kennedy's wrestling empire out of New York was currently the largest and oldest of the three.

"Mr. Kennedy, I have no interest in working out of Miami or on the West Coast. New York is closer to my family and friends in Ohio." My words hung suspended in the air; the truth was I had seldom visited home, much to my regret. I missed Deer Creek Falls, missed the warmth of family gatherings, and, as I saw in Robbie and Page's loving interactions, I sometimes wondered if I had sacrificed the chance to find my lasting love for the relentless pace of the ring.

Kennedy's eyes twinkled with a blend of amusement and business acumen as he remarked, "Freddy, that's so like you. How can you negotiate a new deal by openly saying you're not looking at offers elsewhere?"

Even as he spoke, I knew his concern would be more about my loyalty to him and his bottom line than it would be about my family. My voice faltered as I admitted, "My mind is all over the place right now. My mom's having some medical issues and being placed in a memory care facility. I know my current deal runs out on November 30, but I have to head to Ohio immediately to see her."

Kennedy paused. "I understand. Your deal expires this Sunday, though. I hate to bring up business at a time like this, but… Can we count on you for December? Get a new contract in place before you leave?"

I sighed. "Mr. Kennedy, I appreciate you giving me the rest of the week off to deal with my mom's situation. But until I see what home has in store, I'd rather wait to sign anything new."

His features tightened, then relaxed as he feigned nonchalance. "Fine, Freddy. Here's what I'll do for you: We have the New Year's Eve taping in Cleveland on December 30, where you're the guest referee for the Wrecking Ball versus Vito match and hosting a special New Year's edition of The Foxx Denn. How about you sign a one-day contract for that event, and we'll talk about your new deal when you get into Cleveland?"

"That sounds good. Thanks," I replied.

Kennedy stood abruptly, his hand clapping hard on my shoulder in his trademark, somewhat aggressive manner. "Enjoy your time off," he said, almost forgetting the gravity of my family situation. As I turned to leave, he added, "Oh, and hope your mom turns out all right."

I offered a small smile. "Thanks. Just so you know, while I'm away, Robbie can handle any interactions with Wrecking Ball and Vito."

He raised an eyebrow. "That's a good idea. Robbie can handle the ring work, but we'll miss your voice on The Foxx Denn." With that final remark echoing in my ears, I walked out of his makeshift office and into the thrumming reality of the backstage corridor. In that moment, I realized I was transitioning from a ring warrior to a veteran whose future might lean more toward behind-the-scenes roles.

I quickly packed my belongings, carefully slid my New York apartment keys into Robbie's hand, and made my way to the airport. My first connecting flight would take me from Tacoma to Los Angeles.

As expected, the airport was a microcosm of holiday chaos. Luggage clattered along conveyors, anxious travelers queued at security counters, and every now and then, a die-hard fan recognized me. I found myself pausing amidst a throng of excited onlookers who peppered me with questions and implored me for selfies. I obliged with warm smiles and friendly banter, grateful to each fan—for without their ceaseless energy, the magic of professional wrestling would simply fade.

Today, I donned a Cleveland Guardians hat, partly out of long-time loyalty to Cleveland sports teams but also as a shield, a way to process the heavy thoughts about my mom without drawing any added attention.

Walking into the bustling airport bookstore in Los Angeles to grab the latest Harlan Coben, I felt a small wave of relief that my hat cloaked my identity. But as I turned the corner, I froze when I caught sight of Stuart Tanner, the prominent wrestling promotion owner from Los Angeles. I do not think he saw me.

I turned and continued browsing for the book when a small group of wide-eyed children approached me, voices filled with wonder, asking, "Are you Fabulous Freddy Foxx?"

I looked up, a grin breaking across my face. "I sure am, boss." It was a term of endearment I'd picked up someplace, maybe from my Bruce Springsteen roots or perhaps inspired by Andre the Giant, who referred to his friends in the business as boss.

The children's delight was palpable as they called over their older brother. Before long, we were gathered taking photos and exchanging catch phrases. "We're in your corner!" they exclaimed with genuine excitement.

At that moment, Mr. Tanner stood waiting nearby, dressed with the subtle confidence of a self-made businessman. He approached, greeting me with a polite, "Mr. McClellan, how are you?" Though his tone was respectful and professional, I could sense a personal note of concern when he added, "I am so sorry to hear about your mom."

"Thank you, Mr. Tanner," I replied, softly.

With a hint of insistence, he said, "It's Stuart, call me Stuart. Do you have a few minutes?"

I hesitated for only a moment. "Sure. We can grab a coffee before my flight, but I'm curious: how did you hear about my mom?" After all, my family's situation had been my own private burden until now.

A gentle smile tugged at Stuart's lips as he murmured, "Aaron, nothing stays quiet in the world of social media... or in pro wrestling. It's like that old game of telephone, word spreads, as they say: telephone, tell-a-wrestler."

We slipped into a cozy coffee shop inside the terminal, a quirky little spot fittingly named "Don't Spill the Beans," where I sank into a chair and joined him. Over a warm cup of espresso, his empathy shone through as he asked with genuine concern, "How is your mom? I remember my own mother went through something similar many years ago."

I took a slow breath and admitted, "I'm not sure. I just got the call on the road, and I'm heading back to Ohio now. My sister says she's really struggling."

Stuart's eyes met mine with a depth of compassion, a look that transcended the usual cutthroat business conversation. His story was one of humble beginnings—a man who had grown up in a working-class, predominantly African American neighborhood, earned an academic scholarship, and eventually secured an MBA from Stanford. His success in multiple ventures, especially in marketing, had landed him on lists of America's wealthiest. Yet, despite the glitter of his achievements, he remained grounded and committed to using his fortune for the greater good.

Even as the conversation turned to business, Stuart's voice never lost its empathy. "I know you need to be with your family right now, so I won't keep you long. But I have to say, you were fantastic with those kids back there. It's the real you that everyone sees. It is also the worst-kept secret in wrestling that you're about to become a free agent—very soon, actually."

I was astonished that he knew such intimate details. Stuart continued, "I'd love to have you on our roster. We're expanding our footprint beyond our West Coast stronghold into the Midwest and Southern states. We've even lined up some shows just before Christmas in Ohio, Indiana, and Michigan. Plus, our new contracts in Asia are turning out to be incredibly lucrative. Honestly, you'd be a major asset in our expansion."

I managed to smile through the conflicting surge of gratitude and uncertainty. "I appreciate your offer, but I have a lot on my plate right now. I still have the New Year's Eve show with them, and I need to focus on my family. I can't really make any decisions until after the first of the year."

He nodded, accepting my answer with a warm, "Go be with your family, and call me if you need anything. Let's touch base after the holidays."

I thanked him for his kind words and stepped back into the throng of dashing travelers. I knew I wasn't inclined to work out of the West Coast permanently, but as I grew older, I realized that keeping all doors open might be the wisest course. Stuart's invitation lingered in my mind as I made my way to the departure gate.

As I navigated the crowded holiday-filled terminal, I couldn't help but think about my mother, and the constant sacrifices she made throughout her life for others. My mind alternated between memories of raucous arenas and the tender urgency of family matters.

Professionally, my life has transformed from days of grappling in dimly lit gyms to high-profile appearances in arenas and stadiums filled with adoring fans, and the occasional intense negotiations with the office. I would prefer to just do my thing in the ring and microphone and interact with the fans…though like anywhere else there is a business side to pro wrestling.

But the call about my mom began to give me a different perspective at the moment. My heart, steeled by years in the ring, now pulsed with the worry of a son whose mother now lay in a hospital bed.

As I prepared for my journey, my hat pulled low to obscure my face, I knew the coming days would be a test of both professional resolve and personal courage. The road ahead, filled with connecting flights, tender family reunions, and the looming business of renegotiating a contract, was proving to be unpredictable.

Amid it all, the flashing images of cheering fans, heartfelt goodbyes, and unexpected coffee chats would keep me grounded in the midst of the whirlwind that had become my life.

Chapter 2

As I stepped onto the plane, I could almost feel the familiar warmth of my friendly hometown beckoning me back. I found my seat and buckled in as my thoughts wandered to my mom, my family, and the friends I'd known all my life in Deer Creek Falls—a working-class town that once bustled with the echoes of steel mills and the clanging of auto factories.

What truly makes Deer Creek Falls magical is its people. I often think of songs by singers like Springsteen and Mellencamp and how they poetically describe their hometowns. Despite struggles and challenges experienced by towns like ours, it is the community of people that see us through. Deer Creek Falls is the kind of place where neighbors, friends and family show up for each other, making you feel like you're wrapped up in a great big hug and never going through life alone.

I could still picture myself as an awkward eighth grader. When one of my dad's risky business decisions went sideways, and our rented house started to feel less like home, Robbie's grandpa Hiland, our kindly, weathered landlord, stepped in. He offered me a summer job at his bustling car wash, knowing full well I was saving every penny for an amateur wrestling camp that marked the beginning of my high school wrestling career. His gentle encouragement and the steady presence of my wrestling coach filled the void left by some "Dad gaps" I was feeling.

I smiled and recalled how Robbie's grandpa used to give us advice about the quirky social club next door to the car wash—a rundown bar where old-timers gathered. Leaning down to us conspiratorially, he'd say, "Now boys, a lot of those guys will want you to wash their cars while they're sitting in the bar. Don't be too quick with the hose—they'll tip you better once they're a little buzzed—but don't let them drink too long, or they'll blow through all their cash. Get it just right, find that sweet spot, and the tips will flow." His advice, so simple yet filled with care, was like a warm embrace from the neighborhood itself.

My flight from Los Angeles to Chicago lulled me into a brief doze. I awoke to our flight landing and my fellow passengers looking at their phones as desperation mingled with the scent of stale coffee and recycled air. When I got to the concourse and looked at the departure board, I saw that the connection from Chicago to Cleveland had been cancelled. It was the Tuesday before Thanksgiving, and the airport teemed with anxious travelers. Everyone seemed preoccupied, and the tired faces of airport staff hinted at a mounting sense of overwhelm.

At that moment, I remembered that Page had spent time in Chicago long ago. I reached for my phone and dialed her. Her calm, decisive voice cut through the chaos as she explained, "Get on the South Shore Commuter Rail Line to South Bend International Airport, rent a car, and then drive four and a half hours back to Deer Creek Falls."

Planes, Trains, and Automobiles, hmm? I thought with a half-smile. I calculated aloud, "It's 3 p.m. here; with the train and the car, I should arrive in Deer Creek Falls by 10 or 11 tonight." Then, with a chuckle, Page reminded me that Chicago was an hour behind Ohio, nudging my arrival time closer to midnight.

On the train, I managed to steal some more sleep. I awoke halfway through the journey with my mind drifting to thoughts of how Robbie's eyes lit up when he talked about Page and the subtle ease of their life together. I wished for that. I *wanted* that.

Those memories mingled with recollections of my childhood in Deer Creek Falls, triggering a flashback to the one girl who had captivated my young heart. Though we never dated, she remained the elusive standard of perfection to which I compared every other girl.

I'd neglected my social media accounts and lost touch with her since freshman year of college. Robbie teased me about it, calling me "Analog Aaron" because I preferred pen and paper over digital chatter. Sometimes, I wondered if I should ask Robbie if he'd seen any sign of Abby online, but time always got in the way—or my nerves held me back from finding out she was with someone else.

Abby was a creature of contrast to my own modest upbringing. Abby had grown up in a neighborhood lined with gleaming, new homes, manicured lawns, oversized lots, and garages spacious enough to shelter three cars. In her world of four-bedroom houses with finished basements that boasted dedicated man-caves and meticulously clean mudrooms, my childhood on the other side of the tracks seemed drawn in stark contrast.

My early years passed in cramped apartment complexes and aging post-World War II rental houses; I lived with the creaks of old floors, faded wallpaper, and the constant question of why we were always on the move. It later became clear that our instability was tied to overdue rent, a secret my young mind struggled to understand.

Even as our homes shifted, I was thankful to still attend the same elementary school with my steady circle of friends. I remember one time we moved from one rental home to another that were so close to one another my dad and a buddy of his carried one of those 1970's style aluminum residential swing sets from our current rental house to the new one. Then one day the prospect of yet another move loomed. This one would take us farther away.

I vividly remember the crushing dread I felt at the thought of switching school districts, my entire world built on loyal friendships and familiar streets. Then came the unexpected salvation: Robbie's grandpa arranged for us to rent a new house he just purchased without the burden of a security deposit and with a flexible first month's rent. In exchange, my dad was to handle minor repairs of the place. That lifeline ensured I'd remain in the school and place I loved.

Staying in the same school zone also meant that, when our elementary schools combined into junior high schools, integrating us with students from different parts of town, I would get to meet Abby. Despite our different backgrounds, she treated me not as an outsider but as an equal friend. I still remember how crisp her planner was—a professional looking padfolio transformed by her creative touch: colored tabs, neatly divided sections, and even a dedicated area for tracking her college dreams. She had bold lists of medical schools already researched during our freshman year. I had the school-issued planner with calendar and a portion used as a pass to use the restroom during class, though I did use it to try and keep my life in order.

In a whispered moment during class, while our teacher dissected personality types, I leaned over and murmured, "Abby, you're not just Type A personality—you're a Triple A." The delighted surprise in her eyes sealed the nickname in my heart forever.

Triple A, I wonder where you are right now? I stared out the train window at the passing landscape, thinking of Abby and longing to see her again.

Soon, my thoughts and dreams intermingled with slumber, and I drifted off until awakening in South Bend, Indiana. I retrieved my rental car, a brand-new Ford Fiesta with a curious aroma of freshly-baked gingerbread cookies. As I merged onto the highway, I switched the radio stations between Christmas tunes and the lively chatter of a wrestling podcast. The co-hosts, voices crackling with enthusiasm and deep, reverent affection for the sport, debated whether the legendary Fabulous Freddy Foxx would ever return to the ring, even throwing in a fond shout-out to my mom, affectionately dubbed Momma Foxx. How word does travel fast.

The act of driving stirred up a cocktail of nostalgia and trepidation. Having abandoned driving in my late teens, instead relying on the convenience of college shuttles, cramped rides with wrestlers while working the independent scene and New York's vast transit system, I wasn't accustomed to the tactile pleasure of gripping a steering wheel. Yet here I was, rediscovering the simple thrill of turning corners and tapping into memories of my father's old car that always sputtered at red lights.

Now, a sudden pause at a red light left me jolted and confused. The Fiesta's dashboard indicated a temporary shutdown of power consumption, a modern fuel-saving design that mimicked the ghostly silence of a car on its last leg. *Had the car turned off? Run out of gas?* Gingerly I pressed the pedal, and the car roared back to life, its engine purring like a contented animal. Wow, I was behind the times. Analog Aaron strikes again.

Finally, I arrived in my hometown, and pulling into Deer Creek Falls was like stepping into a living postcard. The town's Courthouse Square was draped in shimmering Christmas lights and holiday decorations, and while there wasn't a flake of snow on the ground, many storefronts had artfully sprayed snow onto their windows. It was well past midnight, and the usually bustling streets lay quiet, with the promise of Thanksgiving Eve festivities looming on the horizon. All I could think about was the comfort of my mom's house, the embrace of family, and the simple joy of sleeping in a real bed.

Although it wasn't the house of my childhood, my mom's place radiated love. The modest 1,200-square-foot ranch, with its three cozy bedrooms and full basement, stood as a monument to my mom's early career in nursing and the hard-won dreams of a first-time homebuyer. She had cared for that house with the same devotion she'd given to my dad, sister Jenny and me over the years.

Yet tonight, for the first time since moving in, she wouldn't be sleeping there.

When I arrived, I was enveloped in the comfort of family—a tight hug from my sister Jenny, her husband Randy's hearty handshake, and a cascade of questions about my journey. Amid jokes about my *Planes, Trains, and Automobiles* saga, we settled with steaming cups of coffee around the kitchen table. Jenny's eyes, usually so lively, now shimmered with tears as she relayed a heavy update about Mom. Her voice trembled as she explained that the dementia was worsening despite new medications and that mom sometimes forgot the names of her grandchildren along with other small, painful details.

"Can she come home?" I asked, my fingers gripping my coffee mug tightly. "To be with family?"

"Yes, thank goodness," Jenny said, and explained that she'd asked the doctors if Mom could come home for one more Thanksgiving. They'd agreed, on the condition that someone stay with her at all times.

We quickly made plans. Tomorrow, we'd scrub the house until it sparkled, stock up on groceries for a traditional Thanksgiving dinner, and visit Mom. As Randy and I exchanged somber reflections on how hard it had been for Jenny to watch

Mom decline, a familiar pang of guilt struck me. *I should've been more present all these years*—a regret magnified now by the loving bond my sister and her family shared.

I went over to Mom's old CD player and slid in The Beach Boys' Christmas album—our family's perennial favorite. The soft, nostalgic strains of "Little Saint Nick" mingled with our hushed conversation and a few bittersweet smiles. Jenny looked at me, her eyes glistening, and whispered, "Thanks, big brother. I really needed that."

I couldn't hold back any longer. "Jenny, I'm so sorry I haven't been around. You ended up shouldering all of this alone, and I wish I could have been here for you."

Jenny reached out to pat my shoulder, her tone gentle. "Aaron, don't be silly. My whole life is here in Deer Creek, and your work has taken you far and wide. Besides, Mom is so proud of her Fabulous Freddy Foxx. She wouldn't have it any other way. You've been a blessing to us."

I tried to speak as tears rose to my eyes, but she continued, "Remember when Dad passed and our finances were in a tailspin? You stepped in and cleared all that debt without a second thought. You helped save this house. Not only that, but I wouldn't have finished college without you pitching in. You sacrificed so much for all of us, Aaron. Don't ever forget that."

Looking deep into her eyes, I replied, "I only did what any son or brother would do."

Her gaze softened, and the weight of our shared history hung in the room. Amid the quiet hum of holiday melodies and the soft clatter of coffee cups, I wished more than ever to be there—to share every struggle and celebration with the ones I loved.

Chapter 3

The next morning, as the pale light of sunrise sneaked through the curtains, we arose and began tidying up the house. I pulled on a pair of old sneakers and offered to head out for groceries. But Jenny, rolling her eyes with a playful smile, reminded me in no uncertain terms that it would be wiser to send Randy instead. After all, with Randy on shopping duty, the task was bound to be completed.

Her tone was light-hearted, hinting that she wasn't questioning my abilities but was instead recalling those times at the local grocery store when Fabulous Freddy Foxx made a surprise entrance. Whether it was me reconnecting with my childhood pals or a gaggle of excited kids clamoring for a picture with Freddy, those errands could easily stretch into an all-day escapade.

While Jenny and I shuffled through dusty living room corners and rearranged mismatched picture frames, the shrill ring of the phone cut through our cleaning rhythm. Randy's voice echoed from the other room, his tone a mixture of bemusement and mild panic. "Jenny, I can't find a turkey…of all things! It's the day before Thanksgiving, and all I see are these enormous 40-pound turkeys!"

Thankfully, Jenny's calm, measured voice reassured him that she'd already purchased a turkey and that once he grabbed the rest of the items, he could stop at home and grab it. True to form, Jenny had planned every detail meticulously.

Later, we made our way to the memory care facility. Outside, remaining late autumn leaves danced in the crisp air as families ambled toward the entrance, eager to see their loved ones. Almost before we stepped through the door, my mom appeared in the corridor, arms wide as she rushed over to us, her eyes twinkling with recognition. With uncontainable joy, she ushered us into her "suite" — a modest room adorned with family photographs and a scattering of postcards I had sent her during my travels as a pro wrestler. Jenny said she wanted some things to feel at home.

Gently touching an armchair, she whispered, "I don't mind being here, but I sure miss our home. I know what's happening around me, yet sometimes I lose track of time, like I'm living in another world." Concern lined her delicate features as Jenny and I wrapped our arms around her and promised with trembling voices that we would always be by her side.

Mom's eyes lit up as she inquired about Jenny's daughters. Her face brightened hearing news of Moira and Margo winning awards at their recent speech and debate contests. Shifting the conversation, she asked about Randy. Jenny explained that he was off on a shopping mission for Thanksgiving.

The moment she mentioned Thanksgiving, a flicker of regret passed over Mom's face. "I wish I was hosting Thanksgiving at the house," she murmured wistfully.

Jenny and I exchanged a look before we reassured her, "Well, Mom, you already are. The doctors confirmed you can come home for Thanksgiving." We deliberately omitted the small caveat that someone would need to be with her throughout her stay. Suddenly, Mom's smile faltered, her eyes darting anxiously. "Well, that's alright… I left the house in such a mess! Between that little fall I had and being here, it might not be tidy enough for everyone," she fretted.

Jenny stepped forward, placing her hands firmly on her hips, the same confident stance she had when we were kids. "Mom, Aaron and I spent the entire day scrubbing, dusting, and organizing. We're headed back to get everything set up for tomorrow. Don't worry about perfection. It's our home, and it's the imperfections make it perfect."

Mom's face softened with tears of joy as she pulled us into another embrace. After a pause, she turned to me with a mischievous glint in her eye, "And what about you, Fabulous Freddy Foxx? What's new in your world? I saw you getting the new kid over with the fans at the last show on television—it was as if you rehearsed every line for that character called Wrecking Ball."

Nothing escaped her notice. At that moment, one of the nursing assistants quietly entered, handing Mom a crinkled schedule of December's events. Studying it carefully, she glanced up at us and asked, "Do you really think I'll be okay this Christmas?"

For a while, Jenny and I lingered with her in the cozy common room, both reassuring her and reminiscing with other families about past Thanksgivings—the pounding of drums from the parade, the aroma of overcooked buns wafting through the air, the texture of dry turkey mishaps, backyard football bouts that ended in laughter, and even the bittersweet memories of the one-time our beloved Cleveland Browns made an appearance on the Thanksgiving football schedule. We chose not to talk about the results of the game.

And we laughed as we recalled the awkward moments when Jenny and I dared to invite friends or new people we were dating to the post-Thanksgiving dinner game night.

Out of the blue, Mom's sunny expression turned into one of serious worry.

"Mom, what is it?" Jenny asked.

Mom's voice quivered with concern. "I...I really wonder if I'll be alright come Christmas," she repeated, her voice barely a whisper.

The three of us clutched each other tightly, tears welling in our eyes, before I broke the silence. "I'm sure you will be, Mom." Glancing at Jenny with a conspiratorial smile, I added, "You remember how, right after wrapping up our Thanksgiving game night, you'd start decorating the house for Christmas?"

Mom's eyes sparkled as she took the bait. "Oh, you two! I'd love nothing more than to have the house decked out for Christmas!"

"Then it's settled," I declared. "We celebrate Thanksgiving on Thursday, Jenny and I will spend the rest of the weekend putting up decorations, and we'll throw a full-on family Christmas party next weekend!"

Jenny's face wavered with a touch of concern, but Mom's radiant glow and her infectious laugh quickly overpowered it. "I love you both so much," she beamed. "I can't wait to be home with my family for the holidays. And will you make me those cutout cookies I adore?"

"Of course, Mom…but only if Aaron helps," Jenny answered before I could even protest, her tone playful and protective. I added, "You should remember my baking skills—nobody makes cookies quite like these hands do."

Our laughter filled the room until Mom's expression turned thoughtful once more. "Wait a minute, Fabulous Freddy Foxx," she began, her brows knitting together, "don't you have wrestling shows this time of year? I don't want you losing your job."

I paused, choosing my words with care. I thought about telling her I was between contracts, but I didn't want her to worry. "It's all under control, Mom. I took a little time off, and Robbie is stepping into the ring for some of my matches while I'm out. I just have to show up for the New Year's Eve show."

Relief washed over her features. "Oh, thank goodness. I'm sorry you won't be here on New Year's Eve, but, Jenny, we should make it a New Year's Eve game night too."

"That sounds like a fantastic idea," Jenny laughed, "and maybe we can watch Freddy here get tossed around in the ring." The room filled with giggles as Mom joined in the teasing at my expense, and in that moment all our worries seemed to melt away into the warmth of family and festive plans.

Chapter 4

The following day, the Thanksgiving parade played on the TV as we scrambled around the house. Randy, Jenny, and I bustled alongside her girls. The kids zoomed through last-minute cleaning while we prepped the turkey and side dishes.

After a brief pause in the front room, I strolled over to the giant bookshelf, its shelves stretching for twenty feet and paired with one of those library-style ladders to reach the top shelf.

"Mom absolutely loved it when you had this built for her," Jenny said, her eyes lingering on the rows of books.

I smiled. "I knew Mom would never ask for such extravagance, as she would call this, but when I was on the road reading one day and thought back to all of those trips to the library when we were kids, I had a vision of having this built here for her. She could finally put all of her books in one place…all of the board games and puzzles too," I said.

Since travel had become such a large part of my life as a professional wrestler, books had become an enjoyable and faithful companion. They filled frequent gaps of loneliness too, having not found a longtime partner to share my life.

I chuckled. "Randy, do you know why I had that ladder installed?"

Randy grinned, "Because it looks cool?"

"It is pretty awesome, but that is not the reason. No, it's so my four-foot-eleven sister can reach the top shelf!" I joked.

Jenny playfully tossed a throw pillow at me. "You're not that tall, big brother!"

I leaned down, opening the cabinet at the base of the bookshelf. Inside lay board games, puzzles, and playing cards arranged neatly. "How about Pit? Ticket to Ride? Yahtzee?" I mused aloud as I gathered the games.

"Don't forget Boggle, Scattergories, and Scrabble," Jenny interjected. Jenny and Mom always excelled at the word and more intellectual games than I did, especially when we were young.

Admittedly, my books of choice when going to the library back then were non-fiction or more of the Jerry Rice and Ken Griffey Jr. kid-friendly bios, books on sports like *Profiles of Wrestling's New World Order* and *Your Modern Baseball Heroes*. My mom was never critical, though, and just continued to encourage me to read.

A playful grin spread across Jenny's face as I rummaged through the games. "You know, Moira and Margo are practically beating me at my own games now!"

The warm scents of turkey roasting and pumpkin pie cooling mixed with the crisp aroma of burning leaves from the open window. That smell always brought back memories of fall in Deer Creek Falls, neighbors burning leaves as they readied their homes for the coming winter.

Meanwhile, Jenny and Randy ruled the kitchen like a well-oiled machine. I remarked over a shared moment, "Mom might have meant well, but her kitchen experiments were always rushed. She preferred a visit to McDonalds rather than preparing meals in the kitchen."

Jenny laughed explaining our typical visit to McDonalds, "The rest of us would order burgers and fries, and Mom would insist on a salad—until she'd eventually say, 'Aaron,

want anything else? Go grab me a Big Mac while you're at it.'"
Apparently, that salad never really cut it.

We both laughed, sharing the nostalgia of simpler times. I loved being with my family, but coming back home also made me think how much I missed all of the people in Deer Creek Falls I'd left behind. For a few seconds, I let my thoughts wander. I wondered if Abby might be in town for the holidays. Did she still live in Deer Creek Falls? Or had she moved away after school? Did she ever marry?

I wondered if I'd see her home for the holidays, if our paths would cross, but I soon set the thought aside. I had other things to focus on.

When it was time to pick up Mom, I asked, "Do you want me to take your car and pick up Mom?"

Before she could answer, Moira chimed in, "Mom, why don't you and Uncle Aaron go get her together?"

Margo added, "Grandma would love that—and Dad can help with the rest of what we need to do.!"

Jenny grabbed her keys and jacket. "Okay," she said. I grabbed my jacket too, and off we went.

As we drove down the maple-lined streets of Deer Creek Falls, I said, "Sis, I'm so proud of you. You're amazing with the girls."

She blushed. "They're my life, Aaron." She paused, then continued, "What about you? Anyone special?"

I could've given her my patented answer of being married to my work, or travel getting in the way of finding true love and having a family, but finally I said honestly, "Seeing you and Randy, being around the girls, connecting with Mom...I miss being home, miss being with family." Of course, as always happened when I thought about such things, my mind went to Abby Rogers.

Jenny waved a hand and teased, "You didn't answer my question...is there a special someone?"

I smiled ruefully. "No. I haven't found the right person yet." And I wondered whether that ship had sailed, and it was too late.

We soon arrived at the lobby where Mom sat, book in hand as usual, waiting patiently. When I started wrestling on the independent circuit, she would get there early to get a front row seat. I would tell her, once I got to know the lay of the land of the independent wrestling scene, not to worry and that it didn't matter what time she got there. I would always get her a front row seat. Even with that, she still insisted on arriving before any of the other fans to get the front spot in line.

She'd once told me her dad, my grandpa, who worked in the steel mills, would say, "If you're on time, you are late…so you better arrive all that much earlier."

Now, giving us both a warm hug, Mom said with the brightest smile, "Let's go home."

We piled into Jenny's light blue SUV and headed back. On the drive, we noticed neighbors already hanging up Christmas decorations in the mild Thanksgiving weather. Our town has a beautiful mix of Victorian downtown architecture and housing options that could accommodate everyone regardless of income. Our region is fortunate to have a low cost of living. Beyond that, it was highlighted by a unique and charming grittiness from its steel and manufacturing history. I looked around in satisfaction. All of it really came alive at Christmas.

Mom asked if we could circle around Courthouse Square, the town's main square, and Jenny obliged. The Square was home to Christmas décor, complete with Santa's log cabin, Deer Creek Coffee Shop, the Falls Amphitheater, Falls Book Store, and Duffy's Pizza rounded out the square that also hosted many festivals, including the Deer Creek Falls Christmas Carnival.

As we drove by, we saw a sign about the Carnival, coming up next week.

"I'd love for us to go to the Carnival this year," Mom remarked.

Jenny and I exchanged a look of agreement. We were recalling that somehow Mom always made magic happen at Christmas, including taking us to the Christmas Carnival. I silently vowed to bring that magic back for her this holiday season.

Chapter 5

We pulled up to the house at dusk. As soon as we stepped into the front room, Mom's eyes lit up when she saw the bookshelf. She slid into her favorite chair in the reading nook and smiled through tears as Moira and Margo rushed in, bringing her a glass of her favorite drink: Southern Sweet Tea.

"Hi, Grandma!" they chimed.

While they shared stories, Jenny, Randy, and I hustled into the kitchen to set the table and bring in food. The dining room flowed right from the kitchen, just like a typical midcentury ranch-style home in the Midwest.

Randy leaned close to Jenny. "Don't forget, high school reunion tomorrow night at the school," he said.

Jenny grinned. "Of course! It's tradition around Deer Creek Falls, right? Reunions the day after Thanksgiving."

I glanced at Randy. We'd graduated together, but our circles never really mixed. I always laughed about how he'd belonged to the techie/Star Wars crew while my friends rocked concert tees and wrestling uniforms.

We chatted about the smallness of our school. "I remember in college hearing some freshmen say their graduating class was over 500," I recalled. "Our class had only about 200, right? You knew everyone."

"I liked it," Jenny said. "It was big enough to find a group of friends you belonged to, but small enough to know everyone."

Soon enough, we gathered around the table, passing dishes and plates. The conversation quickly turned to Moira and Margo's activities.

Moira said, "We're excited about speech and debate and of course high school marching band."

Randy interjected, "What about soccer? Tennis? Basketball?"

We all glanced around and burst into laughter. Jenny stood at 4'11", Mom barely reached 5', and even Randy was a modest 5'6".

"Okay, I get it," Randy mused. "Mathletes, not athletes—except for Aaron, of course."

I laughed. "I got lucky. I found a sport where a decent amount of athleticism and some quick wit keep you in the game."

Jenny nudged me. "Remember your sixth-grade basketball days?"

I grinned at the memory. "Oh yes. Every time one of us got the ball coaches would yell, 'shoot it' Every time I got the ball they yelled, 'Pass it, McClellan!' It was short-lived glory on the court."

Laughter rolled around the table, mingling with memories and food. My thoughts drifted to the future—maybe a family of my own someday. Would I ever have something like this in my own home, at my own dinner table? Or was it too late?

Jenny caught my wandering look. "Aaron, Mom wants to tell you about a project she's been working on," she said.

"It's not a big deal," Mom replied.

Jenny jumped in. "Actually, Mom's volunteering to turn newspaper articles into audio files so the blind can listen. The local paper doesn't have big budgets, but she and her friends make it work at the library."

"Mom, that's wonderful," I said. "You've always helped our community."

Mom waved off the praise. "That's nothing compared to what your nieces are doing. Moira and Margo are collecting 'kindness bags."

"What are kindness bags?" I asked.

Margo hesitated, then looked to Moira. "They're clear bags filled with gloves, hats, snacks, toothpaste, toothbrush, deodorant, a comb—and a five- or ten-dollar bill. We give them to people who pass them on to someone who needs them."

Mom took Margo's hand as we all exchanged grateful looks around the table.

Thanksgiving had always been my favorite holiday. Perhaps it was the fact that we used to get Wednesday through Sunday off from school as a kid, or that I loved the *Charlie Brown Thanksgiving Special* when they ate popcorn and toast for Thanksgiving dinner. Maybe it was the festivities of the parade, or perhaps it was just the fact that it was a more relaxing holiday than Christmas.

But in Mom's house, as soon as Thanksgiving ended, Christmas began.

After dinner, we cranked up the competitive spirit with our Thanksgiving game night. We played a raucous game of Pit, which I won, followed by a round of Boggle where Mom and Jenny completely owned the room.

Between rounds, Mom said, "Let's get the house ready for Christmas tomorrow. I want all the lights up outside and the décor inside set up." In addition to all the other decorations, my mom had a Christmas village she was very proud of. She has accumulated about fifty unique pieces, and it made for a beautiful, festive display.

Last year Moira put it on social media and apparently it went viral.

Mom's excitement was contagious. "And don't forget," I reminded her, "you have to do your Christmas card writing.

The cards always go out the day after Thanksgiving." Our families Christmas cards were always the first our friends and family would receive. Jenny recalled one year our Aunt Donna tried to beat Mom to the punch by sending us a Christmas card at the end of October.

Mom responded, "I told her that does not count. If you are not sending them all out, it's just a gimmick."

As we all laughed, Mom pulled out a bag from her purse. "I have a stack of cards ready to go. I just couldn't get stamps at the facility."

Margo piped up, "Grandma, we have this year's Christmas stamps. Can we help you mail them?"

"Of course," Mom replied warmly.

Jenny brightened. "Tomorrow, we'll decorate early. Then we'll head to that old post office downtown, just like when we were kids, and grab lunch at our favorite coffee house."

Mom's smile lit up the room. The old post office, with its vintage murals of town scenes including steelworkers and our picturesque falls, added a layer of nostalgia to our plans.

We'd also have to see about a tree. Mom preferred a real one and always purchased it from a lot near Courthouse Square the first week of December.

Randy looked at Jenny and then at me. "Don't forget the big night tomorrow. We can't be too wiped out from cleaning. Aaron, you're coming with us, right?"

I looked at him, confused.

"We only get one twenty-year reunion!"

"Oh, right." I hesitated. My mind churned. Should I leave Mom? "I'm not sure," I murmured. "Maybe I should stay home with Mom while you and Jenny dance the night away."

"No way, big brother," Jenny insisted. "The girls will stay with Mom, and Randy's parents are coming over, too. They've heard about our legendary McClellan game nights. Come on!"

Mom agreed, "I will be fine. The girls will be here and I would love to get caught up with Terry and Kim." Mom always got along well with Randy's parents.

Randy clapped his hands. "Then it's settled. Tomorrow, we transform the house into a McClellan family Christmas wonderland during the day, and then we rock out millennial style at night!"

I couldn't resist a joke. "Easy there, Dave Grohl. Is there a band or DJ? Will they play YMCA and the Hokey Pokey? You know, 'that's what it's all about.'"

Jenny's eyes twinkled. "Oh, you didn't know? It's your old band, Nordic Blood."

I corrected her with a grin. "They weren't really my band. I just rang the cowbell and pretended to play bass. That was the extent of my participation. Robbie, Johnny and Mark were kind enough to make me part of what they were doing."

Still, memories flooded back of Johnny, Mark, Robbie, and gigs we did in high school and early college, before wrestling took over my life.

"Johnny and Mark are still performing?" I asked.

Johnny, Mark, Robbie, and I were best friends growing up. We spent a lot of time together practicing and playing gigs as Nordic Blood and also hanging out together. Two better and kinder people you would never meet. While Robbie and I have stayed very close, I could not help but feel bad that I have not stayed in touch with Johnny and Mark back here in Deer Creek Falls. I also knew though that we were also the kind of people that when we did get to catch up it was like we never lost touch. Our bonds would make it so we wouldn't miss a beat.

"They're still around," Randy replied. "Playing shows at coffee shops, wineries, and retro rock nights at local bars. I'm pretty sure they'll knock it out of the park with a killer playlist."

"Then it's settled," I said. Already my mind was racing ahead to tomorrow night, to the reunion and the people I might see after twenty long years.

Chapter 6

Dawn broke as Randy and I lugged out the old-school, multi-colored Christmas lights the following morning. My mom had moved the Frosty and Santa decorations to every apartment and rental house we lived in; they were fixtures of a McClellan family Christmas and meant a lot to us. Outside, in contrast to yesterday's mild weather, light snow sprinkled down, just another late November in Northeast Ohio.

After we strung the lights, we headed inside. Warm music and hot chocolate with marshmallows welcomed us in. The house glowed under the spell of decades of memories.

"Aaron, can you help with the Christmas village?" Mom asked.

"Sure, Mom," I replied, rolling up my sleeves.

Mom spread out over fifty intricate Christmas village pieces. I recalled days of my youth, when she had only a few—the glowing house, a town hall, and a small bookstore. I'd sit for hours, weaving wild tales in my mind of town meetings and adventures in the little bookstore. I'd be the mayor, or part of a happy family living in one of the homes.

Even then, I saw how dearly Mom held these treasures, and how much Jenny and I adored them too. With every hour that passed, I realized more and more how much I loved Deer Creek Falls, and how much I'd missed it while away.

For so long, I'd been off wrestling—first on the independent scene, then with Kennedy's promotion. With more cash in my pocket, I made sure to pick out new pieces for Mom's Christmas Village collection whenever I could. I would hunt for items that fit perfectly with the old ones and buy tables to support her growing display. She crafted snowy scenes from these pieces, always setting them up in the front room by her library.

While helping us arrange the village, Moira and Margo lifted a tiny, familiar sign from the storage bin. They burst into laughter.

It was meant to read "Mom's Village." Instead, it said "Mom's Village Village." Either the maker had a mischievous streak or someone misunderstood the order form.

When I offered to order a new sign back when it came and we noticed the blunder, Mom shook her head and smiled. "No, you will not. I find it charming," she insisted.

That was our mom.

Later, after the village was up, we went to the post office to mail the Christmas cards. I headed back home while the rest of the family went off to a favorite coffee spot. Before parting, I reminded them, "Please bring me back a chicken salad sandwich."

I was concerned if I went to the coffee shop that I might have to answer questions like, "When are you back in the ring?" "How tough is Vito Garramone?" or even more dreaded questions that could come from old friends I would run into, "Are you married? Dating anyone?" This typically would not bother me so much but things have been so non-stop I needed a little break.

I took some time to touch base with Robbie. I needed to update him about life and hear how he and Page were doing.

I dug through my bag, searching for a reunion outfit. Nothing looked right. My choices for what to wear were limited to what I'd thrown in my bag when I headed home. None of it screamed class reunion.

I dashed to the local department store and ended up buying what my nieces called "Daddy duds." True, they were almost identical to what Randy sported, and the other fathers I'd seen in my travels. Still better than my sweatshirt and jeans, I thought.

Minutes later, the door burst open as the family returned. Laughter filled the hallway. "Here you go," Margo said, handing me a takeaway box containing the best chicken salad sandwich on Earth, straight from our favorite coffee house.

"You still remember that place?" Jenny asked, eyes sparkling.

"Of course. Whenever I'm home, it's a must-stop," I said. "Thanks for the sandwich."

Randy stepped forward then. "Guess what? We saw a couple of the guys, and our classmates are buzzing about you coming tonight!" he said, excitement dancing in his eyes.

Moira and Margo chimed in almost simultaneously. "There was a band at the coffee house," Moira announced. "They were playing Dad Rock with some Christmas music mixed in," Margo added, laughing. "Uncle Aaron, they mentioned you and Robbie!" Moira said.

"Nordic Blood was just warming up for tonight," Randy said, nudging the conversation along. "Johnny and Mark are thrilled to see you, though they're bummed that Rockin' Robbie Hiland won't be here."

I couldn't resist a grin at that nickname. *Rockin' Robbie…* still the frontman in my memory. "That mullet—man, he turned it into something over-the-top now." I shook my head.

Robbie's first gimmick when we started in professional wrestling was not *Rockin' Robbie* or even the thankfully short-lived Smiling Robbie Hiland, but something that was about to be more embarrassing for me.

Randy clapped his hands together. "Everyone, sit down and buckle in!" he commanded, waving a remote control. I peered at it. "A VCR? Seriously, who still has one of these?"

Randy grinned. "These tapes hold the first matches of you and Robbie," he explained. He pressed play, and the old footage popped up on the TV.

The screen burst to life with my past. Robbie and I, once high school wrestling teammates, stepped into the ring in tartan kilts, backed by rock-infused bagpipe tunes. The ring announcer thundered, "From the dodgy part of Glasgow, Ian and Prescott Hiland—the Hilanders!" Laughter and cheers filled the room as the scene unfolded.

Our first pro wrestling match flashed before my eyes. Hank Hardway, a mentor and local hero—a retired firefighter who helped coach our high school wrestling team and was a respected pro wrestler who set up his own training gym in his oversized garage—had set us up for a debut we'd never forget.

Hank Hardway had trained all of us taking part in the match that night. As we were getting the crowd going after our introductions, Hank was introduced, scowling at us and the crowd like a classic heel. Suddenly, a hulking figure emerged: Leo the Lumberjack, towering at 6'10", swaggered into the ring with an axe handle in hand. He joined Hank in their corner and our wrestling career began!

After exchanging classic wrestling moves and blows throughout the match, I found myself in the ring with Leo. He lunged at me. I dodged and spun around, but he caught me in the ropes. "Watch out!" Robbie, AKA Ian, shouted. Leo was swinging the axe handle with all his might; I moved as planned and his axe handle rebounded off the ropes. In a twist of fate, the handle violently smacked into his forehead much harder and quicker than he or the rest of us had planned. I had planned to school-boy him as he staggered backwards but he fell straight to the ring apron as he had knocked himself completely out. I covered him for the 1-2-3 as we won our first match in memorable fashion.

Everyone, it seemed, enjoyed the walk down Memory Lane. After the laughter settled, I grabbed my phone and called Robbie. "Hey man, how's life on the tour? How's everything with Page?"

His voice was tinged with a mix of amusement and disbelief as he recounted the Wrecking Ball/Vito Garramone feud heating up on tour. We traded updates about my mom, about old times, and of course, about the upcoming class reunion. "If you were here, you'd be strumming a guitar by now," I teased.

Robbie laughed. "Maybe one day," he replied. Tonight felt like a bridge between past and present, a night where old memories, wild matches, and family banter all converged as I headed toward the glow of my 20th high school reunion.

Chapter 7

Jenny's in-laws arrived like a burst of holiday cheer and were instantly enamored with Mom's exquisite Christmas village display. Every miniature building and tiny figure had a story, and Mom's excitement was almost tangible as she detailed the history and details behind each piece.

Jenny leaned over to me with a half-smile and a knowing look, whispering, "We may be coming home late from the reunion, and Mom will still be showing off her village treasures."

That day, Randy had taken care of our arrival to the reunion in his own unique way. He'd rented what he described as a "vintage" car, a real mood enhancer for our little retro outing. Apparently, there is a car rental place near Cleveland that specializes in this type of thing. Randy's choice for tonight was a 1996 Geo Metro. Though not a luxurious choice, it was the type of cheap used car many were driving while we were in high school.

As he pulled up, the car's faded paint and quirky design drew a mix of amused laughter and playful skepticism. Jenny and I exchanged glances, our laughter quickly shifting to questions like, "How on earth is this still on the road?" and "Is it actually safe to drive?" Many of us recalled our own beat-up high school rides that were falling apart; and as we rolled up to the reunion, similar murmurs of disbelief and nostalgic recollections filled the air.

Arriving at our old high school for the reunion was like stepping back in time. The building's exterior, with its classic red brick and single story, greeted us as if nothing had changed in twenty years. The flagpole at the main entrance and the newly sealed parking lot offered a neat, respectful nod to the past. One subtle change, however, caught my eye: where we once remembered multiple back doors and side exits, there was now just a single, fortified entry—clearly a result of modern, tighter security measures.

Joy McKennzie, who hung around Jenny and Abby a lot in high school, was the first classmate we saw walking in. She caught us up about her life, and we shared details about ours. She had relocated to Columbus, Ohio and has three kids. I so much wanted to ask about Abby. As we walked and got close to the entrance the topic turned back to the limited entrances, "Do you remember when Rokey Wolford rode his motorcycle in through one of the western side entrances, went straight through building, and out the eastern entrance?" Of course, we all did and had a good laugh over it.

Rokey Wolford was someone in school who got along with all the student cliques, and none of us were surprised he would be the one to perform such a senior prank! Joy McKennzie added to her story, "Rokey and I got married ten years ago. He could not make it to the reunion tonight due to work so he is home with the kids. He wanted to say hello." Joy held up her phone and there was Rokey with one of their three kids in his arms. I should not have been surprised, he and Joy dated in school and never missed one Nordic Blood gig. I was so happy to hear they have stayed together and seem as happy as they were back in high school. I also thought to myself how lucky they were to find that one person in one another and know enough not to let go.

We strolled from the main entrance toward the gymnasium, our footsteps echoing along the familiar walkway. The corridor eventually opened into a spacious gym where a sign-up table awaited us. A group of bright-eyed National Honor Society students from the school welcomed us.

Suddenly, amid the low hum of conversation, a voice from my past boomed with familiarity, "Is that Fabulous Freddy Foxx?"

I turned slowly around and found Arlo Ritchie, an old friend from Deer Creek Falls High School. A couple of years my senior and also a high school wrestler, Arlo wore the kind of easy confidence that came from years of shared memories. Our previous team bonds, forged under the loving guidance of our wrestling coach, helped bridge the years instantly.

"Mr. Ritchie! Or should I say, Superintendent Ritchie?" I greeted him with an enthusiastic handshake that quickly turned into a heartfelt embrace. I still couldn't believe he was now head of the entire school district.

"I miss you, man," he said with a sincerity that warmed the chilly reunion evening.

"How is it being Superintendent? How's your family?" I asked, my tone full of genuine curiosity and pride for the path he had taken.

He grinned, shaking his head in disbelief at my presence. "It's good, really good. Family is great. I still can't believe you're here!"

We reminisced about our dreams of being educators and wrestling coaches. Meanwhile, Jenny and Randy went off to mingle in the gym, dancing and laughing among the throngs of former classmates, leaving Arlo and me to continue our conversation in a quieter corner by the high school's Athletic Wall of Fame.

Arlo pointed to the wrestling section of the display, a long timeline of team achievements and black-and-white photos capturing the gritty intensity of our high school battles. "Did you hear about Coach Miller?" he inquired, his finger pausing on a framed picture.

I frowned. "No, what's happening with him?"

With a mix of concern and admiration, Arlo explained, "Coach has to undergo some medical treatments in Cleveland. It isn't fatal, but it will definitely sap his energy."

We both lingered in front of photos that chronicled the golden years of our wrestling team, a dynasty of hard-fought state titles, including an impressive record of 12 state title wins and the groundbreaking triumph of three female wrestlers clinching state titles.

"I wouldn't be the man I am today without Coach," I said, the weight of gratitude in my voice. "I also owe my success in pro wrestling to him and his friend Hank Hardway."

Coach Miller and Hank Hardway go way back. Hank helped coach anytime he needed an extra hand with the wrestling team. Those two grew up in town and were top athletes and inseparable when they were young. We saw it for ourselves when our high school wrestling team traveled with them.

I said to Arlo, "I remember my first plane ride ever. You were the team captain and Coach Miller and Hank Hardway put you in charge of the freshman. You kept us safe and in line. I was nervous never having flown before. I do remember you having to explain to Robbie and I what Coach Miller and Hardway were doing at the luggage carousel."

Arlo looked at me, obviously not recalling that moment that was so memorable to me and Robbie.

"Coach and Hank Hardway told us all to watch the luggage coming out very closely and yell out which one of their suitcases comes out first. I was confused why that was so important and you told us later they made a bet on whose would come out first."

"That's classic." Arlo said. "They made all the difference in my life too." Arlo said in agreement, his eyes reflecting shared respect. "I even got into teaching after I had him for class. He inspired me to coach, too."

I chuckled, "Yeah, I was going to follow that very path, but you know the story—I took that infamous fork in the road."

We slowly made our way back down the hallway toward the wrestling workout room, a space thick with memories. The faded mats lay in neat rows, headgear still hung on racks as if waiting for their next use, and the subtle scent of sweat and old linoleum evoked echoes of my younger self.

I could almost hear Coach Williams' steady, encouraging voice saying, "Aaron, you can do this. Commit one-hundred percent, and that college scholarship will be yours."

Arlo's voice brought me back to the present. "Why don't you come by on Monday to see the team practice? The kids would love to meet Fabulous Freddy Foxx, and it'd be great to catch Coach before his treatments begin."

Hesitantly, I asked, "Monday? What time?"

"1 p.m.," he replied.

I arched an eyebrow in confusion, "1 p.m.? Aren't the kids still in class then?"

A smile crept onto Arlo's face as he explained, "They would be, but a few students came to me when I became superintendent and asked me if I would consider giving the Monday after Thanksgiving off, as their families have the tradition of going hunting the first day of the hunting season."

"Did you have any idea what they were talking about?" I mean, Arlo and I had grown up in the same area and knew nothing about hunting.

"It caught me off guard," he admitted. "I mean, honestly, I never really had any experience with hunting. But these kids were quite persuasive. Even the teachers rallied behind the idea. Those kids thank me every time we cross paths. So, for that Monday, we have wrestling practice during the day since there are no classes."

Made sense to me. I nodded and appreciated Arlo's willingness to listen directly to his students.

Back in the main gym, the atmosphere shifted as the stage lit up and Nordic Blood began to cover Green Day's greatest hits. Arlo and I grabbed a drink and caught up with old friends from our graduating class. The band segued into Green Day's "Boulevard of Broken Dreams," its somber notes inviting us to reflect on our journeys, before picking up the pace with a rousing set of Foo Fighters anthems.

I turned to see Randy approaching while Jenny was deep in discussion with someone sporting dark-reddish hair. The conversation paused as Jenny turned, and there she was—Abby Rogers. My heart leapt into my throat and stayed there.

The red hair, beautiful green eyes, nicest girl I ever met… there she was. Abby was the one who got away. We had never dated but became close to the point where I thought one day it might turn into something more.

Today Abby's vibrant red hair tumbled in soft curls, her green eyes shining with a mix of warmth and mystery. She had been the highlight of my long-ago youth—a quiet crush never fully realized.

She and Jenny had been friends in school, so we had spent a fair amount of time around each other. Once we'd even worked together on a class project, spending evenings at each other's houses. But after high school, life swept me away to college and into the whirlwind of wrestling.

Yet the memories of Abby lingered.

Jenny beamed as she greeted the group, "Look who I found!"

My mind raced with questions: *What had become of Abby? Had she found her calling as a doctor? Was she still single, or*—my heart sank—*had she married?*

Before I could speak, Abby's warm voice reached me, "Hi, Aaron. I'm really sorry about your mom, Jenny was just telling us. I'm glad you made it home…and that you're here tonight."

"Thanks, Abby," I managed, my voice catching on the many unsaid questions swirling beneath the surface, leaving me feeling both nostalgic and tongue-tied in her presence.

Just as I was gathering the courage to speak further, a voice from the past cut sharply into our moment—a voice I had long carried bitter memories of: Richard Bartholomew Dobbins III, or Richie Rich as we called him. Dobbins had arrived. Obnoxious, annoying, demeaning…you get the point. His blonde hair completed his Ken-doll looks.

I could tell tonight by his carefully gelled blonde hair and pretentious mannerisms that he remained a textbook example of arrogance. Even now, his insistence that he be called Richard and not something more approachable like Rich seemed to underscore his persona.

Our gym doubled as a cafeteria, and right then a high school memory came back to me. I remembered Robbie, Johnny, Mark, and I standing in line for a second round of school lunch pizza after an unforgettable pro wrestling show in Cleveland—tickets secured by Coach Miller and our friend and future trainer, Hank Hardway. That is his real name, and what he went by when he wrestled: Hank Hardway. Hank even got us a meet and greet with some of the wrestlers, along with t-shirts…we were all wearing these t-shirts that day.

We were standing in line behind Abby, just after our project collaboration, I silently admiring her, only to have 18-year-old Richie Rich Dobbins cut in line.

He leaned in with an overly casual, "Hey, Abby, can I cut in line?" and before anyone could react, Abby, ever the peacemaker, said, "Maybe you should ask Aaron—you know, it's his turn."

Now, Dobbins had a reputation for being a bit lazy and mouthy. He was also jealous, as his dad had a lot of wrestling success back in his high school days, but "Richie Rich" Richard

Bartholomew Dobbins III had failed to live up to it while Robbie, Arlo, and I had success.

On that day twenty-plus years ago, he took a couple of cheap verbal shots, asking, "Where did you get that shirt, McClellan?"

Still annoyed by his presence, I answered, "Coach Miller and Coach Hardway took us to the show and got us these shirts. We even got to meet…"

He cut me off. "You went and saw *that* wrestling? What a waste of time. And those shirts? What a waste of money."

Abby's calm presence broke the tension as she said, "I like the shirt, Aaron. Richard, why don't we take a walk and let Aaron step ahead in line? We have to get you ready for that math quiz."

For a moment, he looked like he wanted to argue, then reluctantly ambled off with Abby, tossing one last sneering remark, "Coach Miller and Coach Hardway bought you those shirts? My dad says there are two jokers in every deck. My dad is going to be on the school board and get rid of those two." Robbie and I glowered at "Richie Rich" Dobbins as Abby pulled him away. Despite his relentless barbs, we both knew that neither Coach Miller nor Hank Hardway, true legends in their own right, would ever be overthrown by someone like him.

Tonight, years later in that same familiar gym, I find myself beside Abby once more, but this time with the weight of grown-up realities and still having to deal with Dobbins again.

Randy leaned in and whispered, "I don't know if Jenny ever told you, but they got married."

My heart lurched at the thought—Abby with Richard Bartholomew Dobbins III? It felt like a gut punch, a twist of fate I hadn't expected.

Dobbins glanced at Arlo, then at us, and with a derisive tone called out, "Hey, Mr. Superintendent, I need to chat next week. And you…" His eyes locked on mine. His tone dripped with mockery as he said, "Fabulous Freddy Foxx, are you still running around in spandex?" Every word raked at old wounds. Somehow, even after all these years, he managed to ignite the same irritation I had felt back in high school.

At that moment, Mark from Nordic Blood seemed to sense the charged atmosphere and drew everyone's attention to the stage. Mark's voice cut through the commotion as he announced, "We are Nordic Blood," introducing the new members—David on drums and Danny on bass.

"When we started on this journey, we had two good friends with us. Not only friends, our band was like a brotherhood. We had *Rockin' Robbie Hiland*."

That name got our fellow classmates chanting, "Robbie, Robbie," and I looked around, grinning at the crowd.

"Robbie could not be here tonight but sends his best. We do have one of our original members here tonight, and we hope he'll join us for a couple of songs and hopefully say a few words. We all know him as Aaron McClellan, but the world knows him as…" Johnny paused and added, "Say it with me…"

To my surprise, my fellow classmates, led on by Johnny, Mark, and Randy, yelled out, "Fabulous Freddy Foxx." I'd heard that name announced thousands of times in my career, but I admit, it never felt better than hearing my friends from my youth doing it.

The exuberant chant went on for a minute or two, and Randy clapped me on the back as I bowed to all for their support. The applause and cheers from friends washed away the sting of Dobbin's verbal jab. As I stepped toward the stage, Mark shook the cowbell in his hand with a big grin on his face. A familiar sense of belonging took over.

Randy nudged me with a playful grin, knowing that the band defused a potential situation with Dobbins, whispering, "Saved by the bell!" recalling Dobbin's remark, almost like challenging me. I laughed, "Who was saved by the bell, Him or me?" I wasn't sure if Abby had caught our exchange, but we shared a glance as I headed onto the stage. Dobbins, in the meantime, stood there fuming. I don't know what Abby could've seen in him, back then or now. It couldn't be just his money. Abby's family had money; and more importantly she was better than that.

As I handled a Blue Oyster Cult song on the cowbell and hopped to the bass lines on a George Thorogood cover, the buzzing energy of the reunion and the band's music dissolved much of the tension. After the set, while chatting with Jenny, Randy, Johnny, and Mark, more memories of past adventures surfaced.

Johnny recalled in booming tones, "Remember that time we played outside Atlanta at that music festival?"

Mark jumped in with a laugh, "Yeah, the hottest crowd and the hottest temperature—wasn't it 120 degrees?"

I smiled, recalling that epic road trip with friends—an adventure where Robbie, our perennial frugal hero, had booked a cheap campsite instead of a hotel. He had hauled a massive, slightly rusted tent from his garage, declaring "Our Atlanta home for the week." We all knew the sweltering Hotlanta nights would be brutal in that thing compared to the air conditioning of a motel or hotel. We laughed as we remembered Robbie spending an hour to find a water fountain rather than buying a bottle of water, avoiding any extra expense.

Mark added, "Robbie knew every fast-food weekly deal out there to save money." Johnny added, "He did. When you got into his car it smelled like a grease fire from all of the hamburger wrappers." I jumped in, "There were times where I just wanted to go to a restaurant where we weren't ordering from a counter."

Despite our teasing about his penny-pinching ways, Robbie is a true friend who would be the first to help anyone and is always there for his friends.

"The five of us had some epic adventures." I added. Johnny and Mark looked at me confused, "Four of us my brother Aaron…there were four of us." "No, five of us." I contended. "Me, Johnny, Mark, Robbie….and Robbie's hair." The entire table exploded with laughter as Robbie's rock and roll hair was legendary and due to his *Rockin' Robbie* wrestling persona, he still has it to this day.

Johnny and Mark shared more stories. "Remember when we all went into the Seven Eleven while he was pumping gas and when we came out, he had the hose in the air attempting to get every last drop he paid for into the tank?" Mark added. As we all got another laugh at his expense, I finally responded with, "Wait a minute, this isn't right. Robbie isn't here to defend himself!" Everyone frowned at me, so I added, "Let's get him on the phone."

I video called him, and the table continued sharing laughs as Robbie introduced Page to the rest of our crew on the phone. Laughter and recollections flowed freely over pasta and meatballs, the massive cookie table that's a staple of Deer Creek Falls events and the comfortable buzz of old friends reconnecting.

At one point, though, I couldn't help but feel conflicted as I glanced at Abby talking with Dobbins. Their conversation appeared civil, but something in the way Abby looked longingly at us having a good time reminded me of better days. I wondered, as I had during high school, what it was in him that had managed to win her over.

How could she have ended up marrying him? I always felt she was with Dobbins in high school because of her parents, primarily her dad. Abby's dad was a successful attorney in town. He seemed to want to dictate everything about Abby's future, including pushing her towards Dobbins due to his wealthy bloodline and his pushing Abby to become a doctor. Though she did have a passion for helping people, her dad seemed to see medicine as an extension of his family's wealth and status.

I forced myself to look away from them. In my heart I was sure Abby deserved so much more.

Near the end of the night, Arlo joined our table and reminded me about Monday's practice with Coach Williams. "Does 1 p.m. still work for me to come by?" I asked. I couldn't wait to see Coach.

"Absolutely," Arlo replied with a nod.

As the night wore on, I realized the reunion wasn't just about reliving high school memories. It was a tapestry of past dreams, old friendships, lingering regrets, and the unyielding passage of time. Was I too late?

Chapter 8

Monday afternoon found me pulling into the school's parking lot with my heart pounding like a drum. In daylight the familiar facade stirred memories of both bright and some painful days of youth. In just a few short days, my life had shifted. One moment I was in Tacoma, preoccupied with the promise of a new contract, and the next, I received the unexpected news of my mom's diagnosis. Now, back in my hometown, I reconnected with old high school friends who reminded me of the life I always longed for.

I stepped through the heavy front doors and was immediately greeted by Johnny's mom, a woman I'd known since I went to elementary school with Johnny. Wearing the same welcoming smile from years past, she now served as Arlo's administrative assistant. Her warm voice filled the entryway as she recounted how much fun Johnny had at our recent reunion.

"It's wonderful having you back here in town Aaron," she said, adding with pride that both Robbie and I were doing well. I could see her eyes sparkle as she recalled how Johnny's house once hosted our Nordic Blood band practice sessions. She had always been an unwavering supporter of our band.

Just then, Arlo emerged, a file clutched in his hand and an air of authority about him—a school superintendent on a mission. "Let's head to the wrestling gym," he suggested.

I hesitated for a moment before asking, "May I see your office first?"

"Sure...not much to see, really. I spend most of my time out in the buildings," he replied. We walked into a compact office that doubled as a museum of memories. The walls were adorned with framed black-and-white photographs chronicling the school's history, snapshots of wrestling teams from our glory days competing for a state championship, each image echoing past triumphs.

"As you saw last night, there's more memorabilia on the Wall of Fame," he added with pride.

"It's amazing you managed to get a room built just for the wrestling program," I said with admiration. "The kids and Coach have worked so hard. They truly deserve it."

But at that moment, Arlo's expression shifted; his confident demeanor gave way to concern.

"Sorry," I said. "Did I say something wrong?"

With a serious expression, Arlo explained that the gym's reconstruction had been a grueling struggle. For years, they had scrimped and saved, only to reach a breaking point. Then Dobbins stepped in with a generous donation that covered about 80 percent of the costs.

Such a substantial gift always came with a catch, though: a constant reminder of who holds the purse strings. Arlo confided, "Remember how his dad used to throw around his money to show his power? Now Dobbins has that same controlling streak. He's just joined the school board and already wants to dictate who coaches. With Coach off for treatment, I worry about what he might have up his sleeve."

Our footsteps echoed along the corridor as we left the office, the weight of Dobbin's influence heavy in my heart. But as we moved past empty classrooms and quiet halls, I could almost hear the distant laughter of students filling these spaces with life.

Eventually, we entered the Richard Bartholomew Dobbins Wrestling Center. A picture of the I, II and III versions of Richard Bartholomew Dobbins was placed above the name emblazoned on the front-facing wall. I couldn't help but raise an eyebrow at the name, though it did indeed suit the man behind it. Inside, the familiar sounds of clashing teammates and encouraging shouts greeted me. Coach Miller spotted me immediately and bellowed, "Fast Freddy Foxx!" in a mix of humor and affection. I smiled at the nickname, he was close and I chose not to correct him, just glad to be reunited with the man who had made such a difference in my life.

After grabbing me in a warm bear hug, Coach Miller's concerned eyes searched mine. "How's your mom?" he asked.

I paused, then gave him an update before shifting the conversation to his own struggles. In his rugged, no-nonsense way, he admitted, "I've been dealing with a few health issues these past years. The treatments they've planned this time— they're going to knock me down. And it's terrible timing, with wrestling season in full swing."

"I'm sorry, Coach. Do the kids know about it?"

"They know I'll be out for a while. I haven't gone into details, but Superintendent Ritchie probably gave them a heads up. He's stepping in to coach while I'm off."

Arlo stepped forward with a grin, "Happy to do it, Coach."

Though he was smiling, I instantly recognized the stretch this would be for him. Arlo balanced the demands of being a husband, a father, and the superintendent, yet his eyes burned with a passion that made it clear he couldn't stand by and watch the students struggle in the absence of their beloved coach.

Arlo then turned his gaze on me. "I'm also planning to bring in some guest coaches to help out. So, while you're here…" he began, looking straight into my eyes.

I could read his silent request. Without hesitation, I replied, "Yes, of course I'll help." That had always been my plan, from the time I earned my wrestling scholarship at Kent State University to the moments I trained with Hank Hardway, hustling for extra cash on pro wrestling shows. My journey through college had been rapid: by the end of my junior year, I had only one more course and a student teaching stint left before I'd earn that coveted teaching license.

But then life delivered a brutal blow. As Robbie and I were preparing for our last practice of our junior year, I received a call all kids dread. When I answered, my mom's trembling voice told me that my dad had passed away after a prolonged cancer battle. In that moment, surrounded by the sounds of clashing wrestling mats and adrenaline, time seemed to freeze. Despite my frustration with Dad's unreliable work habits and business schemes, I was grateful he'd attended my meets and we'd shared precious moments in his final days. He was a good man and was loyal to my mom and all of his friends and family.

As soon as I told my Coach at Kent, he urged, "Go home, be with your mom and family." With a heavy heart, I drove back to Deer Creek Falls, bracing myself for the emotional storm ahead. I'd always known challenges were part of life—and now Dad's many financial mistakes, though balanced by his kindness, had left Mom facing a mountain of credit card debt and a remortgaged house.

I caught the glimmer of heartbreak in her eyes when I finally arrived home. Her nursing training, combined with her frugal way of living, once promised them stability. Instead, she now had to face the painful fallout of the poor financial decisions that dad had made.

Aunt Donna, our reliable family accountant, soon stepped in to help us sort through the debt. She broke down the bills and arranged for refinancing, though the possibility loomed large that Mom might lose the house. In that moment, I felt a surge of determination. Without a second thought, I called Hank Hardway, accepted an offer of going on a pro wrestling tour this summer that would bring in a great deal of money and let me see many parts of the country I thought I would never see, and then called my coach at Kent to explain that I wouldn't be returning for senior year wrestling. It was the toughest decision of my life to that point, especially since I was on track to be an All-American, but with just one class and student teaching left to complete my degree, I knew there was still a path forward when the time was right.

Later that night, sitting around a kitchen table lit only by the soft glow of a single lamp, I broke the news to my mom and Jenny. "Hank Hardway has secured me a good amount of money to wrestle this summer." The table was quiet as I continued, "With that money, I can help out with the bills. Once the tour is over, I'll finish my coursework and student teaching. Then I can start working as a special education teacher and wrestling coach. There's no way we're losing this house."

My mom's expression, a blend of pride and deep concern, said it all.

"I wish you didn't have to, Aaron. I am worried you will not finish school and be a teacher like you always wanted. You always wanted to do that and help coach with the team, you have talked about this since you were a freshman in high school." She paused, took my hand and squeezed tightly and while looking down, almost apologetically. "Aaron, you doing this will help us, and likely save our house." She kissed me on the forehead and continued, "You were always such a sweet boy, and you are a young man I am proud to call my son." I gave her a hug and let her know I will make sure not to let her down. It seemed like a simple solution, a short detour from my college plans.

What I didn't realize then was how that summer tour would set off a chain reaction—one that led to more wrestling bookings across the country. Robbie chose to hold back on joining the pro circuit to avoid injury and finish his senior year of college and wrestling at KSU. Meanwhile, I found myself pulled further into the fold. Eventually, Robbie joined me after college graduation, and we teamed up, performing under the playful "Ian and Prescott Hiland" gimmick, complete with our signature finishing move: the Scottish Splash. Like all tag teams, we eventually would have an epic split leading to a highly-watched feud, which is when I created the *Fabulous Freddy Foxx* character as Robbie grew out his mullet even more and became *Rockin' Robbie Hiland.*

My mom continued to make it clear that while she wasn't disappointed in my unconventional path, she was still sad about what I'd given up on my dream of becoming a teacher and coach. My wrestling success had helped pull her from the depths of debt—and during my initial stint in New York, I even managed to pay off the house. Yet looking back, I can't deny that a life on the road and my habit of helping others meant I rarely built up much savings despite being paid very well.

Now, standing in my high school gym with a renewed sense of purpose, I couldn't wait to step into a role I'd dreamed of for so long: supporting Coach Miller. The team was assembling, stretching on the polished mat, their gear clinking softly. In the midst of it all, one kid stood out. Coach noticed me watching him and said, "That's Ricky. He's a great kid and a fine wrestler. He's one of our team leaders."

I placed a friendly hand on Arlo's shoulder. "Kind of like those team leaders I looked up to when I first joined the team in high school?" By Arlo's look and gentle slap on my upper back I could tell he knew I was speaking of him.

Coach Miller grinned and replied, "That's right. Now Arlo's

leading the whole school district." Coach may not be 100 percent but he got my reference about Arlo too.

Coach called the team over, and eight boys and three girls gathered in a tight circle. "Alright, team. Great job in Hudson this past weekend—you made us very proud. A big shout out to Michelle for clinching first in the female division and to Ricky for winning the male division for the second consecutive year!"

Cheers erupted, although Ricky's face reddened at the praise.

A true leader, I thought, and liked him even more.

Then Coach's tone turned somber. "I know you all know I'll be out for a while. I'm sorry for the timing, but I've asked Superintendent Ritchie to step in for me." He gestured toward Arlo. "You've seen his photo on our Wall of Fame. He was always a leader, and I have every confidence in him. Superintendent Ritchie, would you like to say a few words?"

Arlo stepped forward, his voice steady and sincere. "Thanks, Coach Miller. I wouldn't be who I am today without you and this wrestling program." He turned to the students. "Coach not only made me a better wrestler but also taught me how to be a better person. He showed me how to treat people, how to be respectful, and, most importantly, how to support your teammates. Please call me Coach Ritchie when we are here and competing. I can never replace Coach Miller, but together we will honor his legacy by giving our best at every practice and every meet."

Just then, Coach interrupted with a chuckle, "You are too kind, Coach Ritchie. And I believe you have a surprise for the team?"

"I sure do." Arlo shot me a knowing look and beckoned me over. "I'm actually going to have him introduce himself, but I'll give you a little background. He, like me, wrestled right here on the Deer Creek Falls wrestling team. He wrestled for Coach Miller too and lived in the same neighborhoods that you live in, went to the same schools and played in the same schoolyards."

Do kids still play in schoolyards? I didn't even know. I walked next to Arlo, giving the wrestlers a tentative wave and a nervous salute. The room held its breath, each face a blend of curiosity and apprehension. I have performed in front of tens of thousands of people, but being in this spot made me nervous.

I took a deep breath. "Please, call me Coach McClellan, or Coach Aaron if that's easier. I wrestled here under Coach Miller's guidance and cherished every moment at Deer Creek Falls High School. I'm here because I want to help you the way he helped me two decades ago." I paused. "Some of you might recognize me from my professional wrestling days. If you have any questions, just ask. I'm here not only to coach but also to help you all be successful."

It wasn't long before the atmosphere lightened. A small, younger boy raised his hand. "Yes? What's your name?" I asked.

"My name's Bobby. Can I ask you something?" It was clear he was much younger than most on the team and a bit undersized. "You're Fabulous Freddy Foxx, right?" I laughed and confirmed, "Yes, that's my name in the ring when I'm a pro wrestler." His face lit up, and I blurted out one of my wrestling catchphrases, "Hey boss, you in my corner?"

Bobby's enthusiastic "YES!" My question and Bobby's answer sent ripples of laughter through the group, easing the tension for us all.

Ricky stepped forward with a small gift bag. "Coach Miller, thank you for all you do. We promise to keep winning while you're away."

Coach untied the ribbon from the gift to reveal a collection of DVDs—every season of the television show MASH. I could almost see his eyes twinkle with surprise and recall the many times he had recounted how he once convinced his wife to drive six hours just to see a real-life exhibit of MASH memorabilia, which he fondly called "The Mashseum."

With genuine appreciation warming his voice, Coach Miller said, "Thank you, team. You all make me very proud. Watching all eleven seasons of these DVDs will keep me occupied as I recover. You're not just a great wrestling team, but great people. Thanks also to Coaches Ritchie and McClellan. Today, let's have a team-building session. Pair up, share with your partner the strategy you plan to use in your next match; and tomorrow, put that plan into motion. We'll be around to help."

The cheer that followed—"Miller, Miller, Miller…"—bounced off the walls as Coach packed his things. Arlo and I stepped forward to embrace him, whispering, "We won't let you down, Coach."

The wrestlers returned to the mats, but before he left, Coach Miller pulled me aside. "Aaron," he said, "you've done so much—not just in the ring but in life. You've always been there for your family and for me. Remember when you rallied almost the entire roster of wrestlers for that video tribute the last time I was sick? Thank you for that. But don't forget to take care of yourself, too."

I know I looked at him with a mixture of admiration and confusion. At that moment, I wasn't sure what to do with that advice.

Coach continued, "My wife picks me up when I'm down. I don't know where I would be right now without her. That is what I mean. Do not neglect yourself. Make sure to find that one person that makes everything better."

I nodded, absorbing every word. "Thanks, Coach."

I accompanied him outside to his car, parked near the entrance. His wife was waiting, her kind smile lighting up the cool evening air. "Hi, Mrs. Miller," I said, unsure if she remembered me from years ago.

"Oh, Aaron! It's so nice to see you again. Please tell your mom we hope she gets better, and thank you for helping with the team," she replied warmly. As they drove away, I couldn't help but wonder—how did she know I was already stepping in to help?

In that moment, I felt a deep resolve. Every cheer, every gentle word, and every memory in that house of wrestling reminded me that maybe I was where I was really meant to be—back at Deer Creek Falls. Not in my wrestling persona, but as a coach and mentor, ready to honor the legacy of those who had shaped my life.

Chapter 9

As I stepped back through the doors of the Richard Bartholomew Dobbins Wrestling Center, my eyes were drawn immediately to the oversized sign dominating the entrance. The sign and portraits of Richard Bartholomew Dobbins I, II and III were a constant visual reminder of his donation, I supposed. I could see Arlo in a tight huddle with a few of the wrestlers, his gestures animated as he discussed strategies, while others laughed and swapped stories near the bench.

Off to one side Bobby was hanging on every word of Ricky's as they discussed the next match.

Just then, Arlo walked over with his phone pressed to his ear. "I'll be there in three minutes," he said, before turning to me. "I have to head to the high school office to sort out an issue. Can you stick around until the kids are all gone? We'll debrief after I finish up."

"Of course," I said as he ended the call and turned his attention to the team.

"Thank you all for honoring Coach today," he said. "He cares so deeply about you and this team, and I know he'd be proud of every one of you. Practice is done for today. Safe travels home. If you need anything, Coach Aaron will be here until everyone is gone."

Wanting to keep the dialogue open, I stepped forward as they started packing up their gear. "I just want to thank you all for being here," I began. "Don't be nervous about me being around—if any of you have questions or want to talk, now's the perfect time."

A few of the athletes approached me asking me the typical questions: *"Does it really hurt?"* *"How mean is Vito Garramone?"* *"How many titles have you had?"* I laughed and admitted, "I'd say I have won around a dozen." Someone asked about the largest crowd I'd performed for, and I shared stories that seemed to fill the air with energy. Soon, even those without questions clamored for selfies, excited to share the news about one of their new, albeit temporary, coaches being one of the more recognizable pro wrestlers of the day.

As the team of wrestlers trickled out, I noticed only Bobby and Ricky remained, and I realized the unmistakable bond between them. Ricky was letting Bobby practice moves on him, so I called out, "Do you need a referee?"

Bobby's eyes sparkled as he shot back, "No, but will you be in my corner?"

His use of my catchphrase made me chuckle, and I replied, "Of course!"

"Bobby, could you grab our water bottles?" Ricky asked after he tumbled around a bit with Bobby on the mat, letting Bobby pin him for the win.

With that, Bobby dashed off without missing a beat. Ricky turned to me and said, "Bobby's my little brother. He was born smaller than most, and we always knew he wasn't built for wrestling. But he's here—making sure everyone stays upbeat, helping out and making us all laugh."

"I suspected he was your brother by the way you take care of him," I said. "When did you start wrestling?"

"My Dad was a wrestler here, and so was my grandpa," he recalled. "I wanted to carry on their legacy while finding my own path. I tried out as a freshman, but I wasn't ready. I remember the disappointment—I could see my dad's disappointment, and he even blamed Coach for it. Then, by my sophomore year, I finally made the team."

Gesturing to the plaques on the wall, I inquired, "And then you went on to win a state title?"

Ricky grinned sheepishly. "I did… or rather, *we* did. Without our team and our coaches, none of it would have been possible. Even Bobby plays a part in our success."

Just then, Bobby reappeared, bounding over with the water bottles clutched in his arms. "Hey, would you referee a match between me and Ricky?"

I agreed but couldn't help asking, "When are you getting picked up? The room's been nearly empty for half an hour."

Ricky explained with a casual shrug, "Our mom will be here in ten minutes or so. Parent-teacher conferences are taking up her day, so she'll be here once they're done."

I grinned and said, "Well, I hope she only gets the highest reports about you two." I wasn't sure how either of them did academically, but I had a feeling they were a joy to have in class.

After a few playful exchanges where the brothers sized each other up, Ricky allowed Bobby to practice a couple of moves on him. At one point, Bobby boldly asked if I could demonstrate a professional wrestling move, so I showed him a basic headlock. In the midst of the mock match, as I began counting a takedown, a teasing voice interrupted, "Hey boys, going at it again, are you?"

I turned to see Abby standing in the doorway, her eyes twinkling with amusement. I felt the blood drain from my face. Ricky and Bobby were Abby's sons?

Bobby extended his fist for a bump, and I returned the gesture before rising to greet Abby. "I'm going to be working with the team while I'm in town," I said. "Arlo and Coach Miller asked me to lend a hand."

"Thanks, Aaron," Abby said warmly. "That's very sweet of you."

At thirty-seven years old, you would think by now I could stop myself from blushing, but my Scotch-Irish face turned all shades of red. The boys had gotten their gear together as I walked up to Abby. "So how are these guys doing in class? Did their teachers give you a good report on them?"

She looked confused for a moment, as did the boys. After a brief pause, she said, "Oh. I wasn't meeting with their teachers. I was holding parent/teacher conferences with my students' parents. I teach high school science here."

I blinked in surprise. It had been so long since I'd been back to Deer Creek Falls, and with my minimal social media I hadn't known Abby was a teacher, or that she might even have children. I knew from the reunion that she'd married Dobbins. What had happened to her dream of becoming a doctor? I bet she'd be a great teacher, though, one that all the kids wanted to have for class.

I was still processing all this information, but finally I found my voice. "That's wonderful. I remember how brilliant you were in science back in the day—I'm sure the kids like you more than we liked our high school science teacher.

Abby's smile widened as she teased, "I hope so. Remember when our teacher once caught his tie on fire?"

I laughed. "Yes, and didn't you grab him and push him under the safety shower?"

"Yep…that was all me," she admitted with a laugh. She had such an enchanting smile.

With the impatient energy of youth, Bobby piped up, "Fabulous Freddy Foxx is our coach, Mom!"

"So, is it Coach Foxx then?"

Ricky quickly clarified, "Actually, it's Coach Aaron. He and Coach Ritchie are filling in for Coach Miller. Coach Ritchie will be around for the rest of the season with some guest coaches assisting, and Coach Aaron is guest coach number one."

The brothers began collecting their bags as Abby turned again to me. "Aaron, thanks for stepping in. It means a lot to me…to the boys, and, of course, to Coach Miller."

I was about to respond when Arlo reentered with none other than Richie Rich himself, Richard Dobbins—the very man I was hoping to avoid. Not only was he the one guy in town I didn't want to run into again, but now I knew he was also the husband of my high school crush and the father of Bobby and Ricky.

Arlo was deep in conversation with Dobbins, emphasizing that strategizing was just as vital as physical drills. Dobbins's face tightened with irritation as he interrupted, "Why can't I be named a guest coach, too, while Coach Miller is away?"

Arlo hesitated, then replied "Since you're on the board, I can't also officially appoint you as a coach of one of our teams."

Annoyance flickered in Dobbins's eyes as he muttered, "Maybe next season, then. If Coach doesn't come back, and if I step down from the board, then I can be the coach." Dobbins was obviously goading Arlo into saying something, but Arlo refrained and redirected his attention back to the boys as his phone rang.

As Ricky and Bobby trailed toward the exit with Dobbins and Abby, Arlo's voice shifted smoothly. "Abby, can you cover Ms. Grant's class tomorrow during your prep period?"

"Sure," Abby replied. "But that's just one period down and six to go, isn't it?"

Arlo sighed, "Yes." He turned to me, explaining, "Substitutes are hard to find these days. Our teachers get extra pay to cover classes during prep, but it's a lot to ask. And it's definitely a challenge with the current teacher shortage."

Richard, seemingly oblivious to the conversation, called out, "Abby, are you coming with the us?"

"Yes," she said, and I gave her a small wave goodbye.

Then, Arlo turned to me with an unexpected glint in his eye. "That's it!"

"What do you mean?"

"How would you like to substitute teach while you're in town?" Arlo asked.

"Substitute teach? But I never finished my student teaching, and I don't have a license. I didn't even finish my bachelor's degree." I responded as I processed this.

Arlo's expression softened as he explained that, given the teacher shortages, a high school diploma combined with some college coursework and county-supplied training would qualify me to step in temporarily. "Plus," he added, "it's a great way for you to get to know the team."

The opportunity piqued my interest, and despite some reservations, I agreed to the short-term arrangement. "I'll have to take care of my mom some days, though," I said, and Arlo nodded. He reassured me it wouldn't be a problem and set me up for the necessary training right on the spot.

Later that evening, I returned home to the familiar scene of my mom, Jenny, and Randy gathered around our kitchen adorned with Christmas decor, working on a nearly completed puzzle. The glow of the lamp made the table warm and inviting while the girls were already asleep. I crossed the room to kiss my mom on the forehead.

"You're still up, Mom?" I teased softly.

"Yup," she replied with a gentle laugh. "Your sister and Randy need my help with this Niagara Falls puzzle. Remember our trip there?"

In unison, Jenny and I responded, "Oh yes! Jinx, you owe me a coke!"—our childhood refrain echoing the fun of simpler times.

Mom smiled wistfully as she recounted, "It was such a fun trip. Sure, the hotel was a dump, but the memories were priceless."

Jenny added, laughing, "Remember how you opened the window curtains only to discover a brick wall staring back at you?" We all took delight in looking back at those simpler times.

"So, how did you feel today, Mom?" I asked.

She beamed, "I had a great day. I felt good all day and I don't remember, well, not remembering anything."

Then she asked, "What were you up to today, Aaron?"

"A lot, actually. I agreed to help out with the wrestling team while I'm in town. I met with the team today, saw Coach… Mom, he said to send you his best," I said. Mom smiled as she always appreciated the presence Coach was in my life.

I continued, "Arlo also said they are having a lot of trouble getting substitute teachers, so he asked me if I could do it while I am in town. He set me up with the required training and background checks for tomorrow morning. It's funny, Mom. I always wanted to be a teacher and a coach, and this week I became a guest coach and a substitute teacher. Kind of like my own little fantasy camp."

Mom smiled and said, "Those kids need people like you, Aaron. Your patient, kind, and want to inspire kids. I've seen you on some of the community service pieces they show during wrestling. You always do so well with kids."

I took her hand, my heart full and my mind already looking ahead to what might await me at the school the next day.

Chapter 10

arrived at the education resource center early the next morning, ready to begin substitute teacher training. The center bustled with activity and served as a hub for schools needing everything from quick background checks to specialized training sessions.

In the crowded room, a speaker stood before us and declared, "You're not going to get rich as a substitute teacher." I looked around and couldn't help but think that none of us had stepped in with dreams of hitting the jackpot.

Among the nine of us gathered there for training, most were noticeably younger, full of nervous energy and wide-eyed anticipation. There were two seasoned educators that I knew there, Mr. Mallory and Mr. Morgan. Bill Mallory, with his kind, weathered face, was known not just as an English teacher but also as the mastermind behind a program that integrated seniors into workplace settings. Despite handling the most challenging students on a regular basis, his patience and warmth won him the endless admiration of his students.

When I asked him why he was heading back to the classroom, he chuckled and explained, "I retired two years ago and let my license lapse. Bruce and I were at our retired teacher holiday get-together and heard the school needed help."

Bruce Morgan had a big heart and an ever-present, slightly absent-minded grin. I remembered his economics class from junior year. Fresh off the discovery of my Scottish heritage, I eagerly raised my hand one day and asked, "What are some exports from Scotland, Mr. Morgan?"

His eyes twinkled as he paused, slowly stroking his graying beard. "Exports from Scotland," he mused, "probably Scotch Whisky." It took a few seconds, but the class broke out in laughter, as we didn't think teachers knew alcohol existed.

In geography, he was known for reading every quiz answer aloud, complete with his memorable missteps. I still recall one day, when he announced, "Number one, the answer is Asia—A-S-I-A. Number two, Canada—C-A-N-A-D-A. Number three, Guatemala—G, G... uh, you can look that one up yourselves."

We could get him on a tangent during class quite easily as well. His love of history shone through with the many stories he would regale us with. Sometimes we would get him talking about more popular culture topics that most kids enjoyed more than the history topics. We got him talking about television one day and I asked him if he liked Friends or Seinfeld. He answered, "I do like that Seinfeld show. I have not seen The Friends." He added, "Whose friends are they?"

Out of respect, we tried to hold in the laughs, but most often it was futile.

Equally unforgettable was his penchant for publicly revealing student scores to the whole class. This was a practice that has long since fallen out of favor but was commonplace at one time. One day, his booming voice listed, "Robbie, 80 percent. Johnny, 90 percent. Aaron, you got 95 percent. Jack, 25 percent." A heavy silence mixed with a few stifled snickers followed until he added, "That's pretty good, Jack. Last time you got 15 percent."

Despite these idiosyncrasies, Mr. Morgan's kindness shone through, and we loved him for it and would work hard in his class. Unlike Mr. Mallory, Bruce had been out of the classroom for many years, only to return after a personal loss. Later, over lukewarm coffee, he confided that after recently losing his wife, he needed something to fill his days. "Stepping back in as a sub isn't just about teaching; it's about helping the community I love in Deer Creek Falls," he said, his voice heavy with both sorrow and resolve.

After the training session, I invited both Mr. Morgan and Mr. Mallory to join me for lunch. They reminisced about their early careers, sharing stories of a time when teaching was less about tests and more about genuine engagement. Bill lamented the rise of standardized testing, saying, "All of these tests started taking the fun out of it for the students…and teachers."

Mr. Morgan agreed. "My school friends and I never had these tests, and our lives turned out fine, and we were all gainfully employed…and never took any standardized tests. Our teachers taught us, engaged us, and were the ones who tested us."

I was not prepared for what came out of lunch, but as I listened, I grew concerned about what all this testing might be doing to teachers and their students – especially the ones who faced extra challenges. The retired teachers' words stirred something within me.

I had long dreamed of becoming a special education teacher, of dedicating myself to helping students who needed the most support. Now, I felt compelled to make sure these vulnerable students wouldn't be left struggling.

"Arlo?" I said when I caught my friend later in the day. "I think I want to substitute teach with the special education department whenever I can."

He grasped my hand and gave an appreciative nod. "Aaron, that means more than you know."

After spending the day learning from those retired educators, I hurried over to 3 p.m. wrestling practice. The corridors buzzed with energy, and the gym resounded with the thudding of tackles. Arlo was in and out, and I assumed control of the practice, organizing drills and sparring sessions. Young Ricky, with a maturity beyond his age, stepped into a leadership role as usual, demonstrating holds and giving pointers to the team.

Midway through practice, Johnny's mom stepped into the gym. "Arlo told me your substitute license came through," she said to me. "Ms. Lynch is out. Do you want to start tomorrow?"

Before I could answer, a soft, earnest voice piped up from behind me. I turned to see young Bobby standing there with a look of concern. "Hi, I'm Bobby. I have Ms. Lynch for class. Is she okay?" His concern was palpable, and Johnny's mom responded, "She's fine, Bobby. She's attending a teacher training class tomorrow."

"So, who's going to be our teacher?" he asked.

As if on cue, Ricky called out, "Hey Bobby, let's let them finish talking," and led his little brother back to the mat. Within seconds, he was letting Bobby pin him as they continued to practice together.

Johnny's mom leaned in and explained to me, "Ms. Lynch is a special education teacher. They're the hardest to find subs for, and Mr. Ritchie mentioned you'd be a good fit for her class." In that moment, I glanced at the undersized boy. I hadn't realized Bobby qualified for intervention services. Still, there was no way I'd let him or the other students in the class down.

"I'd be happy to step in for her tomorrow," I said.

She smiled and clarified, "Actually, we need you for the rest of this week."

I blinked, overwhelmed by the sudden responsibility, then added, "No worries at all. I'll report to the high school office first thing tomorrow."

After another brief pause, she said, "It's at our middle school. Ms. Lynch covers grades six through eight."

I grinned and replied, more confidently than I felt, "Again, no worries. I'm in."

The following day, I dove headlong into substitute teaching, juggling classroom lessons with lunch duty and bus duty. Every part of my day felt alive with purpose. On lunch duty, clattering trays and boisterous conversations filled the cafeteria, and as I strolled the hallways, teachers and students alike called out, "Who are you today?" as each day I could be subbing for a different teacher. The question took on a playful air, almost like a rotating costume party, especially after years of assuming various stage names—from Aaron McClellan to Prescott Hiland to the more outrageous Fabulous Freddy Foxx.

At lunch, students would huddle around me, eyes wide with excitement as they peppered me with questions about professional wrestling. They listened to my past tales and discussed the current spectacle and storied legacy of the sport. I loved every minute of their fascination.

At the end of the week, I headed to Friday's wrestling practice. To my delight, the man who trained me to be a professional wrestler is at practice, Hank Hardway. As a lifelong friend of Coach Miller, he had always volunteered to help the team whenever he could, I had thought though that he had stopped coaching at the school the past couple of years to take care of his wife. Over a few minutes of catching up, Hank revealed that despite having retired from firefighting and on the brink of retiring from training pro wrestlers, he was determined to keep supporting the high school team—especially now that Coach was out.

"Injuries have taken their toll on me," he admitted, "but I plan to be here more often." He'd visited Coach Miller at home after the recent treatments, adding that despite everything, Coach was doing remarkably well. The kids adored Hank; despite his gruff exterior, they absorbed every scrap of wrestling lore he dispensed and respected his undeniable street cred.

After practice, as Arlo and I walked to the parking lot. I mentioned Ricky's unyielding determination and Bobby's newfound enthusiasm in class. Arlo stopped mid-step, looked me in the eye, and said, "Aaron, I really appreciate everything you're doing. These kids need a leader. Abby mentioned that last night, Bobby was talking about school much more than usual—not just wrestling, but what Coach Aaron taught him."

I smiled, though inside I couldn't help but wonder about Abby; hearing her name meant she was thinking of me too. Even though I knew she was married with two wonderful children, I allowed myself a quiet hope, a small, secret dream about what might have been.

"I love what I'm doing, Arlo," I confessed, and he responded, "And it shows."

I grew quiet as we approached our cars. What if I hadn't dropped out of college my senior year to earn the money my family needed? What if I'd finished school and become a full-time teacher? I might have earned less money, but perhaps I would have been happier—and maybe, just maybe, ended up with Abby. I reminded myself that one week of subbing hardly equates to a lifetime in the classroom, yet it was hard not to imagine an alternate universe.

"Are you going to be at the Christmas Carnival on Saturday?" Arlo asked.

"I think so. Tonight, we're making cookies for the Cookie Walk."

"Great. I'll see you there. The school choir is set to sing, and my son always insists on checking out those quirky booths—like the Christmas Creatures display."

"What's that?" I asked with some skepticism.

"You know, those county fair-type attractions like the 'boy with a tail' and the 'world of the spider lady.' I'm secretly hoping he'll outgrow that phase soon. Don't get me wrong—I love the carnival, but I much prefer the traditional parts of Christmas," Arlo added with a chuckle.

I drove home bubbling with enthusiasm about my week of teaching, coaching, and wrestling. Sitting around the dinner table, I relayed my experiences to Randy, Jenny, Moira, Margo and Mom. I could tell as I spoke that they were having the same thoughts I'd had, the "what if" wonderings, contemplating that alternate universe. What might have been if I had chosen a career in teaching from the start?

Before I could drift too deeply into that daydream, Mom interjected, "Aaron, you might not have had all your money and fame, but you would have made a difference here. Who knows? Maybe you'd have even found your true love." Her words hit home, and in that instant, Abby's face fluttered into my mind, followed by the thought, "She is married, Aaron."

Sensing my discomfort, Jenny quickly steered the conversation back to the plans for the Christmas Carnival. "We're all going to be there," she declared, "and tomorrow, we'll be making an entire batch of cookies for the Cookie Walk." She looked around the table and added, "Everyone, get to bed early tonight. We'll need all our energy for tomorrow and the carnival."

Then she leaned over to me with a conspiratorial smile and whispered, "By the way, Abby and the boys will be here tomorrow to help with the cookies."

I blinked in surprise, my heart skipping a beat as I stammered, "Really? What time?"

"Around one o'clock, I think. Abby mentioned that the boys wanted to see a championship belt if you brought one."

A surge of anticipation washed over me. Thankfully, I had arranged for Robbie to send over a few special items to Deer Creek Falls from my apartment in New York. I couldn't wait to see the boys, and Abby, of course, but I also wondered… would Richie Rich Dobbins show up, too? He struck me as an uninvolved dad, the kind that would prioritize his own needs over his family. One never really knew for sure.

Guess I'll find out for sure tomorrow.

Chapter 11

enny, Randy and I piled into the car with Moira and Margo, the girls chattering excitedly as we drove to the neighborhood grocery store. We were on a mission to pick up the last ingredients needed for what promised to be a lively cookie baking session. As we wandered down brightly lit aisles, I asked the girls, "What is the money from the Cookie Walk used for?"

Margo, usually so reserved, piped up and said, "It's for a sensory room they're building at the middle school."

"A sensory room?" I said. "What's that exactly?"

Jenny jumped in. "Imagine a room where the lights change to soothe, where sounds are carefully tuned to stimulate the senses, and soft textures invite you to relax while helping you build motor skills. It's expensive, though, and the regular school budget won't cover it. Abby and a group of teachers have been fundraising for it because Bobby's therapist said it could really help him and many other kids."

"Gotcha. So how much do they need?"

Jenny said, "About $50,000 to fully set one up. It's a big goal, but one that's really close to everyone's hearts."

I thought, *$50,000? That's a lot of cookies to sell.*

But then Margo added, "It's important. Bobby told us how much better he felt when they had a room like that at his summer school."

Without thinking too long, I declared, "We're going to raise that $50,000 mark. I promise."

Randy and Jenny shot me looks of disbelief and concern, but as I looked into Jenny's uncertain eyes, I said, "Remember my favorite Beatles song? 'Don't Let Me Down.'" *I have to help any way I can to make this happen. I will not let Abby or the kids down.*

Before we returned to the cookie-making frenzy, Jenny said, "Big brother, please don't drain your personal bank account for the $50,000 if that's what you meant by not letting us down."

I chuckled and shook my head. "I wouldn't do that. Living in New York, I've never been great at saving. I have a few ideas up my sleeve if the Christmas Carnival doesn't pull in enough funds."

She patted my shoulder and added, "Alright, Aaron. Just keep us in the loop with whatever plan you come up with. And remember, your limited savings aren't just about spending; you've helped many of us along the way."

Back at the kitchen table, we set our workspaces among bowls piled high with cookie dough, icing, and colorful sprinkles. I took charge of cutting out the cookie shapes, and Margo joined me. Jenny told me Margo also wanted to become a teacher. As we carefully stamped shapes into dough on the scatter of flour-dusted countertops, I noticed how confident she was becoming. Every precise cut and every little smile revealed a caring heart and a keen mind. I could imagine her one day standing in front of a classroom, nurturing the very students who needed it most.

Earlier that day, Jenny also mentioned how Moira and Margo helped Abby pitch the fundraiser, standing bravely in front of the Christmas Carnival committee explaining the need for the sensory room project as the charity initiative for this year's fundraiser.

Soon enough, trays of cookies adorned the counter. Suddenly the door burst open with excited noise. Bobby, his eyes gleaming like he'd just won the championship, raced into the room. He barreled toward me, reaching out to give me a bear hug, and shouted in a burst of joyful enthusiasm, "My favorite teacher! And coach! And wrestler!"

Abby and Ricky carefully stepped through the doorway. With a teasing gleam in her eye, Abby said, "Let's not make his head any bigger than it already is!"

Bobby tilted his head in confusion. "Why would it get any bigger?"

Ricky said, "It's not really about his head—but hey, why don't you ask Coach Aaron what you wanted?"

Bobby grinned. "Coach, I mean Fabulous Freddy Foxx—can you sign the box from when I got your action figure?" He pulled a carefully wrapped box from his bag.

"I can, sure, but come with me and we will see if we can do even better than that," I said. "You want to come too, Ricky?"

"Sure."

The room we entered wasn't my childhood bedroom in the strict sense, but it had been lovingly arranged by my mom after she'd moved in here after I went to college. It still held fragments of my past—pro wrestling posters, my high school trophies, and mementos of my high school wrestling and Nordic Blood days.

As we stepped inside, I pulled out a collection of wrestling belts, assorted merchandise, and memorabilia, most of it neatly stored in bags. I selected two of my prized Fabulous Freddy Foxx signature series action figures and inscribed each with, "I will always be in your corner. Fabulous Freddy Foxx." I took my time, as I tended to have lousy handwriting.

Watching Bobby's uncontainable smile and glancing at Ricky, who looked either on the verge of tears or merely overwhelmed with excitement, I knew how much it meant to them.

Then I pulled out three championship belts to show them. The first was a modest belt from my very first win with an independent promotion organized by Hank Hardway, a simple design echoing the early days when wrestling belts were handcrafted and basic.

Then, I revealed the tag team belt that Robbie and I had earned as The Hilanders. That one was the only one Robbie ever held, and it represented our spirited attempt to embrace our "Scottish roots," complete with our comically exaggerated accents—even if one European reporter had dismissively called them "rubbish."

Finally, I showed them the belt I had won at the first-ever New Year's Eve Wrestling Extravaganza, a proud relic from when I was at the peak of my popularity.

Ricky, his eyes shining with recollection, said, "That was an unforgettable match! Coach Aaron delivered four Foxx Trots to The Broadway Brawler before he pinned him!" His excitement echoed through the room, and he explained to Bobby how the Foxx Trot, my signature finishing move, had become synonymous with my persona, much like Bret Hart's Sharpshooter, Stone Cold's Stunner or Razor Ramon's Razor's Edge.

"You're right, Ricky," I said. "The Brawler was a beast. He'd defended his title for nearly a year until I finally got the win that night."

"Wasn't that the match of the year?" Ricky asked.

I was surprised and impressed by his depth of knowledge about wrestling. "Yes, it was, Ricky. Nice work." We fist-bumped as I described how The Broadway Brawler's theatrical pre-match performance, singing Broadway tunes while mixing in playful dance moves, fooled everyone until the match was underway, revealing his true, intense grit.

At that moment, Abby peeked in from the hallway. "Hey, boys, you've taken enough of Coach's time for now."

Smiling at her, I nodded and said, "You're right; we need to get back to those cookies." With wrestling matches still lingering in the back of our minds, we filed out of the bedroom and back to the festive chaos of the kitchen.

The kitchen was alive with holiday cheer. Tables were strewn with trays of cut-out cookies decorated with Santa hats, round, smiling Rudolph faces, and red-cheeked snowmen. I teamed up with Bobby, Ricky, and Abby to ice and decorate each cookie as if it were a miniature work of art. Yet I couldn't help but wonder where Dobbins was. How could someone miss such memories with their kids?

Abby and Ricky's cookies were very neat, and looked like something you would see for sale in the store. Mine and Bobby's were marginal at best. Bobby was young, but what was my excuse?

In the middle of it all, Mom reminded us of our longstanding tradition: we'd each take a person-shaped cookie and decorate it to look like whoever was creating it. I fumbled a few attempts until I managed a borderline resemblance to myself.

We had lots of extra "person" cookies decorated for the sale, and Bobby asked, his eyes alight with curiosity, "Well, who are all these people?"

I began, "Here's a mom and dad, and their sons, Kenny and Frank—Kenny's in fourth grade, always glued to his video games and books, and Frank is off at college. Their mom Debbie was a standout college basketball player who now coaches, and their dad, David, works…"

I barely got the sentence out before Bobby burst into laughter. "Mine's a brother and a sister! They both love reading and are training to be wrestlers!"

Abby looked at us with a smile. "Wait, your cookies have a backstory?"

The room erupted in laughter as I retorted, "Don't yours?"

As Abby's laughter softened into a smile, she touched my forearm, a subtle reminder of feelings I was trying to keep in check. Oh, who was I kidding? I was in deep at this point…

falling in love with my high school crush, who was now a married woman.

Finally, after hours filled with cookie making, we finished up all the icing and sprinkles. As we cleaned up the mess, Bobby asked, "Coach Aaron, will you come with us to the Christmas Carnival tomorrow?"

I planned to, of course, but before I could answer, Abby said, "I'm sure he's already been invited. We can all meet up there."

My pulse quickened, and I wondered again whether Dobbins would show up, too – if only for appearances. Drawing in a deep breath and trying not to meet her gaze directly, I replied, albeit stammering when doing so, "I'll definitely be there. I'll be looking for you…uh, you all. All of you."

Chapter 12

The next morning, Randy, Jenny, and I piled into the car to pick up a life-sized set of gingerbread people for the Christmas Carnival. Randy's hands were steady and skilled, the kind that could fix a leaky faucet or assemble a model kit with ease, while my tools consisted of a butter knife and calling Robbie who'd picked up a fair share of handyman tricks from his Grandpa Hiland.

Randy had crafted these oversized gingerbread figures so that carnival-goers could slip their faces into the holes and snap festive photos. Though donations were welcome, none were required, and like everything else at the Carnival, every dime raised would benefit the sensory room project.

We arrived in the heart of downtown and delivered the gingerbread figures, standing them like colorful giants amid the bustling preparations. The committee bustled about, tying ribbons and draping garlands on a makeshift stage. While Randy climbed a ladder to string twinkling lights on the lampposts, Jenny and I arranged glowing luminaries along the sidewalks. These beacons lined the route from the parking area to the Carnival, inviting townsfolk to wander among the warm, flickering lights. Along the way, we strolled past Deer Creek Falls, a waterfall dressed in red and green holiday lights. The water danced as it tumbled down mossy rocks that gave the town its name.

As we passed a station labeled "Christmas Creatures," my eyes were drawn to a bold sign proclaiming "The Man Who Feels No Pain." I couldn't help but ask, "Who's behind this one?" thinking, *What a great, yet campy, tagline for a wrestler to use.*

Jenny explained, "I heard the mayor called in a favor. She knows someone who's originally from here, who travels the country performing this 'no pain' gimmick. Since we needed an extra draw for the Christmas Creatures, she thought he'd be perfect." I was seriously considering paying the suggested five-dollar donation just to see this mysterious act.

Before I could, though, Jenny's expression darkened with concern. "We better get moving," she said. "Margo and Moira are with Mom, but we should head home to check on her. She's been through a couple of exhausting days already." I nodded in agreement as we hurried back.

By the time we arrived, the house was filled with familiar chatter. To my surprise, Mom was recounting tales of some of the girlfriends I'd had in my younger years. The stories weren't quite serious, but she remembered them fondly. You know how moms can be when their adult children aren't married.

Then Jenny piled on. "Girls, did you know your Uncle Aaron charmed quite a few ladies when he was younger? He was always so sweet—just too shy."

Moira's eyes lit up with curiosity. "Uncle Aaron, you would be a great catch for someone. Did you ever come close to getting engaged?"

Becoming slightly embarrassed by this point I responded, "No, not really. I did have someone I really liked, but like your mom said, I was too shy for my own good…"

Jenny cut in, "He's been planning that perfect proposal for years."

Mom looked over with a smile. "Really? You must share, Aaron."

Jenny shot me a look that said, *'tell them, or I will,'* so I sighed and began.

"Remember the annual Christmas tree display at Carter's Christmas Land?" I began.

Margo piped up with a dreamy smile, "Yes. I love going there. It is a tradition that Mom said started with her grandma taking her, and our grandma continued the tradition, and now our mom takes us. I love that. All of the different trees and you can buy all of the ornaments to decorate trees just like they have them."

Mom added, her tone warm and nostalgic, "Christmas isn't complete until you've wandered through the magic at Carter's. Oh, and we need to get a tree soon."

Hoping to steer the conversation away from proposal plans, I asked, "Is the Christmas tree lot on Main Street still set up this year?"

Randy answered, "They are. I passed it when I picked up Margo's saxophone from the music store."

We had gone to this same Christmas tree lot for many years when I was growing up. Our town is more of a mid-sized city, but we have some classic amenities like a Christmas tree lot on Main Street. I decided to double down on making this about our Christmas tree, rather than go back to the discussion about my planned engagement idea that hasn't materialized.

"Let's go Tuesday after school to pick a tree," I said.

Everyone agreed until Jenny joked, "Alright, Uncle Aaron, are you going to finish telling us about your engagement idea, or should I?"

I chuckled and continued, "Alright, fine. You know, I've always been drawn to the annual Snowman Christmas Tree at Carter's. The idea of a wintertime engagement, right there amid all that sparkling snow and festive cheer, just feels right."

Jenny, who must have either been thinking I needed to get to the point or just that it was tough for me to share these things, jumped in with, "So, your Uncle Aaron wants to take his future bride to the Carter's Christmas tree display, get on one knee in front of the Snowman Tree and ask her to marry him." There were genuine oohs and aahs from all in the room.

Mom smiled. "That is very sweet, Aaron. When the right person comes along, she'll be so lucky."

"Of course," I said, "there's always a long line at the display, and I'd be so worried that when I'm down on one knee, someone might shout, 'Hey, man, keep things moving!' when all I want is an unforgettable moment." Laughter bubbled around the room, along with more oohs and aahs.

Jenny clapped her hands together and announced, "Okay, everyone—tonight we're all staying over to get ready for the Carnival tomorrow. Girls, is the air mattress set up in the front room?" The girls chirped in unison that they had already taken care of that detail, and with warm hugs and goodnight wishes, they headed off. Mom soon joined them, leaving Jenny, Randy, and I alone together.

Later that evening, Jenny asked, "Who's up for some tea?"

Randy and I immediately agreed, and we all settled around the kitchen table, sipping and sharing nostalgic memories.

Jenny remarked, "So, you and Abby seemed to have such a good time today."

I leaned back in my chair, growing more guarded. "What do you mean?"

"When you, Abby, and the boys were in the kitchen making cookies. Lots of laughter, fun…and it looks like those boys really have taken to you."

I couldn't help but grin. "Ricky and Bobby are great kids," I said. "Subbing right now at school and helping coach the wrestling team, I find myself looking forward to seeing them every day." After a pause, I added a verbal jab. "Would be nice if Dobbins could show up to something his kids are involved in.

It's not like he has to help make the cookies but at least show up. I don't know how Abby is still with him."

Randy and Jenny exchanged a quick glance. "What do you mean?" they asked in unison. "Are they back together?"

"Back together? I thought they were married."

Jenny sighed and explained, "They were married, yes. But Abby got tired of the constant back-and-forth between being married and single. Richard was rarely around for the boys—except for the occasional wrestling match—and he took Abby for granted. You know, you won't find a more thoughtful person than Abby. But Richard is aloof, with no real self-awareness."

"Oh, I could go on about Richard Dobbins," I added. "He's just a carbon copy of his dad. Growing up, his dad always used his wealth and power to influence school affairs and the team, and it seems nothing's changed. He even made a threat about Coach Miller the other day. Seriously, how do you kick someone when they're already down? No character."

I stopped for a second, then added softly, "Abby deserves so much more." I cleared my throat, then asked, "So, when did they tie the knot…and when did they call it quits?"

Jenny's eyes sparkled. "Oh, my social media-absent brother. When Abby was at the end of her junior year of college, she found out she and Richard were going to have a baby. She moved back home with her mom and dad and then in with Richard when they got married. They had Ricky and then later had Bobby. It was a tough road for her."

I leaned forward; curiosity piqued. "I bet it was. Abby was always laser-focused on becoming a doctor. That must have been such a curveball. Don't get me wrong though. Ricky and Bobby are special kids, and she seems like a great mom and a great teacher."

Jenny nodded. "Abby is the best. She would do anything for her boys. She even gave up her dream of medical school when

Ricky was born to stay home with him. But after Bobby arrived, things only got worse. Richard grew more detached from the family, barely showing any interest in the kids."

Jenny shook her head. "You know her, though. She made a plan. She decided to divorce Richard, move in with her mom, who could help with the kids, and go back to school. She couldn't afford the time and expense to become a doctor, though. She looked into a lot of options but decided to become a teacher. With all of her science credits at college, she decided to become a science teacher…and your right, she's a great one."

I was stunned by the details of Abby's sacrifice and resilience. The way she'd abandoned a meticulously planned future for the sake of her children—and even turned down the financial safety net provided by Richard Dobbin's family—was a testament to her strength and fortitude.

Wanting to know more, I asked, "Do Abby and the boys still live with her mom?"

"Yes. After Abby's dad passed away, it just made sense for them to stay with her mom. Her mom has been a tremendous help; and given the financial mess her dad left behind, living there benefits everyone."

"Financial mess?" I asked confused. "They were pretty well off from what I could remember." Jenny explained, "They were, but her dad had gotten in some financial trouble, something about over-billing clients. It got really bad for her mom. Abby moving in with her after he had passed away helped her mom too."

I would've been lying to myself if I said I didn't have feelings for Abby. Hearing about what her family went through I found myself wanting to be with her, holding her and making sure she was okay. I'd liked her since we were in junior high school together, spent time with her since she was friends with Jenny, and even went to her house when we worked on the project together. She was kind and caring to everyone and always willing to lend a hand when someone was in need. I'll never understand how she ended up with Richard Dobbins but, thankfully, as pro wrestling's prolific librarian Page Turner's catchphrase states, "That chapter is over."

Finding out all this gave me mixed emotions. I still had some questions for Jenny, but how would I ask them subtly? "Does Dobbins take the boys sometimes? You know, like an every-other-weekend rotation?"

"Yes," Jenny replied, "but sometimes he cancels, and other times the boys are left bored with him. It's always transactional when they spend time with him."

"Did he remarry?" I inquired, trying to gauge the full picture.

"He did," Randy said. "His new wife is younger, and they don't have any kids."

Finally, I blurted out the real question I wanted to ask. "What about Abby? Has she come close to remarrying…or does she date? Is she dating anyone?" I stumbled over the words.

Jenny regarded me with both concern and a glimmer of hope. "Her boys are her whole world. It'll take someone truly special—someone who accepts them as if they were their very own—to win her heart again."

I nodded. "Of course. That's the way it should be."

Chapter 13

efore the carnival, my mom and I settled into a corner booth at our favorite diner. We hadn't had much time together since I arrived back in town. As we sat there with an Alvin and the Chipmunks Christmas classic playing in the background, and a plate of scrambled eggs and buttered toast set before us, my mom leaned in. "Aaron, thanks for coming and staying. I know you are taking time away from your work."

I reached across the table and squeezed her hand. "Mom, stop right there. I can take as much time as I need. You are what is most important right now," I reassured her. "How are you feeling?"

Her gaze wandered over the diner for a moment before she confided, "I'm okay. Physically, I feel great, but I worry I'll keep forgetting things and may not be able to stay in the house." She paused, her knuckles whitening around my hand as she continued, "What will happen to the house? You know…if I can't go back there?"

I held her hand tighter, trying to smooth away her concerns. "Mom, I'm so sorry you're going through this. I've spoken to others dealing with the same issues, and they said the hardest part was not knowing what comes next. The best advice I got was to take things one day at a time. Enjoy the good days…

each of them. Whether it's something simple like waking up to read the paper with a hot cup of tea, or the special events like all things Christmas. I want all of us, especially you, to enjoy each good day we have."

After a moment of silence, Mom's face brightened as she asked, "Am I able to stay home through at least New Year's Day?"

"I believe so," I replied, "You've had all the good days since being home and that's exactly what the doctor said would be our measure." With that, we gathered our things to head for the Christmas Carnival.

Driving toward the carnival, she said with a smile, "You know, Abby is going to be at the carnival with the boys. The Christmas Family Feud trivia teams need teams of five. Maybe you can help them out?"

"It's not wrestling trivia, Mom. How much help can I be?" I teased back.

At the carnival, my mom joined me at a fundraising table where I was busy signing photos of myself adorned in my Fabulous Freddy Foxx wardrobe for a ten-dollar donation. You could snap selfies or have me record a quick video message for twenty dollars apiece. The table was bustling. The steady line of supporters had me busy during the first hour.

Still, I found myself glancing around for Abby and the boys. Suddenly, Bobby burst through the crowd, a blur of excitement with Ricky tugging at his sleeve trying to rein him in so he wouldn't miss out on any of the fun. I could see delight on Ricky's face as he watched his little brother's joyful antics. Clearly, the chaos was a welcome reprieve, especially for someone so young who had been through so much in his short lifetime.

Not long after, Abby appeared, trailing closely behind the boys. She enveloped my mom in a warm hug and, to my surprise, gave me one too. My mom grinned at Abby. "I'm going to take the boys to a few Christmas kiosks, while you help

Aaron remember that his name is Fabulous Freddy Foxx when he's signing autographs or doing selfies."

I nearly choked on my laughter at her authoritative "assignment," and Abby smiled, replying, "I'd be thrilled to help Fabulous Freddy Foxx raise money."

For the next three hours, I stayed at that table as Fabulous Freddy Foxx. The crowd, a mix of locals and devoted wrestling fans who had traveled from miles away, filled the space with constant chatter and clapping applause. I was too busy handling autographs, selfies, and playful quips to talk much to Abby. At one point, leaning in close, she whispered, "Do you think we should add an extra hour so we can reach everyone waiting?"

"Of course," I said with a smile, "as long as you're here with me," hoping she got the message I was sending.

After the meet and greet, Abby and I joined forces for the Christmas Sleigh Race. This was a contest where one person sat in a Christmas Sleigh while their teammate pulled them. Ricky pulled Bobby to victory in a smaller version as part of the "Youth Division" of the contest. The prize was a gift certificate to Duffy's Pizza, a favorite of mine since I was a kid and apparently Bobby's as well. I was winning my heat pulling Abby until Bobby and Ricky jumped into the sleigh which gave us a good bit of humor though not a victory.

As I finally dropped at the finish line carrying three people in my sleigh while everyone else had one, Bobby instantly asked, "Mom, can we invite Coach Aaron over for pizza when we get it?" His eyes were bright with hope.

Abby hesitated, then said, "Of course, Aaron can come over and have pizza with us. We can even let him pick the night."

I grinned. "How about we get pizza after practice on a day your mom is busy? That way, she doesn't have to cook." The boys were in, and Abby slipped her fingers into mine as we held hands, for the first time, and walked to the next kiosk.

There we found a carnival barker attempting to draw a crowd to the outlandish performance we would always remember. His pitch for "The Man Who Feels No Pain" echoed off the purple curtains that lined the sides of the makeshift stage, his voice demanding attention. When he described the act in detail, Bobby turned to Abby.

"Can we do that? Can we do that?" he pleaded. Ricky chuckled at the earnestness of his little brother, and we all laughed.

Inside the room, draped with more velvety purple curtains, a woman stood beside a bed of menacing iron nails and introduced an older man in a black suit with a flowing cape and a top hat. Her theatrical announcement cracked through the hush: "All of us have pain receptors all over our body. All humans. Only one man has been able to use his mind to ignore any pain that his body feels. Please help me welcome, Hardwired Harry!"

That introduction and name made it impossible to keep my laughter to myself. Abby and I tried to hide our chuckles, our eyes meeting in amusement. I leaned in and whispered, "Can this guy really ignore pain?" I added, "If he can, I am getting him in the wrestling ring."

Before we could share more, Harry bellowed, "I need the biggest person in the audience to help us with what you're about to experience!" Surveying the room filled mostly with moms and wide-eyed children, he zeroed in on me. "You," he commanded, pointing directly at me.

I hesitated for a moment before raising my hand. "Who, me?" I managed; despite realizing he meant exactly that.

"Yes, you, sir. What is your name?" Harry insisted.

"I'm Aaron," I said, still trying to process the rapid turn of events.

At that moment, Bobby called out excitedly, "He's also Fabulous Freddy Foxx…and our coach!"

Undeterred by the mix-up between my names, Harry continued in his booming tone, "You, Freddy. Please come up here."

Now, despite my internal protests, I rose to the challenge. I walked toward the stage, heart pounding, aware that I was about to embark on one of the most bizarre stunts of my life, and that says a lot coming from a professional wrestler.

Harry shook my hand warmly and instructed, "Before we proceed, touch these nails and let everyone know they're real." I stepped forward, my fingertips grazing the cold, unforgiving metal, and declared to the modest crowd—about 25 generous donors—"Yep, these nails are very real. And I'm not planning on lying down on them!"

Harry chuckled and then made his next request: "When I lie down on the bed of nails, I need you to stand on me." Shock flickered through me for a split second. "Wait...what?" I asked. "Yes, yes," Harry insisted. But then I recalled the precision and safety of performers like Harry, and with a cautious resolve, I agreed.

His assistant—her name was Julie— introduced me before Harry slowly lowered himself onto the bed of nails. I gingerly placed one foot on his chest, then quickly added the second as my balance wavered. The uneven surface nearly cost me my footing, and almost immediately Harry bellowed in alarm, "Get off! Get off!"

My tenure atop him lasted a mere second or two before I scrambled down. As soon as I stepped away, I noticed my entire family had gathered at the back of the room, barely holding in laughter as Julie hurried over to check on Harry. Despite the brief scare, the performance gave everyone a story they'd laugh about for years—one I already planned to recount whenever I had the chance to tell the tale of Hardwired Harry, The Man Who Feels No Pain. Incidentally, that turned out to be the first, and likely the last, time Harry attempted that specific stunt.

After the performance, Abby and I shared a laugh before heading over to grab hot chocolates for ourselves and the boys. This time, I deliberately linked my fingers with hers, savoring the intimacy. With mugs of steaming cocoa with a generous amount of marshmallows in hand, we made our way to the snow angel-making contest.

The recent snowfall had transformed a giant greenspace near the Deer Creek Falls Amphitheater into an enchanting winter playground, where nearly everyone in town paused to press their arms and legs into the soft snow. Abby, Ricky, Bobby, and I positioned side by side, and by some happy accident, our angels blended into a striking, giant snowflake.

Bobby's art teacher, new to the school but already beloved by the local families, stepped forward as the judge of the contest. After announcing the winners, she approached Abby and me, saying, "Mom and Dad, here are your winnings. I also want to tell you how much I love having Bobby in class. I know I mentioned it during parent-teacher conferences, but I haven't yet had a chance to tell Dad."

I smiled and clarified, "Oh, sorry, I'm not Bobby's dad. I'm just someone who joined the team tonight for some fun."

Abby quickly interjected, "That's okay, Ms. Fisher. You couldn't have known. Aaron here is a wonderful guy who works with my boys on wrestling. He's even subbing at our school this month."

Ms. Fishers' eyes twinkled as she added, "First, call me Jodie. And yes, I do know you from somewhere. Perhaps from your subbing? I have two younger brothers, and they remind me so much of Bobby. I haven't yet met your other son, but I'm sure he's just as kind as Bobby."

I couldn't help but wonder if she had seen me wrestling on television, especially if she had two younger brothers.

Feeling a tug of guilt for my earlier words, I looked to Abby for an opportunity to speak privately. "Can we talk for a minute?" I asked.

"Sure, Aaron. What's up?" she replied, her eyes softening.

"I wanted to apologize for making it sound like I was just joining your team for the night. I love spending time with Bobby and Ricky…and you, of course. I always liked being around you at school when we were younger, when you used to hang around with my sister, and I'm so happy we have had the chance to reconnect these past couple of weeks."

Abby stepped closer to me and said, "Aaron, you're amazing with my boys. You've always been so kind to me, and I'm sorry I never showed how much I think of you." With that, she leaned forward, put her arms around me, and gave me a quick kiss. My heart swelled. I was stunned but thrilled. Here we were, after all this time, finally sharing our first kiss.

Just then, Jenny rounded the corner, starting with an exasperated, "There you—" She stopped short as she saw us, with our arms around each other. Abby and I broke apart in a flurry of surprise and embarrassed laughter, as it was time to join the Christmas Family Feud. Jenny led the way.

My family's team was comprised of my mom, Randy, Moira, Margo, and Jenny. With five members gathered, it looked like I would be sitting out this round. Perhaps that was for the best, since I noticed Richard orchestrating a team of his own family members, and clearly, Bobby and Ricky were meant to be on it.

I glanced over and saw Abby in discussion with Ricky, whose usually confident demeanor now seemed vulnerable, as if tears had threatened to spill. A moment later, she walked over to me.

"I can't believe Richard—he's putting together a team for Christmas Family Feud and just asked Ricky to be on it. When Ricky got excited, thinking Bobby would join, Richard said there was no room for Bobby on the team. He asked me if he had to join his father's team. I told him if he didn't want to, he didn't have to. The thing is though, Ricky looks forward to this contest every year," she said with disappointment."

Worried about the boys, I asked, "Is your mom here?"

"Yes," Abby replied softly.

A light sparked in my mind. "Let me run this by you. What if it's just the five of us, you, me, Bobby, Ricky, and your mom? That way, Ricky gets to be on our team, and Bobby isn't left out."

In that moment, Abby grabbed my hand and gave me an uninterrupted, lingering kiss…one I will never forget. Snow fell gently, the buzz of the crowd surrounded us, yet all I could feel was her lips on mine.

I'm in trouble, I thought. Because with every moment that passed, I was falling more deeply in love with the sweetheart of my dreams, the girl from my past, and the woman I wanted to become part of my future.

Chapter 14

Armed with our new plan, we approached Abby's mom. Abby's dad had never quite warmed up to me. When we were working on a project together in high school we were at her house once and he ended making comments about the side of town I came from. But Abby's mom had always treated me with genuine warmth. When I discovered we were from the same neighborhood, I understood why. When we asked if she'd join our team for Family Feud, she immediately agreed, and just like that, our team of five was set.

The organizer gathered all eight teams of five and explained, "This is a bracket tournament in single elimination style, using traditional Family Feud rules but with Christmas-themed questions."

Suddenly, Richard Dobbins ambled over and asked, "Isn't this supposed to be made up of *families*?" It was a cheap shot to say the least, particularly from a guy who would not include his youngest son on his own family team.

Abby's eyes flashed with hurt, but before she could retort, the organizer said, "Family comes in many forms. Here, for example, I see a mom, a dad, two sons...and a sister!" She gestured toward Abby's mom, who appeared to love the compliment. "Besides, I'm not even sure how official these rules really are!" she added.

Our team ended up placing third in the contest, winning the consolation round against another runner-up team. There was satisfaction in that, especially when I congratulated Ricky. "You were amazing during the modern Christmas movie round. I can't believe you knew all those *Jingle All the Way* questions!"

Ricky beamed. "I love that movie. My mom, Bobby, and I watch it every year. When they asked who was Turbo Man's sidekick, I knew it was Booster!" We exchanged a celebratory fist bump as Bobby leaped into my arms, exclaiming, "Coach, Coach…we did it!" His unbridled joy touched my heart.

Then, to my surprise, Ricky asked his mom, "Can Coach Aaron come over and watch *Jingle All the Way* with us sometime?" Abby and I exchanged a look. We knew there was something stirring here, yet it wasn't the time to bring it up.

"How about we talk about that when we use our Duffy's Pizza Gift Card for pizza this week?" I suggested, and the group seemed to love the idea.

At the end of the day, I volunteered to help Abby and her crew count the money raised from the carnival. Jenny offered to take Bobby and Ricky back to the house with Mom, Randy, and the girls for a hot-chocolate break. In the midst of friendly fist bumps and Bobby's playful attempt to put me in a headlock, it was obvious that the event had brought us all closer together.

Jenny gave me a knowing look as she led the boys toward the car. I'm sure she knew I wanted to spend more time alone with Abby.

After cleanup, we headed into the downtown log cabin. My Aunt Donna, already busy with the numbers, handed us a banker's bag and a meticulously recorded sheet as we moved to a long, wooden table. Abby frowned at the tally. "Oh, no."

"What is it?" I asked, my heart sinking as I realized our ambitions may have overshot our reach.

"It looks like we cleared around $18,000. That's so much less than what we need. I don't get it. I mean, the cookies sold out, and there were so many people," Abby explained, tapping her pen against the sheet. After a pause, she added, "Maybe it was counted wrong?"

"Sorry, Abby. I doubt Aunt Donna made a mistake. She's an accountant. Honestly, raising $18,000 is a lot of money to make from cookies and carnival activities." Looking to lighten the moment, I joked, "Maybe if the Man Who Feels No Pain had charged a hundred bucks a person?"

Abby sighed, "I know. It's just so disappointing."

"Let's head to the bank and get this deposited. Where did you park?"

"Over by the Falls and Amphitheater," she replied.

On our walk to her car, we detoured onto a bridge overlooking the glowing Falls, now illuminated with brilliant, shifting colors. Moments like these stirred old memories.

"I love how they light up the Falls now," Abby said. "They didn't do that when we were kids, but it was still beautiful then." She turned to me, her cheeks pink from the cold and her eyes bright. "I still remember when you and Robbie were on the state wrestling championship team—right here in front of the Falls, they presented Coach and the team with the trophy."

I was touched she remembered that. "Were you here when that happened?" I asked, already wondering if I had seen her in the crowd. "Sorry, it was so busy, but if you were there, I'm sure I saw you," I added sheepishly.

"I wouldn't have missed it for anything," she replied. "I was so proud of you and the team. I wanted to become closer friends with you, though I know it bothered Richard. I'm sorry he was always so rude to you and the rest of the team. I should have seen him for who he was—just like his dad."

I gently put my fingertip to her lips. "It's okay, really. We can't control everything that happens. I learned that early on, but I still struggle with it sometimes. Being back here brings up memories of when I had to make a decision about my future when my dad passed away. I had to decide if I would go after money now and be able to help my family, or stay in school." I looked at the waterfall for a few seconds. "I'm still not sure whether I made the right choice."

Abby's voice grew soft, "Aaron, that whole situation was thrust upon you. You had to make a difficult decision, and your choice came from kindness and love for your family." She smiled, "And then you went on to fame and fortune..."

I opened my mouth to respond, but Abby continued, "My future was dictated to me too, in many ways. Having Ricky and Bobby has brought so much joy into my life. They have given it real meaning. It wasn't planned, just as your dad passing away was not planned. But you stepped up and helped not only your mom but also helped Jenny pay for college. That's very selfless, Aaron, and one of the things I love about you."

Her words struck deep. *She just said the word love – about me? Or about my actions?* Did it matter? For a moment we just stood there, an intimacy born of shared trials and triumphs. Then, hesitantly, I asked, "Can I ask you something?"

"Of course."

"I've always wondered...why did you give up on your dream of becoming a doctor? I know raising Ricky and Bobby made it tough to consider med school, but with Dobbins's money, I thought it might have been an option." My voice trailed off in apology as I realized the probing nature of the question. "I'm sorry, that's too personal."

"No, no...it's fine. Just hard to talk about," Abby continued, "Richard really didn't want me going to school or working. Like his dad, he wanted to spend his days working and his nights socializing to make connections that would benefit him, or, as he would claim, our family. That didn't really lend itself to me finishing my degree or going to medical school."

"But you were always so passionate about helping people. How did you end up moving into teaching and earning that degree?"

She smiled, a bittersweet expression in her eyes. "I always loved school as a kid, loved our teachers, and having children of my own showed me how important education is to kids and their parents. I figured I could still have a positive impact on other people's lives as a teacher, just as I would have as a doctor. The college told me that I had a lot of science credits, so the quickest pathway to a degree was to be a science teacher."

She sighed, then went on. "All that was great, but Richard still didn't want me taking the time away to go back to school. I continued to put it on hold for a long time. Then, when I lost my dad…well, you know, you do a lot of reflecting."

I knew what she was talking about, of course. My own loss of my dad charted the course of my life for the next twenty years.

Abby leaned closer, snuggling into my coat. "After all of that reflection and grief, the boys and I spent a lot of time with my mom, and less and less time with Richard. He always seemed to have other places to be and other things to do. It got to a point where I decided to leave Richard. The boys and I moved in with my mom. I finished school, got my teaching degree, and became a science teacher. I'm just lucky to be doing it at Deer Creek Falls, where I grew up."

We embraced as she finished her explanation, and eventually, she lifted her face to me in the chilly air, and I kissed her again. For the next few minutes, time held its breath, and we kissed under the gentle cascade of green and red lights illuminating the Falls, a silent promise of shared hope and understanding. I didn't want to stop. I didn't want to let her go or lose the magic of the moment.

Reluctantly, we broke apart and continued on toward her car, hand in hand. Abby stared up at the dark sky. "It's so disappointing we couldn't raise enough money for the sensory room. I was really hoping we could fund it—and maybe even help other buildings get one too—but we're short."

Wanting to find a solution, I asked, "What about Arlo? Didn't he say the school might cover it out of their budget?"

"He actually did. He went before the board and argued that the design and engineering costs should be on the school's budget. That's really all they can afford," she explained. "There's much more that's involved, though."

Standing at the car, with the Courthouse Square dazzling under holiday lights in the distance, an idea began stirring inside me. "What if we put on a wrestling show as a holiday fundraiser? I could call in wrestlers, hold it in the high school gym, attract sponsors, do autograph signings and meet-and-greets—and put all that money into the sensory room project."

Abby's face lit up with excitement. "Aaron, that's an incredible idea. You are too much! Do you think there's even enough time for that?"

"You don't know until you try," I replied. "I'll talk to Arlo tomorrow at school and see what he thinks. If he's on board, I'll get to work on every little detail."

Chapter 15

I arrived at school the next morning with extra pep in my step. My mind buzzed with excitement, not only about teaching and coaching, but also about the possibility of organizing a wrestling fundraiser to fund a sensory room. I typed a quick text to Arlo, asking if he had a few minutes to meet. We arranged to meet during lunch, meaning we supervised the students at lunch and talked while we were there.

At lunch, I shared my idea. He listened intently but furrowed his brow. "Aaron," he said as we walked back to his office, "I love you, man. But is this even possible? A holiday fundraiser? I mean, it would be in three and a half weeks. I don't want to go there, but I feel like I need to—are you doing this to prove something to Abby?"

His question caught me off guard. Leaning forward, I responded, "No. I've spent a lot of time with Abby and the boys lately, yes, but my desire to help with the sensory room is about helping all kids, not about showing off."

He gave a small, understanding nod. "Alright, I had to ask." He leaned back in his chair. "Now, I have another question, nothing about wrestling or Abby at all."

I waited, curious.

"The state of Ohio is launching an academy for second-career teachers," he explained. "They're putting together a program where you can take your existing credits and work experience, and then they fast track you towards getting a full teaching license. Based on how quickly you've made an impression here, your passion for teaching and coaching, I'd love to see you try it. Each district can sponsor up to five people, and I need to give them a head's up by early January. The training is set for this summer, which means you could be fully licensed by the fall."

I sat there, taken aback by the opportunity laid before me. "Wow. Yes, I am interested," I admitted. "But I'll need some time to think everything through…though obviously not too much time."

Arlo smiled. "Keep in mind since you pretty much had all of your teaching coursework done and only needed student teaching, if you stayed on as a sub the rest of the year, it looks like you'd just need a couple courses, and you'll be licensed by next fall," he finished, clearly trying to convince me.

My mind spun with the possibilities of changing careers and staying in Deer Creek Falls full-time. Could I do it? Did I really want to?

My mind shifted back to the fundraiser. "Thanks, Arlo. I'll think about it, I promise. But, back to the fundraiser—are we set to use the gym?"

He gave a playful wink. "Absolutely. Just don't let this new information distract you."

Later that day, during my prep period, I walked to Abby's classroom. Today, fate had granted both of us a free period, a rare moment where neither of us was rushing off to substitute for another teacher. I asked if we could share lunch, eager both to update her on the fundraiser and to relay Arlo's news.

"Arlo said we can use the gym for the wrestling fundraiser," I began with excitement. "I'll get on the phone after practice tonight to see who I can get to come. We can use the gym for the show, but the common room could be a Fan Fest area where fans can get autographs and photos with wrestlers. I know it's a short time frame, but wrestling fans are some of the most loyal fanbases, and I'm pretty sure they'll come out for something like this. I'll ask Hank tonight at practice if we can use his ring, and if he would help with booking and managing the night's action."

Realizing I was diving too deep into details, I chuckled and apologized, "Sorry. I'm a little lost in my own head with all these ideas."

She smiled and squeezed my hand. "It's okay. Just tell me what you need help with."

Without missing a beat, I replied, "Your Triple A organizational skills, for sure." We both laughed at the reference, and I was relieved she remembered the nickname I'd given her all those years ago.

"So, what was that other thing Arlo mentioned?" she asked.

"He mentioned a state program for those who took college courses in education but never finished. The idea is to fast-track people like me into getting licensed. They're addressing the teacher shortage and, with my credits, I could be done as early as this summer and start teaching in the fall."

Her eyes widened with concern. "Is that really what you want?" she asked.

I'd expected immediate enthusiasm, but her tone was measured, as if urging me to consider every possible consequence.

"Absolutely," I insisted. "From day one, this has been what I wanted. Serving as a coach and sub has only made me more determined to become a teacher."

Abby glanced around the room. "I know, but I just want you to be absolutely sure. You're making a big shift—your whole lifestyle, your location, even your income."

I couldn't help but laugh at that. Everyone knew teachers didn't make top dollar. Leaning closer, I added, "I already spend all my money anyway. And what really changes for me isn't just what I do or how much I earn." I caught her gaze with mine and held it steadily. "It's about spending time with the ones I love."

Practice later that day went off without a hitch. The energy on the mat was infectious, and I couldn't help recalling the day's earlier conversations as I wiped sweat from my brow. After practice, Hank Hardway swung by with his booming laugh and a friendly slap on my back. His presence was reassuring. Seizing the moment, I asked him about the possibility of using his ring, along with his help in booking the show.

"Do you have time to grab some wings tonight after practice?" I asked. "We could go to McClellan's Pub."

"Absolutely," he replied, "but I'd better have something of the non-breaded, non-fried variety. Doctor says I need to mix in more salads and less fried foods."

I laughed and said, "No worries. We make sure the wings at McClellan's Pub have zero fat and zero calories." I laughed at the recurring misconception that my family-owned McClellan's Pub, a regional chain from St. Paul, Minnesota that had become as much a part of our town as the local diner.

After practice, Hank and I settled into a cozy booth at McClellan's. There, I explained the fundraiser in detail—how Abby and the school were working together to fund a sensory room that could help a student like Bobby thrive. I unfolded my plan for a wrestling fundraiser, outlining the idea of using the gym for the matches and converting the common room into a space where fans could get autographs and photos as part of a Fan Fest.

Hank listened intently, nodding as he recalled his own days running charity shows with community-driven events. "Sure, I can help," he said. "You can use my ring, and I'll pull in some of the guys I trained to help set it up. I'd be honored to be your booker and produce the show. It's not every day I get to be a part of something like this."

After a moment, his tone turned thoughtful. "After this show, I'm likely going to sell the ring. I'm hanging it up. No better way to go out than for a great cause like this. So, thank you!"

I shook my head. "No, thank *you*, Hank. You broke both me and Robbie in. You saw something in us and got more out of us than I knew either of us had. I cannot thank you enough." I took another crispy wing and asked, "So, what will be next for you? After this show and wrestling season?"

Hank's eyes softened. "This is the hard part for me. After this year, I'm going to sell my house and move to Vermont with my sister. Her husband passed away, and she could use some help around her house and property. We're close, and her kids all live up that way. I'll sure miss my family here though."

I looked puzzled as I knew he had lost his wife and they had no other family living in town. "My wrestling family, Aaron. The kids at Deer Creek Falls High School, Coach Miller, and all of those I coached and trained."

I absorbed his words, then said, "I get that. You deserve nothing more than to ride off into the sunset and enjoy the time with your sister and her family." I paused and added, "I'm off to see Abby, and I'll start calling around about the show."

At my words, Hank had as big a grin as I had even seen on his wide mug of a face.

"What?" I asked.

He laughed. "We've been sitting here for over an hour, and not a minute seems to go by without you mentioning Abby, Ricky, or Bobby."

"Okay, okay…," I answered. I felt my face redden.

"By the way, do you have a name for the show yet?" he said.

I admitted I hadn't come up with one and knew I needed to work on that soon. Wrestling promotions love to come up with names for their shows. I thought to myself we need to come up with some kind of holiday-themed name for this one.

Later, with the excitement of a kid on Christmas break, I headed to Abby's house. For the first time, I could picture a future where Abby and I would share not just family moments but also a career in teaching and coaching—a dream I'd always wanted.

Inside her welcoming home, I found her sitting at the kitchen table alongside Ricky and Bobby, who were busy doing their homework. I updated her about my conversation with Hank Hardway about the show: we had a ring secured, a booker/producer on board, and a venue for the show. I laid out my plans to reach out to several wrestlers, while stressing the need for a catchy, holiday-themed name for the fundraiser.

Together, we all brainstormed names around the table. Christmas Clash? Winter Wars? Nothing sounded quite right. Just then, Karen Carpenter's "Home for the Holidays" was playing. Bobby leaped up and put me in a headlock, shouting, "It's a holiday headlock!" Looking at everyone, I immediately shouted, "That's it, Bobby! 'Holiday Headlock' is the perfect name for this show!"

Chapter 16

Abby's knack for organization was nothing short of inspiring. Within days, she'd already begun contacting local businesses for sponsorships, gathering volunteers for the show, and coordinating meet-and-greet sessions for the Fan Fest. Things that could be done that didn't require knowing which wrestlers were going to be on the match card. With the calendar now reading December 6 and the show scheduled for December 27, we needed to finalize the card to move on to advertising and other logistical plans.

Besides Hank Hardway, the next person I knew I had to call was Robbie. Although he was under contract with Kennedy's wrestling company, I knew he might be available, especially since Kennedy's crew would be in Cleveland for the December 30 event. I thought of roping in Robbie as he would be a favorite of the hometown Deer Creek Falls crowd. I hoped to tap some other top talent for guest appearances, but I needed to act fast.

When I called Robbie, he was in London where he and Page were attending a press event for an upcoming Premium Live Event. He was excited to hear about the Holiday Headlock wrestling fundraiser and said he would love to take part, provided he could speak with Kennedy first. I suggested that if it was okay with him, I'd reach out to Kennedy directly and make the ask. Perhaps it being for charity, and the fact that I'd already signed on for the December 30 event, would convince him to help out with this good deed.

We then moved the call to FaceTime. Robbie knew I loved London and wanted to show me where they were. On the screen, I saw Robbie and Page were framed with a view of Baker Street, since they were huge fans of Sherlock Holmes. I remembered Abby was a big fan, too, and asked them to send me some pictures I could share with her.

I updated them on my work as a sub, coach, and the unexpected opportunity to fast-track my way into teaching. Their expressions were encouraging, though they understood how hard it would be to leave behind the world of wrestling.

"By the way," Page asked as we started to wrap up the call, "how are things with Abby?"

"We've been spending a lot of time together," I admitted. "And it's been great."

Robbie grinned. "Interesting how your path toward becoming a full-time teacher intersects with finally stepping up with Abby. I'm happy for you, man. It seems like everything is coming together."

After an early wrestling practice the next day, Abby, the boys, and I spread out our well-earned Duffy's Pizza on the kitchen table for lunch. As we ate, Abby took out a well-worn clipboard and began sketching out a detailed seating chart for the wrestling show. Bobby and Ricky crowded around, helping with printed ticket designs and a neatly drawn table layout for the upcoming Fan Fest.

With her phone pressed tight to her ear, Abby coordinated with potential local and regional sponsors, jotting down every detail in a faded leather-bound padfolio. "We've got to track every expense, not just count the revenue," she said, glancing at the clipboard as she balanced projected costs against hopeful gains.

I watched her with quiet admiration, losing myself in the shimmer of her green eyes and the determined set of her jaw. *You amaze me in every way,* I thought. The quiet but determined teenage girl had turned into a force of nature, a beautiful, accomplished woman who cared deeply about everyone around her.

I felt like the luckiest man alive, to be spending time with her. When I reached out to take her hand, I saw Ricky and Bobby both take notice.

In that brief moment, a thousand questions flickered in my mind: What were Abby's intentions? When would we tell the boys about our growing connection? Or did they already know?

Knowing that our fundraiser depended on every careful detail, I realized it was time to start making calls. My first task was contacting Don Kennedy. He was still my boss, of course, and controlled the biggest professional wrestling association in the world. If we could just get some of his wrestlers on the *Holiday Headlock* card, that would be huge.

I envisioned fans streaming in from New York City, Chicago, and even farther away, drawn by the promise of a festive wrestling card during the holiday break right in Northeast Ohio. With nearly half the nation within a 500-mile radius, the event was perfectly poised to be a magnet for crowds and a huge boost for our sensory room project.

I dialed the number for Don Kennedy's assistant, Pat, whose caring tone was a refreshing contrast to Kennedy's callous demeanor. "Aaron, how's your mom?" she asked, and as she spoke, her own tender memories of her parents, both stricken with early-onset Alzheimer's in their late 60s, colored her words with understanding.

"She has good days and bad days, but mostly good as of late." I shared.

"With all the modern medicine and technology now, I'm sure your moms in good hands," she assured me.

She checked the schedule and offered, "Mr. Kennedy has an opening at 4 p.m. today, before the talent arrives for tonight's house show in Madison, Wisconsin. Will that work for you?" My pulse quickened in surprise at how swiftly she had arranged things. "Yes, absolutely."

"I'll dial you in and connect you," she said before ending the call. "Take care, Aaron, and please give my best to your mom."

The thought of speaking with Kennedy swirled in my mind. I'd only have his "undivided" attention for a few precious minutes to pitch our fundraiser idea calmly and clearly, unburdened by the chaos of a live event.

I then began making a series of calls to independent wrestlers who weren't currently contractually tied to Kennedy. One call in particular connected me with Turnpike Mac, a wrestler who had carved out a niche for himself with a trucker gimmick, a role I had once been urged to take on.

I still remembered the awkward costume: an oversized Mac Truck hat, faded blue jean overalls with a belt buckle as big as a license plate, and a road map poking out of the back pocket. Thankfully, Kennedy had let me retain the more vibrant Fabulous Freddy Foxx persona, giving the truck driver character to someone who could make it more successful.

I sent Turnpike Mac a quick text so he'd know I was calling, and his reply came almost immediately: "Aaron, how can I help my wrestling brother out?"

I explained the purpose behind the fundraiser and outlined how the proceeds would be channeled into a project that mattered. I told Mac all about the kids it would be helping and of course mentioned Abby to him a time or two. Mac listened and requested that only his travel expenses be covered. I explained to him we wanted to make sure everyone taking part was fairly compensated. Guys like Mac never got some of the more lucrative, guaranteed contracts you see more now. Mac was all in and he would bring his rugged charm to both the wrestling show and the Fan Fest, making the card all the more attractive for the wrestling fans.

I went to find Abby to talk numbers and budget details and found her standing in the doorway, watching me. A soft smile played on her lips. "I heard you on the phone, explaining why we're doing this show," she said. "Thank you. I can't tell you what it all means to me."

Without warning, she closed the distance between us. She snuggled up to me in a bear-like hug and planted a kiss on my lips that made my heart stutter. I looked down, lost in the brilliance of her green eyes.

There was so much I wanted to say, yet I could barely find words for it all. "Would it be too presumptuous to tell you…"

But she put one hand on my lips, cutting me off. "I love you, too, Aaron," she said, her voice tender. "I think in some way, I always have."

"Oh, Abby, I love you too." My mind spun at the fact that she'd said it first. "When should we tell the boys?"

"Soon, I think. It's important to me that they're part of all this." She slipped one hand into mine. "I do have some exciting news on the financial front."

"Oh, yeah? What's that?"

"Carter's Christmas Land just donated $5,000 in sponsorship, and Duffy's Pizza is catering a meal for all of the wrestlers and volunteers—no cost at all!"

"Already? Abby, you're amazing!"

Just then, the boys ran into the room, holding Abby's phone. "Mom, look! We got another text!" Bobby exclaimed as Abby leaned in to read the screen.

Her face lit up. "Superintendent Ritchie is donating $5,000!"

Good ol' Arlo. First, he got the planning and design done for the sensory room through the school's budget, and now he was personally helping make this happen.

"Honestly, he's the best superintendent our school has ever had," Abby said. "Everyone, from long-time teachers to those just starting out, says it because he's so authentic and truly cares about the kids and the staff."

I reached out to hold Abby's hand again and realized the boys were right there.

Abby glanced at me and then began, "Boys, you know sometimes people date—hold hands, hug, and show affection."

"Don't go any further, Mom, we get it," Ricky said with a grin, while Bobby asked, "What are you talking about?"

"It means that Coach Aaron and I are going to be seeing each other a lot from now on."

Bobby grinned. "So, does that mean you'll be around more often?"

"Yes, I will."

He considered this for a moment. "I have a follow up," he said after a beat.

"A follow up? What is this, a press conference?" I joked looking at Bobby.

Unabated, Bobby continued. "Can I still put you in a headlock?"

I laughed too. "You sure can, buddy."

My phone started buzzing again, and I glanced at the screen with bated breath, half-expecting Don Kennedy's call. The caller ID read "Beer Town." I recognized it immediately, not as a local brewery, but as Milwaukee Mike, a veteran of the independent wrestling circuit. Milwaukee Mike had a classic fireplug build. His reputation as a brawler preceded him. When Mike came to the ring, he would always bring a six pack of Milwaukee's Best beer. At some shows, he would use it as a weapon, hitting his opponent over the head.

I explained our fundraiser and the reason for it. Without hesitation, Mike agreed to join, though he requested a straightforward flat rate, noting that his wife works for an Atlanta-based airline and he could get to us through her employee pricing cheaper than us paying to get him there. I said no worries and joked about while him being called Milwaukee Mike and being based in Atlanta as it is similar to Hank Aaron, referring to the Milwaukee Braves moving to Atlanta. My attempt at a joke fell rather flat with Mike. Perhaps he was not a baseball fan, or he was a few beers into a six pack already?

Before I could catch a breath, another call came in. This time, it was Pat with news from Kennedy. "Hi, Aaron. My apologies. Mr. Kennedy's schedule went a little sideways for later this afternoon, but he has time right now if you do."

My fingers trembled with anticipation. I had no idea how this call, or my proposition, would go. "Yes, I can talk now. Thanks, Pat."

True to her word, exactly two minutes later, my phone rang and I answered with a steady, "This is Aaron."

There was a brief pause before Kennedy began in his typically measured tone: "Freddy, Pat mentioned you needed to talk. I think I know what this is about. Robbie asked if he and Page could take a couple of days off before the New Year's Eve Extravaganza to join your fundraiser."

I kept my voice steady despite the rapid beating of my heart: "Yes. Do you want the full explanation, or the thumbnail version?"

"Just sum it up for me."

I took a breath and laid out the essence of our plan. I explained that I was hoping to secure some of his talent to strengthen the card, making the show a must-see event for fans nationwide. I detailed the arrangements for transportation and housing. Finally, I told him we would love to have Robbie and Page, but anyone else he could spare as well.

He paused for a long moment when I finished. Finally, just when I was sure he'd say no to the whole thing, he said, "Freddy, you can have Robbie and Page join you. When Vito heard about it, he wanted to help out too."

Hearing those words, relief and excitement washed over me. Kennedy's tone turned firm: "Here are my rules. Robbie and Page can wrestle on your card, but make sure nothing happens to them. Vito can attend, but he cannot wrestle. He can take part talking in the show, but he's a big boy and knows what he can and cannot do. That's all we can do for you and your fundraiser. I hope it's enough."

"Oh, it is, sir. Thank you so much." I exhaled deeply, grateful that Robbie and Page were on board and excited about Vito's potential contributions. I envisioned him doing a live *Foxx Denn* segment during the show and playing a key role drawing fans to the Fan Fest. I thanked Kennedy, but before I could broach the subject of additional sponsorships, he hung up. No asking about my mom, and still calling me Freddy instead of Aaron. Oh well, that was typical for Kennedy.

No sooner had I set the phone down than Robbie's excited voice rang through the line again. He'd just gotten the confirmation from Kennedy and couldn't wait to join our show. "Vito's a standup guy, and I'm glad he's coming too," he added.

Before I could say anything else, Robbie confided in a low voice, "I'm going to ask Page to marry me by the Falls while we are in town, Aaron."

"No way, man. That's incredible. I can't wait for that!"

"Well, I'm asking her, not you," he joked, and we both started laughing.

Then Robbie's tone grew concerned. "Aaron, how's your mom, your family? And what's happening with your contract negotiations? Kennedy seemed nervous about you potentially heading to Los Angeles."

I thought back to my unexpected encounter with Stuart Tanner at the airport. "I'm not sure what to do yet," I admitted. "I ran into

Stuart Tanner at the airport when coming home and he sounded like he's going to make me an offer. Not sure I want to go to LA, but I have a lot of respect for him. Kennedy sounded like he was going to make me an offer to stay with New York. We'll see what happens, but I told you where my mind is right now."

Just then, as if on cue, Abby walked into the room.

"Robbie, Abby just walked in. Let me put you on speaker."

"Hey, Abby," Robbie said. "Can't wait to see you when we come into town, and I can't wait to introduce you to Page. I hear your boys are awesome. Can't wait to meet them too."

Abby shot me a glance but then said, "Hey, *Rockin' Robbie*. My boys have your action figure and will be excited to meet you and Page. Your tag team partner here has been keeping us all busy."

"Can't wait. Listen, I gotta go. Page and I are doing a meet and greet at a children's hospital here in London. It is the Great Ormon Street Children's Hospital, the one that all of the proceeds from Peter Pan books benefit. Tell Jenny I remember she loved that book and how she named Moira after Wendy from Peter Pan."

"Jenny will absolutely love that," I said. "I'm glad you guys got to spend extra days in London."

Robbie laughed and said, "Can't wait to see you all very soon."

As we wrapped up, Abby reminded me of the pressing tasks we still faced. She reached out, touching my hand, and in that moment, I felt an unmistakable spark, just like back in our high school days when everything seemed possible. I wished I'd told her back then how I felt, but maybe Robbie was right. Maybe waiting to have true love in my life was meant to be.

I took a deep breath. "Abby, I love being back here. I love spending time with Bobby and Ricky and I have strong feelings for you. You know that. I always have."

Her eyes softened. "I feel the same way, Aaron," she replied quietly, "you are the kindest person I've ever known. I'm thrilled to have you here with my boys, but I also know you have big decisions coming up, and I don't want to distract you."

"You aren't a distraction at all. I haven't been this happy in years," I responded.

After a tender pause, Abby shifted gears. "We've still got a lot to do, don't we? I have a couple more calls to make, and you still need to update Hank Hardway, right?"

I gave Abby a shrewd look. "Are you double-checking my schedule to make sure I don't miss another call? You're such a planner, my Triple A."

She giggled, planting a quick kiss on my cheek before heading off to finalize more fundraiser details. In some ways it felt like an ordinary day, filled with the excitement of planning a school function—and yet after the words we'd exchanged, I knew nothing would ever be the same between us.

Chapter 17

I called Hank Hardway to update him about the show. His voice crackled over the line, alive with as much excitement that a grizzled veteran of the wrestling business could muster. When his generation of pro wrestlers were coming up the business exemplified the word gritty.

"Hank, what's the plan?" I asked.

"I've got Turnpike Mac facing Milwaukee Mike in a Grudge Match. Turnpike Mac will be announced from the Pittsburgh side of the Pennsylvania Turnpike. Think Steelers versus Packers, as they seem to be on a collision course for the Big Game this year."

I knew where Hank was going with this. Our town is dead set in the middle of Cleveland and Pittsburgh and despite being a long-suffering but loyal Cleveland Brown's fan many of my friends growing up supported what my dad referred to as the evil empire: The Pittsburgh Steelers.

Hank continued, "Pittsburgh's own Turnpike Mac will be decked out in full Steelers gear, waving the Terrible Towel like a battle flag. Meanwhile, Milwaukee Mike will roll in with his signature six-pack of Milwaukee's Best, all while sporting full Packer colors and a cheesehead hat."

I knew some people might find this over-the-top aspect of professional wrestling a bit much, to be sure, but I also knew that, when seeing the crowd's reaction, you could suspend disbelief and get lost in the moment. I figured, like any other entertainment, people deserved to forget about the struggles of life and just enjoy themselves for a while. Much like all art forms, we provide a well-deserved distraction from life's challenges and struggles for our fans.

I joked, sort of, "Just make sure he doesn't hit Turnpike Mac with that six-pack. It's a family show, after all."

Hank laughed. "Don't worry. I've got it under control."

A moment later, Hank's tone shifted. "Hey, I heard Page Turner is on the card. That got me thinking. Why not call Dynamite Destiny? She and Page worked together on the indie scene and Destiny even mentored her. With Destiny living outside Chicago, this fundraiser is accessible and the cause is right up her alley. Their matches from five years ago stirred the wrestling world when they swapped the women's world title back and forth. I'll call her, if you think it's a good idea."

"Good idea? I think it's a great idea!" I affirmed.

Our conversation moved quickly to a gimmick match. Hank said, "I can line up a couple of my newest students for a holiday-themed bout. They're older—forty-ish—and always said wrestling was on their bucket list. I trained them and had them perform at my buddy Jimmy Styer's show near Akron. They asked if they could do one more match but under a mask or some type of disguise."

"What's the angle?"

"I thought we could call it The Christmas Throwdown," Hank replied. "Mistletoe Mauler versus Kris the Kringle. I'll referee, and the two students will battle it out for Christmas supremacy.

He paused, then added, "I once saw a Grinch versus Santa match. It went over with the crowd but Grinch is trademarked and no one wants to see Santa get thrown around the ring, and Santa would be a little too on the nose anyway. This works better."

I nodded. "It's over-the-top—and that's exactly what we need."

After wrapping up with Hank, my phone buzzed again, and I saw Vito's name. I had worked with him for years. Vito's strength and the manner in which he carried himself made him a leader in the locker room among the other wrestlers. He has become one of the most respected wrestlers in the business, while at the same time positioning himself as one of the biggest heels with the fans.

On many occasions, Vito had spoken up when one of the wrestlers was being mistreated by the office. One time, he even threatened to walk out before one of the biggest Premium Live Events of the year. One of the female wrestlers, who went by the name of "Stacy's Mom from the Suburbs," complete with the Fountains of Wayne song as her theme music, was obviously being targeted by owner of the company, Don Kennedy.

Despite being known as one of the best female wrestlers in the world, Kennedy fired her right on the spot before the big show. This is someone who received Wrestler of the Year honors multiple times in her career and was always willing to help up and coming wrestlers. Kennedy's daughter Ashley, who was working as an assistant in the company, had been dating "Stacy's Mom," whose real name is Stephanie Keaton.

Vito had heard Kennedy made his daughter break things off with Stacy's Mom/Stephanie Keaton, and then fired her. Kennedy contended that it was due to Stacy's Mom/Stephanie Keaton's diminishing skills, but we all knew better. Kennedy never liked his daughter dating one of the "talent," as he often referred to us. Vito was scheduled to be in the main event and went into Kennedy's office and threatened to walk out if he went through with firing her. When Robbie, myself and several other wrestlers found out we backed up Vito to support her. Kennedy called the firing off, and even had *Stacy's Mom from the Suburbs* in Page's corner for a match that night.

While Kennedy never forgave Vito for taking such a stand, Stacy's Mom/Stephanie Keaton and Kennedy's daughter were married within a couple of years…with Vito Garramone's brother serving as officiant. Don Kennedy did not attend. We felt bad for Ashley, Kennedy's daughter. All of the wrestlers took her in like family as she traveled on the road with us and she seemed thrilled we were all there to celebrate the big day. Eventually, *Stacy's Mom from the Suburbs* contract expired and she went to work for Stuart Tanner. Even Kennedy's daughter Ashley took a job as a producer with Tanner and has moved up in Tanner's business. I am sure this infuriates Kennedy even more.

As I was quickly recalling Vito's standing up for other wrestlers, I picked up Vito's call. He immediately made me forget he is one of the best wrestling heels ever.

"Hey, Aaron," he said as I picked up "How's the family?"

"They're good, thanks. And yours?"

"My dad had dementia," Vito admitted softly. "It is terrible to see someone you love go through that. You are doing right by trying to spend as much time as you can with your mom."

"Thank you, Vito," I responded.

"Listen, since Kennedy won't let you wrestle at the show, we're bringing in The Foxx Denn for a live segment. You always know how to get the crowd fired up, and I don't want to put you in a bad spot with Kennedy."

"That sounds great. I'll be at the Fanfest, too. I hope we raise enough for the sensory room. My nephew's school just got one and my sister said it has been a godsend."

Then, with a mischievous laugh, Vito surprised me. "And about the match—I'm not sitting this one out. I know we can only advertise that I'll be on *The Foxx Denn* for the show, but how about having someone come out and challenge me, and we can have a match later in the show? By the time Kennedy hears about it…well, it'll be too late."

I hesitated. "Are you sure? Kennedy has a long memory when he's crossed."

Vito's voice carried a confident heel smirk. "*Fuhgeddaboudit,*" he said in his signature Italian accent. "Helping the kids means more to me than that old man."

"Alright, Vito," I agreed. "Thanks, man. I'll see you soon."

"Happy Holidays, Aaron, to you and your family. And my thoughts to your mom," he added.

"Thanks. Happy Holidays to you, too."

Later, Abby, the boys, and I grabbed a quick bite before we hurried off to meet the others and get our Christmas tree. Everyone was buzzing with holiday spirit.

Bobby tugged my arm. "Come see my tree!" he insisted.

We walked through the living room, and each ornament whispered a story—hand-painted baubles, snapshots of the boys growing up, even a photo of Abby in her cap and gown. I stopped beside the tree. "Is this when you got your teaching degree?" I asked.

"Yep," Abby replied with a proud smile, hugging her mom. "I moved in with her and went back to school. Mom was amazing. I couldn't have done it without her."

I squeezed her hand. "I may not have been around, but I'm so proud of you. I heard you worked at the library too, and you were raising the boys…finishing your license—that's incredible." In the background, Ricky zipped up his jacket while Bobby tugged on his winter gear. Soon, they reappeared, ready to go.

Bobby piped up, "Are we chopping down the tree?"

I laughed. "Not chopping it down, buddy. We always got our tree from a friend near Courthouse Square. I need your help to pick the perfect one."

Bobby grinned. "I remember when Dad took Ricky to cut down a tree in the forest."

Ricky wrapped an arm around Bobby. "I didn't even get to pick the tree or decorate anything back then." Ricky explained, in a disappointed tone. "It will be better this time, helping Coach Aaron pick his tree. And we will be doing it together."

Bobby hugged him tight. "You're the best big brother, Ricky."

Their bond shone through, a reflection of Abby's care. The boys dashed outside to check on the snowman we'd built the day before. Bobby even proudly fastened his play wrestling belt onto it. Walking up to the car, I smiled at Abby. "Your boys are amazing. You're doing such a fantastic job raising them."

Abby sighed. "Thanks. There were tough times, though. I should've let Richard go long ago. I tried keeping him involved, but he just stays in the loop without really engaging. Last Christmas, when they went to get that tree, Ricky was crushed. He felt like he was an afterthought. Not only was Bobby not included, but he was ignored by Richard. Ever since, things haven't been the same. I feel so awful for him. With the divorce and his dad always letting him down, he's had to face so much."

I gently touched her cheek. "I'm sorry you had to handle all that. Your cheeks are getting as red as your hair in the cold! Reminds me of that tobogganing trip."

Abby grinned. "That was the best. I felt sorry you were the only boy on that trip. We had Jenny, me, our friends…and you. You drove, got us hot chocolate, and even let me borrow your scarf."

I raised an eyebrow. "You remember that?"

"Of course," she replied with a tender smile. "You were always the sweetest."

I hesitated before confessing, "I have to admit, I had the Music Express plan in mind."

"The what?" she asked, puzzled.

"Remember the Music Express ride at Lake Amusement Park? Jenny and the girls crowded one car, and you and I were alone in the next. At full speed, you were pressed right into me. I figured if I went tobogganing with you, by chance the same thing could happen again."

Abby laughed and kissed my cheek. "Well, well…you were smoother than I gave you credit for."

From the back, Ricky shouted, "Let's go!" He jumped into a van. Abby's dad had a 14-passenger van he would use when he was alive to help the community's Chamber of Commerce transport dignitaries around. Her mom had kept it for some reason, and it was perfect for our purposes tonight.

Abby snatched the keys from me. "You're riding shotgun this time, Fabulous Freddy Foxx," she joked. Ricky and I helped Bobby buckle up, and I settled into the front seat. When we reached Mom's house, I slipped inside to get the rest of the family while Abby and the boys waited in the car.

"Hello, family!" I called as I stepped inside. In the living room, Mom, Jenny, Moira, and Margo were poring over photo albums.

"We're looking at Christmas photos from years past," Mom announced. Her tone was confident, and it warmed my heart to see her doing so well.

Moira pointed to a photo. "What's happening in this one?"

Jenny grinned. "That's a classic! Remember this, big brother?" I glanced at the picture: I looked about seven or eight, and Jenny was just a couple of years younger.

Mom explained, "This is from Christmas Eve. I always let your mom and Uncle Aaron open one gift each."

Margo cocked her head. "What were the gifts? Mom didn't seem too happy with hers."

I blushed. "I got a generic superhero action figure, but I look like I'm hoisting the Stanley Cup, I was so excited."

Jenny chuckled as we looked at the picture with her sad face, that looked like she'd lost a puppy. "I ended up with new towels. I kind of got short-changed that Christmas Eve," she added. "It's a hilarious picture, though. I even have the old school curlers in my hair."

Mom reminisced, "Remember how we always took pictures of everyone who came over to our house during the holidays standing in front of our Christmas tree?"

Margo added, "My Mom still snaps pics of anyone who stops by at Christmas time!"

Mom's eyes lit up. "Look at this one, Aaron." I sat beside her as she showed me a photo of young me with Dad and Mom in front of a tinsel-draped tree at one of our old apartments.

"Wow, Mom. Look at that—and now look at all you have." I could not help but sit there in disbelief in how far we'd come from where we began.

Mom smiled. "It was only me, you and your dad in that tiny apartment. Now I have you, Jenny, Moira, Margo, Randy—" She stopped as a puppy, who I had not seen before, came running up to her and barking, but in a small Yorkie bark, and licking my mom. "…and, of course, Dasher here."

"Uh, Who's Dasher? Where did Dasher come from? A new addition to our family?

Margo explained, "This is Dasher. He's a rescue Dad heard about from a friend. We're fostering him temporarily for now, but we want to keep him."

Dasher leaped into Mom's lap, her huge, soulful eyes melting everyone's heart. I joked, "Maybe she'll end up living with Grandma!" Laughter filled the room as we all knew how much joy this little pup brought Mom.

I glanced at my watch. "Are we ready to go? Abby and the boys are in the van."

Moira raised a picture. "Uncle Aaron, look at this!" She handed me a photo of Abby and me in front of a Christmas tree from over twenty years ago. I remembered this photo being taken. I'd kept it up in my room, often wondering why I couldn't be Abby's boyfriend instead of just her friend.

Teasing, I said, "Hey, did you see what I did to this photo?" I passed it to Jenny, who carefully unfolded a corner.

"I see what you did, but don't worry. I know it wasn't because you didn't want me in the picture," Jenny said, pausing for a moment. "It was because you wanted a photo of you and Abby together." Long ago I took the picture of Jenny, Abby and I in front of the Christmas tree and folded it so that it only showed Abby and I.

I felt my cheeks burn, and the family burst into laughter. Just then, Abby and the boys came in. "Hey, McClellan family," Abby said.

No sooner had they all stepped inside than someone yelled, "Abby, you have to look at this picture."

Jenny explained the now dog-eared appearance of the picture and, yes, my Scotch-Irish heritage turned my face more shades of red than John Cena had championship runs in wrestling.

"Okay, okay. You got Uncle Aaron," I said. Abby, sensing my embarrassment, came over, kissed me on the cheek in front of everyone, and said in a low voice, "Now, look how red *your* cheeks are. They're the color of my hair."

As we all laughed, Mom declared, "Once the tree is up, I want a picture of you two in front of it. We can even put your old one and the new one in a nice little frame."

I grinned as Randy arrived from work. He glanced at the photo and teased, "There's Uncle Aaron in his hair band phase—like you're in a Whitesnake cover band!" He was right, my hair at the time was beginning to rival Robbie's classic mullet.

More laughter followed, and soon we all boarded the van. Bobby then suggested, "Let's sing some Christmas carols on our way to get the tree!" Abby's angelic voice filled the air as we drove to the Christmas tree lot downtown.

We parked at the small lot run by Ralph—a friend of my dad's as long as I could remember. Without a word, each of us chose the same tree: not too big, not too small, perfectly shaped with strong, green needles. Ralph talked fondly about Dad, how they grew up together and how Dad had helped him when he returned from the military. I listened as he talked about the bond he and my dad had. I nodded. "Friends stick together," I added.

Ralph protested that we shouldn't pay for the tree, but we insisted. While the rest of the family fetched the van, Ralph and I hoisted the tree onto its roof and secured it with rope.

As the van was brought over, Ralph leaned closer. "Back in the day, your dad and I went to watch the greats—Bruno Sammartino, Rocky Johnson, Ivan Putski, Bobo Brazil, The Original Sheik. They all wrestled at the Falls Music Hall."

I smiled. "I remember that from Hank Hardway's stories. And now there's Holiday Headlock coming up, a fundraiser I'm helping put on at the school."

Ralph's eyes lit up, though I could tell times were tough. "Wow, that sounds amazing. I'd love to come, but…" He didn't finish.

"Ralph, thanks for being such a good friend to my dad," I said, extending my hand. Ralph shook my hand and then hugged me.

"Listen, we have some complimentary tickets we can give out for the fundraiser. I will make sure you get some. Do you have any family here?"

"I appreciate that. My son gets his son and daughter for the holidays. I'm sure they'd love to go," he responded.

"Then it's settled. I'll make sure we get you ten tickets to the show. That way the kids can bring friends if they want to."

Soon, Randy strolled up to see if we needed any help. Being the handy one in our family, he inspected the sturdy rope, making certain it had adequately secured the tree. Randy shook Ralph's hand. "I'm Randy, Aaron's brother-in-law."

"You married Jenny? Their dad was so proud of you both," Ralph said warmly.

I promised Ralph we'd be in touch about the *Holiday Headlock* tickets. Then, we headed back to Mom's house to decorate the family tree.

Ricky and I worked on getting the tree off the van's roof while everyone else scurried inside to set up lights and ornaments. Bobby offered to help, but shivered in the cold and led Abby to get hot chocolate instead. We needed a ladder for the high van, so I headed into the garage. There, Randy was pulling out trays of cookies stored in a spare fridge.

I frowned, wondering if we even had a ladder. After years away, I felt bad that I hardly knew what was in Mom's garage. Randy noticed. "Hey, Aaron, need something?"

"I'm looking for a ladder. It'd take Andre the Giant to reach the top of that van without one."

Randy scratched his head. "I think Jenny and I borrowed the ladder for some painting. I'll run home to get it."

While we chatted, a car door slammed. Looking up, I saw Ricky at the back of the van holding a ladder. It was the same one Ralph and I used when putting the tree on the top of the van. "Coach, this might work!" he yelled with a grin.

Ricky's calm, happy demeanor reminded me of that first day in the wrestling room. Abby had once confided to me, "Ricky always promises to take care of me and Bobby." He always seemed to have the look of someone that had the weight of the world on his shoulders. Truly, he had an old soul and a maturity beyond his years.

I shouted, "Brilliant!" in a playful, old Prescott Hiland style as Ricky held the ladder high, like a trophy. "I'll be right there."

I grinned at Randy. "Ralph must have stashed that ladder in the van for us."

Randy nodded. "I'm sure he did. You know, Ralph actually called Jenny when he heard about your mom having memory issues. He said if we needed anything to give him a call. He said he would have a tree delivered to our house and your mom's house if things got too busy for everyone."

My Dad had his challenges, but you don't build bonds like the one he did with Ralph without being a good friend.

Randy pointed at Ricky as he untied the rope securing the tree. "What a young man," he observed.

I smiled. "He is. So is Bobby." I paused. "Abby is one of a kind. To have so much thrown at her and raising those two boys so well."

Randy's tone grew serious. "Jenny and I are happy for you both. You deserve that love. But...do you know what you're going to do?" he asked

I looked puzzled. "What do you mean?"

He sighed. "Sorry, Aaron. I don't mean to pry. Jenny and I were talking. We're just worried about you as well as Abby and the boys. You all are getting so close, and we're worried that once you sign a new contract, you'll be gone again. Abby mentioned to Jenny that she heard you on the phone talking about it."

Seeing my discomfort, Randy patted my shoulder. "Sorry, man. I didn't mean to stick my nose in your business. We know you've thought about this. No matter what, we're here for you."

Randy and Jenny were right. Since returning to Deer Creek Falls, I'd wrestled with my choices. I hadn't planned to get this close to Abby and the boys. I confided, "I care so much about them. I don't want to hurt anyone by leaving. Can I tell you something in confidence?"

"Of course...it's in the vault...Dig It!" Randy says, trying his best to become Macho Man Randy Savage at that moment, attempting to lighten the moment.

I took a deep breath. "I'm seriously thinking of getting my teaching license and moving back here for good. Arlo said there's a huge need for special ed teachers. I love subbing and helping with the wrestling team. I've got a meeting with my boss, Don Kennedy, right after the *Holiday Headlock* show to decide my future."

Randy's eyes softened with concern. "That's a heavy load, Aaron. But I know you'll make the right decision. Jenny and I will be here for you, no matter what you decide."

Just then, Ricky rejoined us, clutching the ladder. "All set to get it off the van. Is this the family ladder?" he asked.

"No, it belongs to Ralph—the guy who sold us the tree," I replied.

"I'll return it," Randy offered. "His lot is on my way to work."

"Thanks, Randy," I said. Then I nudged Ricky, "Did your mom print the tickets for *Holiday Headlock*?"

"Yep. They look great, too. I told her no one has paper tickets anymore and then she went into a rant about the difference between an independent wrestling show and large-scale shows…I asked her who she was and how she knows so much about the wrestling business all of a sudden," Ricky said as the three of us shared a laugh.

"Randy, when you take the ladder back to Ralph, could you take him fifty complimentary tickets, instead of just ten? Tell him he can use them for his family, but if he wants to give some away to help his tree sales, that's cool too."

With that decided, we all headed back to the van. We unloaded the tree, took it inside, and set it up on the stand—ready to start our family Christmas celebration.

Chapter 18

We were gathered around the tree, surrounded by boxes of ornaments, when Mom grinned and said, "Remember when you were little? When we said, 'Let's trim the tree,' and you nearly bawled your eyes out the first time you heard that because you thought we were going to cut it all up?"

I remembered being about six or seven and too literal for my own good. "Don't remind me!" I said as laughter all around softened any sting of the story.

"From that day on," Mom continued with a twinkle in her eye, "we never called it trimming the tree, but decorating the tree instead."

Bursts of laughter mingled with shared stories as memories danced in the warm light of the room.

My mom always used a variety of decorations rather than a themed-based tree, or "mixing it all up" as she referred to it. Our tree was like a scrapbook of our lives. Handmade ornaments, commercial ornaments that characterized a popular moment in time like the *Sesame Street* character ornaments we had, and even a couple from when my mom was growing up.

Mom's fingers worked delicately as she hung each ornament. "Our tree is like a scrapbook," she explained, patting a glittered, round bulb. "My mom and grandma gathered the kids every year. They'd buy round green and red bulbs, each getting one with a kid's name in glitter. I still have two of them left, one green and one red."

I exchanged a meaningful look with the others, knowing this was one of Mom's good days. It did me good, hearing her tell the story.

When her hand began to tremble while placing another bulb, Bobby stepped forward. "Can I help?" he asked gently.

"Absolutely!" Mom replied, looking down with a smile. "Could you hang this one for me?"

Bobby reached up to the perfect spot. At that moment, Abby squeezed my hand, and Mom clapped her hands to announce, "Let's listen to some Christmas music!"

Randy fumbled with a CD, but Mom waved him off. "Margo, Moira, why don't you play some carols at the piano instead?"

The girls were happy to oblige. "Of course, Grandma. As long as you play with us!" they chorused, and soon the room filled with the twinkle of piano keys.

I recalled with pride how Mom once had been one of the best piano players in Ohio, as my aunt had once told me. Even with all her duties, music wove through our home. After I found success in the world of pro wrestling, I bought her the piano she had dreamed of owning. Jenny told me she played it often, so I was surprised she didn't sit right down and start playing. Tonight, she hesitated, and I wondered if she was worried about remembering the notes or simply wanted the spotlight on Moira and Margo.

We all sang and danced and laughed. Bobby dashed off to round up the Santa hats, and soon we were snapping photos by the tree.

Bobby then examined the red Christmas stockings, each one neatly tagged with a family name: Mom, Jenny, Aaron, Moira, Margo, and Randy. I smiled, remembering how, despite my time on the road, Mom and Jenny found a way to keep me a part of every cherished tradition.

Looking at Bobby, Mom said, "There are some missing stockings. Don't you agree, girls?"

Moira and Margo, still on the piano, nodded as Mom continued, "Girls, head to the basement. There's a bin marked 'Stockings' along with a craft box of glue and glitter. Bobby, why don't you, along with Ricky, help create stockings for you, Ricky, and your mom?"

Bobby's eyes lit up. "Really? Will you help, Ricky?" he asked.

"Of course, little brother."

Just then, Abby stepped in. "You don't have to do that. Your stockings are lovely and it is very nice of you to offer, but the boys have stockings at home. It's not necessary."

"Don't be silly," Mom insisted. "You three are family to us. Besides, it's always possible that someone could leave something here for any member of our family at Christmas…so we'd better have stockings ready."

Abby hugged Mom, and my heart felt like it might burst.

Soon, Moira, Margo, Ricky, and Bobby gathered around the kitchen table with craft supplies. "We got this!" they declared in confidence.

I glanced around, soaking in the pure happiness—Mom's joyful eyes, Abby's radiant smile, and the tender looks exchanged between Randy and Jenny. In that instant, I wished to bottle up the magic of Christmas so I could keep it close forever.

"Remember that Christmas Eve party?" Mom asked. "The one when your dad dressed as Santa and handed out gifts to every kid in the family."

"That was Dad?" I said teasingly.

Jenny and I burst into laughter. "Well, Mom, Santa was smoking the same brand of cigarettes as Dad, and drove us home in our station wagon after the party. So, we figured it out pretty quickly."

I didn't want Mom to think Dad's efforts had been in vain, so I added, "I loved it. I even asked Dad if I could be his elf the next year. He winked and said, 'Santa will have to think about that' in a warm voice I can still hear coming from my dad."

Mom smiled, and I continued, "The best part was when we got home and Santa and my mom put me and Jenny to bed. A few minutes later we heard a loud noise, like stomping on the floor or a man in a red suit going up a chimney. Of course, in our case it would've been one of those fake red corrugated cardboard brick fireplaces. About 10 seconds after the sound, my mom came in and said, "Santa left, Dad's home," and Dad walked into the room.

Even when I got older and wised up, I continued the playful mystery for Jenny. I turned to Mom and said, "You and Dad made Christmas magical."

Mom clapped her hands. "We should drive around and look at lights tonight like we used to. We still have the van here. Everyone can go."

Randy agreed at once, saying, "Absolutely! Let's check on the kids and head out when they're ready."

Time had flown by as we relived those cherished memories. In the kitchen, Jenny grabbed my arm. "Mom is really doing well. Being at home helps her," she said.

"It really does," I agreed.

Jenny's tone grew thoughtful. "But what about after the holidays? I worry about her care once work and school resume. Overnight stays might be an issue. I just hope it doesn't all slip back."

"I know. I worry too."

"What's your plan? "Jenny asked.

I smiled and explained, "I'm exploring a few options. I have a meeting with Kennedy in New York, and Tanner from LA has reached out. Miami is in the mix, too. They're all making a pitch."

Jenny raised her eyebrow. "Really? That sounds like a bidding war."

I laughed, "Not exactly. It's more like weighing my options. Honestly, Miami is offering everyone crazy money right now to steal them away from the big two in New York and LA. I have to follow up with New York and LA after *Holiday Headlock*. We'll see what happens."

Before I could explain further, Abby appeared. I wondered how much she had heard. She gave me a puzzled look but recovered quickly and said, "Your mom is wonderful, and she's always so kind with my boys."

Jenny hugged Abby tightly. "Are we ready to see some lights?" I asked.

"Yes," Abby said eagerly. "But later, can you drop us off at home? We started the day at my house in the van."

"Of course," I replied. "Is your mom home? We can pick her up and ride together."

"I'll call her now," Abby said.

We gathered everyone and drove to Abby's house. As Abby headed inside with the boys to fetch her mom, we admired the brilliant yard of lights and festive decorations.

Randy remarked, "Why don't any single bulbs ever go out anymore? LED lights, perhaps? I remember as a kid everyone who put up lights had some go out."

Jenny, Mom, and I giggled. Randy turned to us and said, "Oh boy, I think I'm in for another McClellan family story."

I laughed even more and said, "When we were kids, Dad and his buddy Ralph pranked each other all the time. One night when we got home from looking at lights, every other bulb on our string of Christmas lights was off! Dad inspected them, totally confused. On the door, Mom found a note from Ralph: 'Fix your lights—they're an embarrassment!' with a tiny smiley face wearing a Santa hat.

"We thought Dad was going to lose it for a minute, but he burst out laughing. He went out and screwed every other bulb back in. When he finished, he called Ralph and said, 'Well done, my good man.' It was all in good fun."

Laughter filled the van as we drove through Deer Creek Falls and neighboring towns, marveling at dazzling displays, from quaint old neighborhoods to lively suburban streets and peaceful rural roads.

Sharing this with someone I was falling in love with was magical. Abby and I held hands the entire trip around town as Bobby and Ricky looked at the lights in wonder. Moira and Margo provided a running commentary, no doubt sharing stories they'd picked up over the years from their parents.

Jenny reminded us of the year Mom invented fake holidays. "Remember when you came home for your freshman year at Christmas? Mom had just finished her nursing shift. She told us she'd be working on Christmas Day, so we celebrated on December 26—our very first 'Fake Christmas' as it came to be known. It even spread to Fake Easter and Fake New Year's some years, all the while Mom worked hard taking care of people at the hospital and her family."

I did remember it well. My freshman year of college was the year fake holidays were born.

Chapter 19

It was late when we pulled up to Abby's place and as I went for a goodbye kiss with Abby, my phone rang. I frowned, wondering who could be calling so late. When I glanced at the screen, though, the California area code made sense. I saw Stuart Tanner's name, labeled "Tanner West Coast Wrestling" in my contacts, Abby noticed it too.

I hesitated. "I have to take this call," I said, glancing at Abby with worry. She seemed a little put out but nodded. "It's okay, Aaron. See you soon. Good night."

As I answered Stuart's call, I stopped, sensing something was amiss. "Abby. Sorry. I just have to…"

"It's okay," she said, one hand already opening the door. "You have things to do, contracts to discuss, negotiate. I get it. We can catch up when you have time."

But I didn't want to wait for later. I asked Tanner if I could call him back in a half hour, and he agreed. I hung up and turned around to the door, but Abby had already closed it. My heart sank.

I climbed back into the van, silent. Jenny and Randy were chatting, but I just sat there, quiet and lost in thought.

"Earth to Aaron, you there?" Jenny asked.

"Yeah, I'm here."

"Are you going to see Abby tomorrow?" she asked.

"Not sure," I admitted, worried about how things had been left with Abby just now. I knew we would be in touch again about the *Holiday Headlock* fundraiser but really was not sure how soon to contact her with how the night had just ended.

Then Moira chimed in. "Uncle Aaron, can I post our picture on social media? One of my friends doesn't believe my uncle is Fabulous Freddy Foxx. I can text it to you."

I chuckled. "Sure." I did hope Abby would see the photo of all of us from Moira's post and remember the good times we have been having.

Jenny turned to the girls. "Hey, before we drop off Uncle Aaron and Grandma, do you want to give him the gift you made?"

I looked around, confused. "It's not Christmas yet. Are you sure?"

"Yes," Jenny insisted and leaned closer. "You look like you need it."

Margo handed me a small package. Inside was a picture frame holding the old picture of Abby and me alongside the newer one. "Wow. How'd you do this so fast?" I asked, impressed.

"We didn't spend the whole time making stockings," Margo explained with a grin. "Dad had an extra frame that worked, and Moira and I printed the photos. Do you like it?"

"I love it," I said, smiling.

And when I got home, I put it on the end table beside me. I hoped I wasn't ruining everything, but I had some calls to make.

I picked up the phone and dialed.

"Stuart Tanner."

I always thought it was interesting that he answered directly. I had to get Don Kennedy through his assistant, but Stuart answered himself. It might've been the upbringing he had. I remember reading about him for the first time in a college business class. He was being honored by an African American business organization for using his success to help other African American-owned businesses. He'd created company after company, each one more successful than the last. The best part was that he'd paid off his parent's mortgage after his first business success.

"Mr. Tanner, how are you?" I began.

"I'm good, Aaron," he replied. "Remember buddy, its Stuart. How is your mom? I hope she's doing well?"

"She has had some really good days as of late. My sister and I are surprised—you wouldn't notice any problem from a visit."

"That's wonderful. Is she home for the holidays?"

"Yes," I answered. "We asked if she could spend them with us in her home. The nurses agreed, as long as she is not left alone." I paused. "I fear the good days she's having are because she is in such a familiar and comfortable environment."

His voice softened with empathy. "My brothers and I struggled with our parents too. I feel for you, my friend."

After a pause, he went on. "I know you have a lot on your plate, but I wanted to call and check in." I was waiting for the follow up question.

What was my decision on the contract? Did I have any interest in signing with him? I braced myself, unsure how to answer.

But it was then he continued to both surprise me and, in many ways, show me there was still humanity in people. "Aaron, I wish I could make things easier for you and your family. I know you're going through a lot right now. I support a few causes in memory care and dementia. Just let me know."

It was then I began to believe his kindness wasn't trans-actional. I thought of a story I'd heard about him years ago. A wrestler I have known for many years named Cal Muccio went to work for Stuart after he and I had worked together in New York. Cal was a great worker but never made it past mid-card status in New York.

Stuart saw the talent Cal had and "repackaged" him into a slicked back, smooth talking, gold chain wearing, unbeatable superstar that would forever be known to wrestling fans as one name: Calderone. Cal, or as everyone now knows him as Calderone, became the top star for Tanner's wrestling promotion making millions for him and the company, which makes what Tanner did for him even more altruistic.

Cal had called me about a year ago to check in and see how things were, and I found out his older sister needed a kidney transplant. He told me how Stuart Tanner pulled him off the road and sent him home to help with his sister and that he never missed a paycheck the entire time. Tanner also was instrumental in using his resources to help find a transplant match which saved his sister's life.

Cal said Stuart wanted nothing in return. No pressure to sign a longer-term exclusive deal. Just a nice gesture that changed the lives of the wrestler known as Calderone and his family for the better.

"I appreciate it, Stuart," I answered, still thinking of the life-changing kindness he showed Cal and his family. "Actually, I'm putting together a charity wrestling show for my hometown school. We're raising money to build a sensory room for special needs kids. Any help would mean a lot."

He answered at once. "Aaron, I'd be glad to help. Let me look into a few things and get back to you tomorrow. My first thought is sending you a few of our wrestlers to put on the card, hopefully help you drive up ticket sales. We're in your region that week with some of our team. We'll make something work."

"Thanks, Stuart. This means a lot," I said, feeling a bit overwhelmed.

"Happy to help. I'll be in touch tomorrow," he responded.

The next morning, we had wrestling practice at the school. High school sports never stopped for the holidays. I was supposed to meet Abby after practice to check on ticket sales. But before that, I decided to visit Arlo in his office.

Inside, I found Abby with Johnny's mom. I asked, "What are you two up to?"

Abby smiled and said, "There are so many ticket calls for the show. I'm here returning calls and handling requests." Johnny's mom added, "I wanted to help as much as I can too. Johnny and Mark are excited to be part of this Aaron, what a nice way to give back to your hometown."

"We could not do it without everyone's help," I said, which is for sure the case. There are as many moving parts to this as Chris Jericho has wrestling holds.

"Now we know why Ticketmaster replaced calling in for tickets," Arlo said as he walked out of his office and into the common area. "Remember, back in the day, how we had to stand in line for tickets outside to get tickets for a show when they went on sale? Those days are long gone, aren't they?" he added.

Abby shrugged. "Well, even though selling tickets from the office and phone calls is old school, it seems to be working. We've sold half of the gym out already and many tickets for the Fan Fest. You were right, Aaron. When we announced Vito Garramone was going to be here, the Fan Fest show ticket requests went crazy. We may need to move it to another location but keep the wrestling show in the gym," she added.

"That's great news. Remember though, its pronounced Gar-a-MOAN-A" I joked using Vito's over the top Italian accent.

I sensed she was keeping business and personal feelings separate, after the awkwardness of the other night. What was happening with our budding romance? I wanted to ask, but I knew there was a better time and place.

Instead, I turned to Arlo and asked, "What do you think about the Fan Fest location?"

"How about using the elementary school?" he suggested. "It has its own gym and auditorium, and it's right here in the same complex."

"That's a great idea," Abby agreed. "Is that okay, Aaron?"

"Of course," I said with a smile. "Thank you both."

"Time for practice," Arlo said. On our way to the wrestling room, I asked, "Listen, if I'm sponsored by the school and use substitute teaching time for classroom hours, do you really think I'll have my full teaching license by the end of summer?"

He looked at me and grinned. "I guarantee it. I've helped other people on similar paths. You were almost licensed before, remember? Even though it was twenty years ago," he added with a joking smile.

We stopped outside the gym. "So, you're really thinking of doing this?" he asked.

"I'm strongly considering it," I admitted. "I love working with kids and the wrestling team. I might miss the ring, but I was thinking about talking with Hank Hardway about buying his ring and pro wrestling academy when he moves to Vermont."

He nodded; his joking smile gone. "It's a lot to think about. With your mom's recent health issues, you coming off the road, having to think about your next contract…That's a lot for anyone to deal with." He opened the door to the wrestling room, and we could see Ricky working with Bobby on the mat. "And, of course, I know there's Abby and the boys." Arlo emphasized.

Arlo put his hand on my shoulder and gave me a look of encouragement and confidence.

Spending a couple of hours working with the team was just what I needed. Time flew by. The team was thriving. There was

Michelle, who looked set to be a state champion, and Ricky, who was performing high enough to earn a wrestling scholarship. I was working with some of the team in my role as Substitute Teacher and it really made me feel like I was making a difference. Pro wrestling has been great to me financially which has provided me the opportunity to help my family and friends, as well as meet so many great fans and see the world. I could not help my mind continuing to wander thinking about a new life as a teacher and coach in my hometown, with my dream girl by my side. I thought, maybe the idea of an Aaron 2.0 was what I have been after all along.

After practice, Abby asked if I'd bring the boys to the office where she was still coordinating the fundraiser. Ricky was doing some post-practice cooldown stretches while I worked with Bobby. Bobby asked me about coming over to play with his wrestling action figures with him. "I have some of Ricky's wrestling dolls from when he was little. Sometimes he'll still play with me," Bobby said as Ricky looked over.

I grinned. "What do you have planned?"

Ricky walked over before his brother could answer and said, "We should do that Main Event you wanted to do."

"Main Event…what Main Event?" I asked.

Bobby grinned as he jumped up. "You'll see. Can you come over today?"

"Let's see what your mom has to say," I answered. I was not sure if Abby was ready for me to head back over to their house so soon.

Ricky followed us with worry in his eyes. "Coach Aaron, is my mom okay? She's been quieter than usual."

"I'm sure she's busy, Ricky. We've got a lot going on for the fundraiser."

We walked up to the superintendent's office together. Abby had just finished a phone call when Bobby ran over to her. "Mom, can Coach Aaron come play wrestling dolls with me?" he asked.

"Sure, Bobby." Then she looked at me. "Ticket sales are going great. We did some budget planning and it looks like the sponsorships and Fan Fest will clear a profit. It may not be fifty grand, but it will help a ton."

"I'm supposed to get another call from Stuart Tanner. He is thinking about letting us use some of his talent at the show. That would be huge. If they come in for the Fan Fest and the wrestling show, we may get to our $50,000 after all."

Abby's face brightened at first, but each time I mentioned Tanner or Kennedy, a flicker of concern crossed her eyes.

As we headed to her house, Abby explained we could use her mom's 14-passenger van to pick up the wrestlers. "Randy will drive," she told me. "I'm planning the seating and ticket layout. Jenny, Moira, and Margo are on Fan Fest admissions. Moira and Margo even came up with a Golden Ticket idea—one ticket for the show plus an autograph from every wrestler. She thinks we should price it at $250. Is that too steep?" she asked.

"It provides a choice to the fans. I don't think there is anything to lose going with a Golden Ticket option," I answered.

Abby was amazing with details. With her business sense and Hank Hardway booking the show, my confidence soared.

At Abby's house, before checking out Bobby's wrestling dolls, I spoke with her mom while Abby prepared hot chocolate for the boys. Her mom recalled, "You know, I took Bobby and Ricky to one of your shows in Youngstown a few years ago."

"Really?" I said. "I wish I'd known you were there. I would've upgraded your seats, brought you all to the back to meet the wrestlers."

"It's okay. The boys loved it. They couldn't believe you went to their school. They even made signs at home to take in with them."

Bobby couldn't wait anymore. I followed him to his room where he had set up an entrance for his action figures. Ricky came in and asked, "Is this the Main Event you've been talking about?"

Bobby proudly displayed his dolls, Robbie and me represented in action figures from our Ian and Prescott Hiland days. Honestly, I still had trouble believing there were action figures of me in the world.

"Look, you're against Jason and Justin Journey—the Journey Boys!" Bobby declared.

They were top tag champs under Stuart Tanner. Their high-flying style had always been a draw, and fans loved the fantasy matchups. Bobby was onto something.

Bobby used his best ring announcer voice: "The match is set: Journey Boys versus Hilanders!"

Robbie and I were finishing our run of tag team champions in Don Kennedy's wrestling promotion about the time the Journey Boys swept on the scene in Stuart Tanner's promotion. Unfortunately, we have never crossed paths in the ring. There were always dream matches talked about and The Hilanders vs The Journey Boys was a top one for wrestling fans everywhere.

Ricky helped Bobby, creating an entrance podium and Bobby played our rockin' Hilander bagpipe theme as the opposing Journey Boy's action figure team entered with a fast-paced pop anthem. I watched, amused. I couldn't remember the last time I'd done anything like this. The imagination that Bobby had was invigorating. It wasn't about winning for him; it was pure fun.

Bobby gathered all his vintage figures. He even had some early AWA wrestling dolls that were a couple of generations older than the new ones he had. I remembered these well, as my dad passed his down to me when I was a kid. They all used the same bodies as He Man and the Masters of the Universe action figures. It was obvious to me that they used the same molds when making the AWA wrestling dolls as they did the Masters of the Universe. Legendary wrestler Larry Zbyszko's action figure had the same body style, complete with ripped abs, as

He Man villain Skeletor, while the real Larry Zbyszko was built more like an everyman.

Soon, we were caught up in a whirlwind of matches. Time flew as Bobby had me do a *Foxx Denn* in the ring using my Fabulous Freddy Foxx action figure to interview several different wrestlers one at a time.

Then Abby called out, "One more match, Bobby. It's dinner time, and I'm sure Coach Aaron has a lot to do."

I looked at Bobby and said, "What do you think, my man? Who will be in our last match?"

"How about champion vs. champion?" Ricky suggested. "Vivo Garramone versus Shady Shelby Peters?"

Bobby beamed as this was another match wrestling fans dreamed would one day happen.

About fifteen minutes later, Abby appeared at the door. "Dinner's ready, boys." She paused, then asked quietly, "Aaron, would you like to stay for dinner?"

I was surprised by the gentle tone in her voice. "Absolutely," I replied.

We all headed downstairs together, ready to share a meal after an evening filled with calls, promises, and a bit of wrestling magic, as well as the hope of things to come.

Chapter 20

We sat down for dinner, and my phone buzzed. It was a text from Stuart Tanner. Abby's eyes flicked to my screen and her expression told me everything I needed to know. I hesitated. I wanted to focus on Abby and the boys, and I worried she might think Tanner's calls were about my future contract rather than anything else.

I quickly replied, **I'll call you in 30 minutes.**

Bobby and Ricky were still riding the high from our impromptu wrestling show. "Remember that awesome Scottish Splash?" Bobby cheered, and Ricky chimed in with ideas about who should go head-to-head next. Their innocent excitement was contagious.

"Ticket sales are through the roof," Abby said as we ate. "People are coming from all over, both for the show and Fan Fest." She slid a budget sheet across the table. "Talent isn't cheap, though, I do worry about clearing enough of a profit," she added.

I remembered my early days in the business. "I once told a promoter I'd work for free in my early days, just to get some experience," I said. "But he pulled me aside and said, 'No one works for me for free. You earn every dollar you make.' I never forgot that. When paying for talent, and you add in travel and other expenses, it does get expensive."

Abby sighed. "We're looking likely to break even at this point, Aaron," she admitted, disappointment filling her tone.

"Food and merchandise might pull us ahead. I'll try and reach out to some others. Come up with some different ideas. Maybe there's a miracle yet," I said

Abby waved off my concern with a gentle smile. "Go ahead and make your calls, Aaron. Even if we don't meet our goal, the boys, the school, and the town will have a great time watching the show and meeting the wrestlers."

I started to respond, but she added, "I know Bobby and Ricky will love every minute of it. Now, I need to grab the boys and take them to Richard's." Her tone was quiet—the kind I hadn't heard from Abby since I returned to Deer Creek Falls.

I sensed that Abby was steering clear of a heavier conversation. Maybe she worried that if I left, the boys would be hurt all over again. I swallowed my concern and said nothing. I had a lot to consider, and I wasn't close to deciding yet. I said my goodbyes and left, heading home.

The familiar creak as I walked up to Mom's porch reminded me why home always felt right. *Moms always know what to do.* Stepping inside, I found my mother waiting for me with a warm embrace.

"What's up, Fabulous Freddy Foxx? You're a bit off today," she said, her eyes searching mine.

I managed a small smile. "You're right, Mom. I'm sorry. But first, how are you? How was your day?" I knew she'd spent a good bit of the day alone. It was unexpected as Moira and Margo had a holiday speech and debate party and Jenny had to work. Randy had planned to be home all day, but was called away for an issue at his job.

Mom confessed, "I spent most of it by myself. I missed having someone around, you know?" Her concern was palpable in every word.

"I understand, Mom."

"Are you okay?" she asked.

I hesitated, then said, "We're just breaking even on the wrestling show. I was really hoping it would do better and fund the sensory room for the kids." The weight of my words hung heavy between us.

"And?" Her voice dropped, "What about Abby?"

I paused, choosing my words carefully. "I don't want to hurt Abby…or the boys."

Mom squeezed my hand. "What do you mean? You and Abby seem to be getting along so well, working together on the show and raising money for a good cause. You two are the cutest couple, by the way. You know I always wanted you to get together when you were in high school. When she married Richard, it turned my stomach."

I rubbed the back of my neck. "She's great. I love Bobby and Ricky. But if I go back on the road with wrestling, I worry I won't come back much. I fear I'll disappoint them like Richard did. She overheard me talking to some of the promoters, and I'm sure she's thinking, '*Here we go*. He comes in, gains the trust and love of my kids, and then decides to leave.'"

I looked down. "I don't blame her for feeling that way."

"*Are* you going back on the road?" she pressed gently.

I shook my head, steadying my voice. "I don't think so. I really love teaching and coaching, and being back home in Deer Creek Falls where my friends and family are. It's hard to imagine being away from all of this. And Abby and the boys…I'm not sure I would be able to be out on the road without missing them. It would be hard to maintain the kind of edge I need as a pro wrestler, knowing the ones I love are back home."

I took both her hands in mine. "That includes you, Mom. You are doing so well. I was thinking…if I come back for good, I could live here. Maybe the doctors would let you move back home?"

Mom's eyes sparkled with warmth. "Do what feels best, Aaron. You've built a phenomenal career. You have fans everywhere. You run all over the world with Robbie. I'm no expert, but I read, and I know you're one of the best wrestling personalities of all time. It is not going to be easy for you to give that up…and I'm sure there will be a bidding war for that one last contract, so good you may never have to work again."

She paused as she continued looking me straight in the eyes, saying all of this. "My sweet son, whatever you decide will be the right decision." She kissed me on the forehead.

I managed a grateful smile. "Thanks, Mom. I've got a few calls to return about the show. You relax, okay?"

She laughed softly. "I have tea, a new cozy mystery, and Dasher is snuggled at my feet. Go on, then."

I sent Stuart Tanner a quick text to let him know I'd call. When I did call, he answered right away.

"Hey Aaron, how's your mom?" he asked.

"She's doing great. Home suits her well," I replied.

"That's good to hear," he said. "Listen, we'll be in your area when this tour wraps up, just before your show. And by the way, *Holiday Headlock* is a killer name!"

I chuckled. "Thank you, Mr. Tanner."

"It's Stuart." He reminded me.

"I just don't think I could call you anything but Mr. Tanner," I said.

He laughed. "Fair enough, Mr. Foxx. I've been thinking, Aaron. I'm giving the roster the rest of the year off after that last show. I met with them the other day to go over things and a few of them asked about taking part in *Holiday Headlock*. I asked if they were serious, just to make sure, as you know how nice having a few days off in this business is, and how rare it can be."

"I appreciate that."

"Once many of them knew I was okay with it, they signed up, I mean literally signed up. Shady Shelby Peters literally created the sheet and hung it up…signing it first," Tanner shared.

I raised my eyebrows. I knew Shady, but we weren't really close. Vito always raved that Shady was one of the best heels in the business, arguably the meanest of them all, and that's coming from a legendary heel himself.

There's a classic story about Shady wrestling at the Sea World Ski Stadium, which they'd convert into a wrestling venue once a year. It already had the perfect setup—lights, pyrotechnics, and sound. When I first heard the story, it reminded me of the yearly trips my grandparents took us on to Sea World, where the Super Friends-themed ski show was a highlight. I truly believed I was seeing Batman, Superman, and my favorite of all, Robin.

I'll never forget the last time we went, when I was about ten. I had the best seat ever and couldn't wait for the show. But as the boat approached, I realized something was off—no superheroes. No Batman, No Robin…not even Aquaman! Just guys in straw hats and bibbed overalls yelling "HATFIELDS!" and "MCCOYS!" I was crushed. My mom always told the story of how I sat there pouting, arms crossed, completely unimpressed with the hillbilly replacements for my beloved Super Friends.

Stuart went on, bringing me back to the present, his voice animated. "Remember Shady's infamous night at the Sea World Ski Stadium when he was facing the Broadway Brawler? Shady strutted in, grabbed the mic from the announcer, and the crowd roared with boos as he sneered. 'Are you all here for the Broadway Brawler?' he asked as cheers broke out."

The Broadway Brawler was a popular world champion at the time, so the match was going to be a classic good vs evil battle. Brawler had just made the save of another beloved fan favorite earlier in the night and as part of a video package shown before his introduction, they showed him visiting a community center near Sea World that many in the crowd were familiar with. Broadway Brawler, introduced hailing from Broadway in the Heart of Manhattan, as opposed to Shady hailing from the Island of Alcatraz, comes out with a mini Rockette-style kick line when introduced…pure showmanship.

I recalled the scene vividly, and affirmed to Tanner as he continued, "Of course I remember. And we know what happened next?"

"Oh, yeah," Tanner replied, excited to continue the story. "Shady continued yelling at fans for supporting the Broadway Brawler, 'Everyone is a Broadway Brawler fan. Like you over there, you, old lady.' Then he turned his attention to an unassuming young boy in the audience. 'Hey kid. Yes, you. Did you hear the news? Did you all hear the news? All you snotty-nosed little brats. Your pathetic parents probably brought you hear today to see the otters, sea lions, seals, and oh yeah, Shamu…well you have to have heard the news though. Shamu's dead. He died. DEAD.'"

Tanner paused. "Now, I wasn't there to see it, but like everyone else in the business, I heard about it immediately. Plastic bottles being thrown at him, kids crying, adult fans yelling at him and some of the more passionate moms and dads rushing the stage trying to get their hands on him! Parents were furious."

"And the match didn't even happen," I chimed in, "as Brawler was attending to the child, Shady was pointing at the child who would likely be traumatized for life. Shady was banned from the property for life, right?"

"Indeed," Stuart said. Then his tone brightened. "Despite all that, getting Shady on the card for *Holiday Headlock* is a huge win."

Then his voice softened. "Aaron, before I list the others coming to help the cause, I have big news. My board just approved a $50,000 sponsorship donation for *Holiday Headlock*."

I nearly dropped the phone. "Stuart, I—thank you. This is unbelievable. It means we might actually fund the sensory room!"

His voice was warm and sincere. "You're welcome, Aaron. You've done so much for this business and the fans. It's the least we can do. And no strings attached—this is all for the kids in your hometown."

He added quickly, "I'll email you the details. Justin and Jason Journey are coming too. Could you call them to set everything up?"

"Absolutely," I said. "Thank you so much, Stuart. Please thank everyone for me."

"Will you be able to attend?" I asked, hoping our kids and community could show him our appreciation in person.

"I'm not sure yet. I have to meet with my family to see what things look like for the holiday season. Keep in touch, Aaron, and let me know if you need anything else. Take care, my friend," he said, ending the call.

"Thank you again. You're the best," I said to him, and meant it. Sitting there, I couldn't wait to tell Abby about all that had happened.

Chapter 21

I woke up the next morning feeling like I had finally slept soundly for the first time in years. The light crept in, and I murmured, "This is it, a real night's sleep in a real bed." Tanner's generous donation had lifted a huge weight off our shoulders. Mom was having good day after good day. I was heading to my high school alma mater to teach for the day, followed by coaching after school. Abby had texted and asked to have dinner that night as the boys were going shopping with Abby's mom to shop for Christmas gifts for Abby.

I couldn't help but grin at the promise of sharing the good news with Abby and warm moments later that night.

The day sped by. After practice, I pulled Arlo aside. In a hushed voice, I confided, "Tanner donated $50,000. Keep it under your hat for now."

His eyes lit up with excitement as he replied, "You're kidding? This is huge!" Later, I drove Bobby and Ricky over to Abby's mom's place. When Abby arrived, we headed out together.

Our first stop was our hometown chocolate shop. "Which chocolate Santa is it today?" I asked, holding up plain Santas, peanut butter Santas, all the different choices on display. Abby laughed and said, "Bobby only loves the peanut butter ones, and if it is not from Falls Chocolate Shoppe, he will know." We tucked it safely in the car, joking, "The cold does the job better than a fridge." No chance of the chocolate melting tonight. In our part of the country though you must be ever vigilant when preparing for weather. As the saying goes, if you do not like the weather, wait just a minute, it will change.

We then headed downtown to the Vintage Vinyl shop. Amidst the bustle of Deer Creek Falls' busy sidewalks, Abby's eyes were sparkling as she flipped through classic albums. She told me that Ricky's taste in music definitely matched his old soul nature. She scored an REO Speedwagon album to put under the tree.

As we strolled on through the crisp winter air, I couldn't hold the secret any longer. "Abby," I blurted out, "Tanner donated a massive fifty thousand dollars to our fundraiser!"

She stopped suddenly and pulled me into an embrace. Without a word, she took my face in her hands and pressed a long, soft kiss against my lips. When we finally pulled apart, she squeezed my hand and said, "Aaron, this is overwhelming—in all the best ways."

Not long after, we bumped into Johnny and Mark who, when we showed them the albums we just bought at Vintage Vinyl, shared with us that they had bought Vintage Vinyl a few years back and were heading there now. Mark added, "We're gearing up for *Holiday Headlock*. Need extra hands?" Johnny and Mark, much like Abby, have obviously become staples of the Deer Creek Falls community. Everyone knows them and many count on them for things large and small.

Abby had a job hand-picked for them. "You're on sound duty now. Meet us Friday in the gym for a volunteer meeting." Johnny and Mark of course were up to the challenge. They both said they would bring their families and their sound equipment to the show.

As we chatted, I couldn't help but think, *Triple A is really in the zone tonight.*

Before leaving, I couldn't help myself and went back into the record shop with Johnny and Mark. Them purchasing Vintage Vinyl had added meaning, as this was where we had our first Nordic Blood gig many years ago. Before I left, I grabbed a few more albums for Ricky—old favorites like Greetings from Asbury Park, Rumours, and Purple Rain—a nod to his timeless taste.

That evening, we settled into Deer Creek Falls' best Italian restaurant. Maybe I should've left well enough alone, but I couldn't help myself. I told Abby again, "I am so grateful to Stuart Tanner. This donation finally gives us room to breathe."

Her smile remained soft but quiet. No words.

"Aren't you excited about it?" I asked. "I just thought…" I trailed off, searching her eyes for reassurance.

She reached out, took my hands, and fixed her gaze on me. "Aaron," she said, voice steady, "Tanner's generosity is something I'll never forget. But I know you have your dreams too."

Before I could answer, she went on, "I know Tanner thinks a lot of you. I'm sure he hopes by doing this it will convince you to sign with him. It's okay. I understand. That's how business works. I stand by whatever decision you make. If you go back and work for New York, sign with Stuart…whatever you decide."

My heart felt like it might explode and my mind was racing. She knew so much, sensed things I hadn't spoken aloud. Finally, I stuttered, "I love teaching…and I love your boys...and I love you."

Her gaze caught mine and held it for what felt like forever. Tears shimmered below the surface, but she was smiling. Her gentle reply came almost as a whisper, "I love you too, Aaron. So much. But I don't want me, my boys, or anything else standing in your way."

"It's not like that," I began, but just then, Arlo approached, introducing his wife with a friendly smile. We stayed for a long time, closing down the restaurant. And once we got back to the car and it was just the two of us, I decided not to bring it all back up, but to talk instead about the gifts she bought for the boys and plans for Christmas.

After our final wrestling practice before break, Hank, Arlo, and I gathered with the team. We surprised them with a visit from Coach Miller. He was looking a bit thinner than before his medical treatments, but still filled with energy, he lingered to chat. Hank and I discussed Tanner's new talent for the upcoming event. Coach Miller spoke up, smiling despite his obvious fatigue. "You all are doing such a nice thing for our kids. Can't wait to see this."

Before leaving, he announced, "I'm retiring on January 1st. I want to do right by the team." He'd wanted to stay longer, he explained, but the treatments were wiping out his energy. We thanked him warmly and planned to continue dedicating the season to his influence on so many wrestlers and the school.

On our way out, Arlo and I stopped by the display of trophies and photos from our Coach's heyday. "I'm thinking of setting up a scholarship in his name," I said. "It's the least I could do."

Arlo grinned. "That would be nice," he said. "Maybe we could also rename the wrestling room for Coach Miller instead of Dobbins?"

I agreed wholeheartedly.

That evening, Abby presided over a spirited volunteer meeting for *Holiday Headlock* in the school's commons. Christmas music played lightly in the background and chatter filled the room as she coordinated arrangements for transportation, security, seating, lighting, and sound. "Hotels are full, and fans are coming in droves," she announced. "Thank you, everyone. These kids will soon have a sensory room, thanks to all of your efforts."

Abby called me forward. I cleared my throat for the gathered volunteers. "Stuart Tanner donated fifty thousand dollars," I announced. The room erupted in cheers and gasps of astonishment. I worried for a moment that the drive to raise money might fizzle out, that with the news of such a large donation, we would all become complacent. In true Deer Creek Falls fashion, the volunteers were fired up even more to make this the best fundraising event ever. There was talk of starting a fund for a sensory room at each building.

As the meeting wound down, a few students and volunteers started cleaning up.

"Triple A, you never miss a detail," I said as she explained how local radio and TV stations had reached out for interviews about both the wrestling event and the new sensory room.

She smiled and blushed. "I'm lining up as many Zoom spots as I can," she said with determination.

I glanced at my watch. Christmas was a mere six days away, and *Holiday Headlock* was a mere eight! My mind raced with final plans—the card needed refining, media releases had to roll out, and I still had to get Abby a Christmas gift. Hank and I agreed to meet the next day to finalize the card, while I planned to pick up Abby's present on Sunday.

The following day, Arlo, Hank, and I journeyed with the team to Cleveland for a pivotal match. The stakes were high, as the best wrestlers from our region were about to vie for a state championship spot. "We've got real talent this year," I remarked as we prepared for the competition.

Among our brightest were Michelle Stephens and Ricky. Michelle was the daughter of a friend I'd had in high school. He'd been on the wrestling team with us. He was a little older, Arlo's age, and Michelle had obviously inherited some of her father's skills, but, most of all, she had his work ethic. No one was going to outwork Michelle Stephens. She reminded me in many ways of Ricky, who worked as hard as anyone in the state of Ohio towards the goal of a state championship.

It was good to hang out with Abby and Bobby all day as we waited for Michelle and Ricky to compete. We all kept each other busy, laughing, singing Christmas carols, and trying not to eat too many cookies while Michelle and Ricky stayed in the zone. At one point, Abby and I slipped into a quiet room at the arena for a Zoom interview with a local NBC affiliate.

The reporter's eyes widened in disbelief as he blurted, "Sold out? That's incredible!" Abby smiled and told him, "We keep getting calls for tickets, even though none are left. But don't forget the Fan Fest—everyone's invited!"

After returning to the busy main hall, we noted that there were only minutes until Michelle's match and a few more before Ricky took the mat. Abby leaned close and whispered, "Should we try shifting the event to a bigger venue?"

I shook my head. "I don't think we can. Too short of a notice, and the much larger ones are a bit of a drive away from Deer Creek Falls," I answered. "It's too bad we couldn't do closed circuit."

Arlo's laugh rang out. "That's why they call you Analog Aaron! Closed circuit isn't really a thing anymore, my man."

He was right, of course. My mom would tell me her grandma took her whole family to watch the first WrestleMania on closed circuit at the local music hall right in Deer Creek Falls. I heard the story so much I felt like I'd been there. I smiled to myself and shook my head in amusement. I loved this memory.

The high school wrestling performance ignited the gym. Both Michelle and Ricky triumphed, earning their spots in the state championships. The high school bus rocked with celebration as we drove home. Team members sang, cheered, and recounted their favorite moments of the competition, adding another layer of excitement to the holiday season.

Riding on a school bus home wasn't the optimum environment for working, especially with teenagers celebrating. Actually, it didn't feel much like work. Laughing and planning the full wrestling card with Hank just made me feel happy—more happy than I had in years.

In between the laughter, Hank and I scribbled ideas for upcoming matches. We already had showdowns lined up: The Teacher vs. Student trope with Dynamite Destiny taking on Page Turner; and a Grudge Match pitting "Pittsburg's own" Turnpike Mac against Milwaukee Mike. Hank said he was adding managers to the Destiny and Page match. It was as much to tap into a recent altercation Page had with Magnificent Melissa who had left the company without any resolution to their feud. Missy, as the wrestlers referred to Magnificent Melissa, will be in Destiny's corner and Stacy's Mom from the Suburbs will even things out and be in Page's corner.

"Hey, guess what?" Hanks's eyes lit up as he announced, "I was able to book Hot Ricky Rahde!"

I raised an eyebrow. "Hot Ricky Rahde?" I have heard some about Hot Ricky Rahde, a young upstart who was working hard and waiting for his big break.

Hank grinned broadly. "Yes. Gotta love his surfer vibe, complete with his outrageous Hawaiian shirts. His manager comes out wearing a 'Hot Rahde' t-shirt reminiscent of the legendary Rowdy Roddy Piper's Hot Rod shirts. The gall of him comparing himself to such a legend helped to infuriate the crowd."

I added, "I have heard ever since he added legendary manager Tremendous Travis Pruitt to guide his career he has really taken off. Of course, it helps when Tremendous Travis uses the surf board Rahde brings out to the ring to take out his opponent."

"You bet," Hank agreed. "Tremendous Travis gets the entire crowd yelling 'beach bum' at Rahde by insisting that he isn't one as he overreacts when the crowd starts chanting 'beach bum' as loud as possible. It is amazing what having the right person in your corner can do for some wrestlers."

Hank leaned in conspiratorially, "He hails from the Beaches of the Far East, you know."

"And where is he really coming in from?" I asked.

Hank burst out laughing, "Atlantic City, New Jersey."

I shook my head. "Well, that's east of Deer Creek Falls."

He continued with excitement, "I also booked Tenacious Norman Thomas, 'The TNT Kid,' for Ricky's opponent. They haven't clashed before, but their styles will create fireworks. Both are ripe for a big break. Thomas is from Youngstown so returning home for the big match"

As if that weren't enough, Hank laid out another match for me. "Remember Jacques Juggernaut? The gigantic Frenchman from Grenoble with his dark beret and goatee?"

"Sure." The guy was 6'10" and had become one of the most sought-after wrestling big men in the industry. Not many wrestlers kept the same name and gimmick their entire run, but Juggernaut was one who did. He always came out with a dark black dyed and manicured goatee, black beret, and a heavy dose of French arrogance.

"Jacques's opponent will be the wrestling chef," Pete said.

"Broscheff. Really?" I hadn't expected that.

The wrestling chef and ring veteran Willie Broscheff had tried gimmick after gimmick on the circuit, but none had stuck. Honestly, from what I knew, he was just an honest, salt-of-the-earth kind of guy that could really put on a great match. The problem was, no persona he tried got over with the fans. When we signed on with the West Coast, Tanner said to him, "With a name like Broscheff, you'd think you'd be a wrestling chef."

Initially skeptical, Broscheff finally embraced the gimmick, reintroducing himself as "The Culinary Grappler, Chef Derek Cooke from Le Cordon Bleu in Paris France." Coming out with his chef's hat and coat, and invoking terms like "I am going to skewer you," he had been working as the Culinary Grappler for the past few years and seemed to be making it a success. Over the top, yes…but a great fit in the world of professional wrestling.

Hank was excited about the storytelling that he could put together with the Holiday Headlock card. He mused, "I think I am going to make the Culinary Grappler and Jaques Juggernaut match a 'French Street Fight' match." A large, toothy grin shown brightly on Hank's face. I was glad knowing that this would likely be his last big show to put together that he was having so much fun with it.

Hank reminded me, "Don't forget about Kris the Kringle vs. The Mistletoe Mauler on the card—a nod to the holidays and a guaranteed crowd-pleaser." I could already picture the festive chaos and laughter.

As our conversation wrapped up, we realized we had a few holes in the lineup. Since Abby wanted to get the card released and Hank wanted to have it to get the booking tied down, we agreed that Shady Shelby Peters – of the legendary "Shamu is dead" fame – would be in the Main Event and wrestle a mystery opponent.

"There's something else I wanted to run by you," I said. "Bobby had an idea."

"He did?" Hank asked. "What was that?"

I recounted the Dream Match Bobby had come up with while we were playing with his wrestling dolls. The Journey Boys vs. Ian and Prescott Hiland, The Hilanders, could be a Main Event on any wrestling card in the world.

Hank Hardway stood straight up, even though the bus was still rolling down the highway. "I love it! I was thinking about having Robbie be the mystery opponent for Shady Shelby Peters, but this would be epic, having you and Robbie get back together and face the team that beat your record."

Hank's words reminded me not only had the Journey Boys and Hilanders never faced one another in the ring, but that Justin and Jason Journey beat our record of holding the tag team world championship the longest.

Hank sat back down, said he would work on the lineup, finalize it, and let me and Abby know by morning so we could release it. He would also be contacting the wrestlers to go over their matches, so they knew before getting into town.

Abby, who'd been sitting beside us, quietly absorbing every word, leaned across the aisle and gently squeezed Hank's hand. "You've always been there for our team, Coach Miller, for the school, and for me," she said warmly. "Thank you for everything."

Hank blushed and modestly replied, "Ah, it's nothing, really."

Abby got that spark in her eyes that said she had a plan! "Let's set up some Zoom sessions with the wrestlers. Build some pre-match heat!" I exchanged a surprised look with Hank, impressed by how quickly she had learned the pro wrestling business and the lingo. Pre-match buzz indeed.

"It was partly Ricky's idea," she explained, "to release short video streams of the wrestlers calling out their opponents."

Hank nodded in agreement, promising, "I'll work that into our schedule."

As we arrived back at the school and the night drew to a close, I marveled at how the day had unfolded—from Tanner's surprise and much needed donation to high school wrestling championships to a fundraising line-up that promised explosive matches. I looked at the kids on the bus I was surrounded by, at Abby and Hank and thought about all my friends and family here pitching in and realized that thanks to shared dreams and relentless hard work, we were truly making magic happen.

Chapter 22

I got home and fell into a long chat with Mom. We caught up on my day, and she beamed as she told me about Christmas shopping with Jenny.

"Oh, man, I've really got to get on that," I laughed.

"Aaron, it's just days away," she replied with a smile, then asked, "What are you getting Abby?"

"Not sure yet. I've got an idea, but I need to call someone first."

Mom's eyes lit up. "Are you coming with us to Carter's Christmas Land on Monday?"

A surge of nostalgia hit me. I remembered Christmas Tree Lane and the engagement plan I had when I was younger, where I'd one day get on one knee at the base of the snowman Christmas tree and ask my future bride to marry me. "I wouldn't miss it for the world," I said. Then I blurted, "Mom, did anyone ask...?"

Before I could finish, she grinned. "Yes, Aaron. Abby and the boys are joining us Monday." Mom gave me a knowing smile, and I headed off to bed.

The next day, I wrapped gifts for Mom, Jenny, Randy, and the girls that I got for them while I was on the road. But I still needed something special for Abby, and time was slipping away. I knew Abby loved the Falls, and I wanted to see if I could get an artist in town to draw a picture of her and the boys in front of it at Christmas time.

Ryan Duffy, the town's local artist in residence, was the man for the job. With family connections to Duffy's Pizza, he had roots in Deer Creek Falls going back generations.

I met him later at his pop-up downtown studio. As soon as I walked in, though, he quickly draped a cover over his canvas. "Gotta respect my other clients' privacy," he explained with a wink.

We settled into easy conversation. He gushed about his family's newfound love for wrestling. I told him we could get him some tickets for the show, but he had already bought some from Abby.

"Really?" I asked, surprised. "You saw her?"

He stuttered, "Uh… yeah. She was in the store earlier."

I outlined my vision: a drawing of Abby and the boys at the Falls, shimmering with Christmas lights. I watched his eyes spark as he imagined it. It is fun working with an artist. You can see their wheels turning when you tell them what you are envisioning.

"Do you think you can finish it by Christmas?" I asked, a little embarrassed by my request.

"For Fabulous Freddy Foxx? Absolutely," he joked back, and soon his busy workday called him away.

I dashed to a local store for wrestling-themed wrapping paper. I browsed eagerly, then I heard the checkout clerk say, "Sorry, but we've sold out of all the Fabulous Freddy Foxx wrapping paper." I was not so vain that I would purchase wrapping paper with my own face on it, but I knew she was joking with me.

She shared an amusing tidbit about her little brother's wrestling fanaticism and even asked me to sign an autograph. I scribbled my signature and gave her tickets for her and her family to attend *Holiday Headlock*. Then she handed me some

Christmas wrapping paper with wrestling rings mixed with holiday décor and colors. I knew that would be perfect for Bobby and Ricky's gifts.

At home, I unwrapped the package Robbie had sent me, custom-made championship belts for both Bobby and Ricky. I'd tried to incorporate their interests on the side panels and had their names each emblazoned on the front design of each belt. I smiled – the manufacturers had outdone themselves with the quality and care they took in making the belts.

I wrapped the gifts carefully and placed them under the tree.

The next morning, Mom, Moira, and Margo treated us to a waffle breakfast. The sweet, warm scent of maple syrup actually woke me up before my alarm did. I stumbled into the kitchen without doing a thing to my unruly hair.

"There's Einstein!" Mom teased.

I grinned. "I'll take that as a compliment on my brain, not a comment about my hair," I replied, and we all burst into laughter.

Jenny updated me on our plan for the day. "I called Abby. She said she, the boys, and even her mom are riding with us to Carter's. We're leaving in about fifteen minutes. You know it's always crazy busy this time of year."

As we hustled to get ready, Jenny leaned in to me. "I know you've already been thinking about this a lot, but I can tell Abby is worried. You know, you getting close with the boys and then leaving when you sign a new contract."

I frowned. "Jenny, I would never do anything to hurt them."

"I know, big brother. But with the fundraiser, Mom, and contract decisions weighing on you, I worry you might lose sight of some things. It is a lot to deal with."

Angst crept into my stomach. I hated that Abby still worried about me hurting her or the boys. "You know I wouldn't do that. I really am working on making a decision," I said. "Besides, you forgot one important thing." Just then, my phone buzzed. It was Stuart Tanner. "Hang on. I need to take this."

I stepped into the next room, my thoughts swirling with worries about whether Jenny and Abby truly understood my dream of teaching and moving back home. I thought they both knew I was serious about it, but now I wasn't sure.

Jenny seeing that I was taking a call from Tanner right now might also lead to her thinking that I was leaning towards heading back out on the road. Would she say something to Abby about it? I knew how close they were as friends. I also knew that Jenny wanted her brother and her best friend to end up together.

Decisions pulled at me, my head buzzing.

Tanner's voice filled my ear as I turned away from my sister to take the call. "How's your mom? And your family? By the way, congratulations on selling out *Holiday Headlock*. You and your team, your family…your town, have done such a great job, Aaron. I want to help."

"Mr. Tanner, you have done so much already. Letting your wrestlers take part, your huge donation. I could never ask you for anything else," I said.

"Thanks, Aaron, but this is a great cause. We have the technology to livestream events on our platform and, if you want, we could livestream *Holiday Headlock*. Since you can't fit any other fans in your gym, and I imagine it is too late and impractical to move the show, what do you think about our tech team coming and livestreaming it? All advertising revenue that comes in would be donated to your efforts as well," Tanner explained.

I was stunned, and for a moment I couldn't speak. This was beyond generous. "I – uh, Mr. Tanner, I don't know what to say," I finally responded.

"Aaron…say yes," Tanner answered with light laughter. "You would also be doing me a favor. I would like to watch it but will be back West that night, so this way I can watch the livestream. Our guys are already in the region, so it is no problem on our end."

"Well, yes, of course. We would love that."

"Great! I'll text you the contact info for my tech and social media teams. Just have someone on your end coordinate," he instructed.

"Will do. Thanks again for everything," I replied. I could barely imagine what kind of reach our event could get, with the livestreaming added in. And yet with everything Stuart Tanner had done for me, he'd never once used any of it to lean on me to come work for him.

When I joined everyone in the kitchen, Abby and the boys had just arrived. I asked, "Can someone else drive? I need to talk with Abby about the conversation I just had with Stuart Tanner."

Randy jumped in, "Sure, I can drive. But, hey, if Tanner called to offer you millions to join his wrestling league, it's gonna cost you!" His joking tone couldn't mask the concern in Abby and Jenny's eyes.

I just smiled, knowing that once I explained the call to Abby, she wouldn't worry.

In the car, I bantered with Bobby and cheered Ricky, who proudly recounted an article about the team's recent wrestling performance. Then I leaned toward Abby. "Listen to this. Stuart Tanner's going to livestream *Holiday Headlock*! And all ad revenue will go to the fundraiser."

She blinked. "What! Really? That will work?"

"Yes," I said. "He said to give the contact information to my team...I guess that's you," I added with a smile.

Abby leaned towards me and whispered, "Thank you, Aaron. Thank you for everything. I can't even tell you how much I love you."

Her words shot through me, warming me from inside out. *...how much I love you...*

"This has all just been so –" Abby went on before Ricky cranked up the radio and interrupted us.

"Turn it up! This is my favorite Christmas song! Let's sing!"

She didn't finish, but it didn't matter. We linked our fingers together, holding hands as we all joined in a spontaneous chorus of "Up on the Housetop," with Abby and Bobby doing all the silly hand gestures from when we were kids.

The van pulled up to Carter's Christmas Land, and I felt an old familiar thrill. The vintage exterior and brilliant decor took me back to childhood trips. Inside, the store bustled like a festive department store setting. There were gifts, toys, and treats for sale, a full greenhouse and an avenue of Christmas scenes and decorated Christmas trees known as Christmas Tree Lane. People came from all over to see the new displays each year.

We finally entered and saw the dazzling trees and displays, each with unique themes—Sesame Street, Rudolph, Harry Potter, trains, candy, Wizard of Oz. Then, as we got close to the end, there it was…the Snowman Christmas Tree. They always had a Frosty the Snowman tree filled with snowman decorations, snowman lights, and a snowman tree topper.

Always my favorite, and, yes, as Randy would kid me again, this was the tree. "Hey, brother-in-law. Is this it?"

I shot him a look with an expression of "not now." I didn't want to be teased about that right now, especially with Abby there.

Jenny decided to bail me out. "Okay, Randy, go easy on him. I think it's sweet."

Abby, Ricky, and Bobby looked momentarily puzzled by the wedding banter. It was all good-natured, but Jenny was right, I didn't want to go down any road that had wedding engagement talk. First, I didn't want to make Abby uncomfortable, and second, I wanted to surprise her one day, if I was ever so lucky.

Soon after, we left Christmas Tree Lane for an old-school pizza parlor just across the street called Vito's Pizza, of all things. Christmas Tree Lane is a bit of a drive from the center of Deer Creek Falls, so we didn't feel like we were cheating on Duffy's Pizza.

At Vito's, we rehashed our Carter's memories from years past and devoured our dinner. My phone rang. Abby and I glanced at the screen simultaneously. To my utter shock, it was Don Kennedy calling directly. This was unprecedented! Kennedy typically had Pat call ahead and set up calls. I knew I'd better take the call, even though Abby was frowning at me.

Excusing myself, I stepped out into a softly falling Ohio snow.

"Mr. Kennedy," I answered

"Freddy, we need to talk," he began sharply. "I saw today that my competition is broadcasting this *Holiday Headlock* thing you are doing," he said accusingly. Before I could explain, he continued, "I can't let my talent be part of this, knowing my competitor is broadcasting it."

I stared up into the star-filled sky. "Mr. Kennedy, that is not the case. They are going to stream it using their technology and their platform, but all advertising revenue is going to the fundraiser."

Kennedy scoffed. "That's what they told you, Freddy. I'm not sure that's the whole truth."

I took a breath. "I'm nobody's fool, Mr. Kennedy."

After a tense pause, he said, "I'm disappointed, but here's what I'm willing to do. "I'm switching things up with the Main Event for the New Year's Eve show. Fast Frankie Folsom will be going up against Brent "Wrecking Ball" Haynie."

I was stunned. Folsom hadn't worked for Kennedy in years. I loved Folsom, but, since we'd ended our feud battling over the right to use the nickname Triple F name a few years ago, he'd been a mid-carder despite being more talented than many in front of him. It seemed odd these two would now be the Main Event for the New Year's Eve show…and what did this have to do with *Holiday Headlock*?

Kennedy continued, "I want you to put Folsom on The Foxx Denn and put him over as your guest for *Holiday Headlock*. I want to see that livestreamed on my competitor's platform. And you'll be managing Fast Frankie Folsom at the New Year's Eve show, so whatever you have to do on that *Foxx Denn* to forge an alliance between the two of you…make it happen."

I gritted my teeth. "Mr. Kennedy, I manage my own show."

He didn't answer.

I sighed. I didn't want to jeopardize any part of the fundraiser. I figured I could talk to Hank Hardway and he would have some ideas on how to make this work and all make sense for our show. "Okay, Mr. Kennedy. I'll reach out to Folsom and work this out before I have him on."

Without another word, in typical fashion, he ended the call.

I texted Fast Frankie Folsom immediately to set up a talk for tomorrow.

Sounds good, can't wait, he responded.

I bet, I thought. *He's now Main Eventing one of the biggest Premium Live Events of the year!*

What confused me was how Vito's match with Wrecking Ball Brent Haynie, the hottest feud of the year, had been dropped from the Main Event. Vito is the top heel and current champion. I went back into Vito's Pizza and made sure to buy the largest sized Vito's Pizza t-shirt I could. I couldn't wait to surprise Vito with it.

At our table, I paused to watch my family laugh and reminisce over holiday stories as soft Christmas tunes floated in the background. This was what really mattered, everyone together and enjoying the festivities and each other's company.

Abby's eyes searched mine, as if asking about Kennedy's call. "We'll talk tomorrow," I promised. I didn't want her to worry or make false assumptions, like he'd been calling about my contract.

Before leaving, the restaurant owner snapped a picture for his celebrity wall and then took a group photo. I asked him to text it to me and gave him my number. My nieces started to tell me to "just grab it off of your Instagram" and then remembered I was Uncle Analog Aaron.

The owner laughed, then said, "If I give you Vito's Pizza hats for your whole family here, can you give one to Vito Garramone? He's my favorite wrestler. No offense."

I never took offense to another wrestler being a fan's individual favorite. If I was to lose that title to anyone, Vito was right up there with the best. In fact, Robbie and I used to joke that our tag team, The Hilanders, was everyone's third favorite tag team. I answered Vito as I looked around the table, "I sure will. Vito's Pizza hats for everyone!" We all put on the hats and took another group photo. I sent it to an amused Vito Garramone, and we all headed home in the van.

On the ride back, I filled Abby in on Kennedy's attempt to meddle with The Foxx Denn booking.

"Can he do that?" she asked indignantly. "You're not under contract with him. Your deal ended November 30, and you only have a one-day New Year's Eve show contract." Abby's tone was both protective and scornful. "I don't know how you work for that guy." It was a shot at Kennedy, but likely she was also taking the opportunity to remind me that she did not want me leaving and going back to work for him.

Just before Randy pulled into the driveway, I received a text from Vito again thanking me for the photo of my family adorned in Vito's Pizza hats with are bit more ominous ending to the text: **Can we talk tomorrow morning?**

I texted back affirmatively curious what was going on with the Main Event of the New Year's Eve show.

"Christmas Eve Eve" had arrived—December 23, also known to fans of Seinfeld as "Festivus." The kids were buzzing with excitement. Jenny announced we'd spend Christmas Eve and Christmas Day at Mom's. After breakfast with Mom, I called Abby. She told me the boys were with Richard and invited me over for dinner – chicken marsala and classic Christmas music.

"I'll be over around six," I promised and then called Vito.

"Aaron, my friend—ciao!" Vito greeted in his Italian accent, seemingly in character.

"Vito, how are you? I'm excited for our card. We planned to have you on The Foxx Denn, just as we discussed. Oddly enough though, Kennedy called me last night and told me to put Fast Frankie Folsom on *The Foxx Denn* to promote the Main Event match at the New Year's Eve show with Wrecking Ball Haynie. I thought you were going to be putting the strap up against Haynie? I'm going to work with Hank Hardway, who's booking the show, so he can create a card and storylines that make sense out of all of it."

Vito let out a hearty laugh. "Hardway is a good man. If anyone can make it work, he can. I learned plenty from him in the ring back in the day. I just hope he can find a match for me that makes sense."

"Don't worry—I don't want you in Kennedy's crosshairs," I said. "Maybe we can open with a Foxx Denn with Folsom, then slot you in mid-show."

Vito hesitated for a moment, then said, "You must not have heard yet. I'm not sure who knows. Kennedy changed his mind and said I can't come, which is why he is sending you Folsom."

I was stunned. Before I could respond, Vito went on. "He's upset you're going to be livestreamed by Tanner's outfit. He said the only ones who can come are Robbie, Page, and Fast Frankie Folsom."

As I listened with utmost disappointment, Vito hit me with a major shocker. "When I told him I was going to be on *Holiday Headlock* anyway, he said he would fire me if I do. I told him, 'Well, then get ready to fire me'."

I shook my head. "Vito, you don't have to do that. We want you here, the fans want you here, but I don't want you to lose your job," I said.

His voice turned firm. "I'm coming, and I am coming to wrestle. I'll only take yes for an answer."

I countered, "How about this? We pit you one-on-one against Shady Shelby Peters—heel versus heel, champion versus champion. Tanner is sending him in and we have him advertised against a 'Mystery Opponent.'"

A spark lit up his tone. "That's perfect, Aaron. I've wanted this match since he broke through in Los Angeles."

I called Hank Hardway to fill him in about Vito. He wasn't surprised by Kennedy's actions, but he too was shocked that Vito would be willing to walk away like that.

As I was talking to Hank, Vito texted me. **Kennedy just stripped the title from me. Said he is putting it up at the Main Event at the New Year's Eve show between Folsom and Brent "Wrecking Ball" Haynie.**

I quickly typed in response, **Sorry, man. This whole thing is crazy.**

He followed up. **I will be there for the show, ready to fight the Shady man and give the crowd a show they will never forget.**

I relayed all this to Hank, and we immediately began plotting. "We'll start the show with the Foxx Denn with Fast Frankie Folsom—reminding everyone of our legendary Fabulous Freddy Foxx vs Fast Frankie Folsom battle over the right to use the Triple F moniker. Then, Folsom reveals he will be wrestling for the vacant World Title against Brent 'Wrecking Ball' Haynie in the Main Event at the New Year's Eve show."

Hank Hardway continued, "We'll have Vito Garramone in a Foxx Denn segment to build heat for him being revealed as the mystery opponent for Shady Shelby Peters. This will work." Hank said confidently.

On Christmas Eve morning, Mom treated everyone to a pancake breakfast. Abby and the boys soon joined us. Abby had me booked for one of the world's most popular wrestling podcasts right after breakfast, and she planned to push the final card out to the media.

The podcast host was a friend of mine and was very supportive of what we were doing. The first time I was on his show, On the Mat with Matt: The Wrestling Podcast, I referred to him as Mattropolitan. I thought I was being clever combining his name with metropolitan as I knew he lived in New York City. Matt liked it, and as evidenced by his merchandise sales, his listeners absolutely loved it. I was happy for him that he now is able to make a living talking about pro wrestling and loves it.

After the podcast we would enjoy a quiet Christmas Eve and Christmas Day. On December 26, wrestlers and fans would swarm in for Fan Fest, with Holiday Headlock set for Saturday the 27th.

I absorbed every moment—every laugh, every conversation—as I juggled phone calls, texts, and last-minute adjustments. Amid the festive chaos, the warmth of family, the buzz of wrestling, and the spirit of the holidays intermingled to create an experience I knew I'd never forget.

HOLIDAY HEADLOCK

DEER CREEK FALLS HIGH SCHOOL
DEER CREEK FALLS, OHIO

DEC. 27

MAIN EVENT
WORLD CHAMPIONSHIP MATCH
SHADY SHELBY PETERS
CHAMPION - ALCATRAZ, BY WAY OF SAN FRANCISCO, CALIFORNIA
• VERSUS •
VITO GARRAMONE
FORMER WORLD CHAMPION - FLORENCE, ITALY

TAG TEAM DREAM MATCH
JASON AND JUSTIN JOURNEY: THE JOURNEY BOYS
TAG TEAM CHAMPIONS - LAS VEGAS, NEVADA
• VERSUS •
IAN AND PRESCOTT HILAND: THE HILANDERS
THE DODGY PART OF GLASGOW, SCOTLAND

TEACHER VS. STUDENT
DYNAMITE DESTINY
FORMER WORLD CHAMPION - CHICAGO, ILLINOIS
MANAGED BY MAGNIFICENT MELISSA
• VERSUS •
PAGE TURNER
FORMER WORLD CHAMPION
LIBRARY OF CONGRESS, BY WAY OF WASHINGTON DC
MANAGED BY STACY'S MOM FROM THE SUBURBS

GRUDGE MATCH
TURNPIKE MAC
THE PITTSBURGH END OF THE PENNSYLVANIA TURNPIKE
• VERSUS •
MILWAUKEE MIKE
GREEN BAY, WISCONSIN, BY WAY OF MILWAUKEE, WISCONSIN

FOXX DENN
FEATURING
FABULOUS FREDDY FOXX
WITH VITO GARRAMONE
AND SHADY SHELBY PETERS

THE CHRISTMAS THROWDOWN
KRIS THE KRINGLE
FROM THE NORTH POLE
• VERSUS •
THE MISTLETOE MAULER
FROM PARTS UNKNOWN

BATTLE FOR INDY SUPREMACY
HOT RICKY RAHDE
V.S.
THE TNT KID:
TENACIOUS NORMAN THOMAS
FROM THE BEACHES OF THE FAR EAST
MANAGED BY THE LEGENDARY TREMENDOUS TRAVIS PRUITT
YOUNGSTOWN, OHIO

FRENCH STREET FIGHT RULES
FRENCHMAN JACQUES JUGGERNAUT
V.S.
THE CULINARY GRAPPLER, DEREK COOKE
GRENOBLE, FRANCE
FROM LE CORDON BLEU CULINARY SCHOOL IN PARIS, FRANCE

FEATURING
FABULOUS FREDDY FOXX
INTERVIEWING
FAST FRANKIE FOLSOM
FOXX DENN

Chapter 23

bby told me we'd likely clear enough funds to create sensory rooms in three of our schools. I felt a deep sense of relief knowing we were going to help so many kids of Deer Creek Falls, and I was able to relax and enjoy the holiday.

The food at our Christmas Eve celebration was a spread of appetizers and pub-style fare. I'd always wondered what it would be like to be part of a family celebration that was more ethnic in nature—like the Feast of the Seven Fishes. I remembered my childhood friends describing massive family gatherings with dozens of cousins, and though that sounded exotic to me (especially given Mom's limited cooking skills), I knew I wouldn't have it any other way.

The music, the laughs, the stories…this was what a family Christmas meant to me. And now, with Abby and the boys in the mix, everything felt nearly perfect.

After dinner, we broke out the games and played most of the night. Bobby had brought along some of his wrestling action figures, so Ricky and I were often roped into playing with him. At one point, Ricky stopped me and said, "Coach, Mom showed me the card for Holiday Headlock. Thanks for taking Bobby's ideas and making them real. When he's old enough, he'll understand that his dream matches with his wrestling dolls came to life as part of all this. Thank you."

Though Ricky wasn't usually one for much emotion, he hugged me as he added, "You're a good man. I appreciate how kind you've been to my mom too."

I smiled and replied, "I know I've said this before, but you're a young man with an old soul and maturity beyond your years. You, your mom, and Bobby are special to me and always will be. Thank you for making me feel so welcome." We fist bumped and headed over to join Bobby.

It was time for our guests to head home. Mom and I stayed behind to clean up. Then each of us grabbed a cup of tea as we settled in the front room. Mom asked, "Aaron, have you made any decisions?"

Not entirely sure what she meant, I answered, "I'm going to bring out the gifts I got for everyone. Jenny talked Abby into bringing the boys over around noon. Hope it's okay if they stay for dinner. I got something for Abby and the boys for Christmas, so they'll probably open it here. Is that alright, Mom?" I was a bit worried that too many people two days in a row might be too much for her.

"Oh, it's fine. The more the merrier," she replied, then added, "But that's not really what I was asking about. Do you know what you're going to do with the wrestling contracts? Have you decided what you're going to tell Abby?"

I sensed her concern—she was asking because she cared. I admitted, "I'm not sure yet. I've been thinking about Abby more than the contract decision. I'm not even sure what kind of offer Kennedy will make, and I don't know what Tanner has in mind either. It will all happen soon, that much is for sure. I just want to do the right thing."

She squeezed my hand and said, "I know you do, Aaron... and you will. It's a tough decision. Randy mentioned one of the wrestling blogs said you might be offered $1,000,000 a year for five years. I know you've never made that kind of money, and you've spent a lot helping me, your dad, and your sister. We all understand if you decide to hit the road again and work for any of those companies. Such an offer would set you up for life. But remember, you'll always have a home in Deer Creek Falls."

I sighed. "It's really a tough call. I've truly loved teaching and coaching. The kids are fantastic. The kids I work with still have the same hopes and dreams I had at their age. Even though it's only been a short time, it will be incredibly hard to walk away from them."

"I know, Aaron," Mom said softly, and reached over to squeeze my hand.

I chuckled and added, "But a million dollars a year... I mean..." We both laughed, finished our teas, and I headed to bed while Mom curled up with a book. As I left the room, I joked, "I've got to get to bed—I don't want Santa passing our house by!"

Christmas morning arrived, and it was my first time in years spending Christmas with Mom and my sister—and now, for the first time ever, with my two nieces. My nieces were so attentive to Mom, which was incredibly sweet. Even Dasher, the dog, got into the spirit and received his share of doggie Christmas gifts.

I must have looked like the proverbial kid on Christmas morning when I heard the door and Abby's voice shout, "Merry Christmas, McClellan family!" followed by Ricky echoing the greeting. Before I could even process it, Bobby had dashed into the front room and declared, "Holiday Headlock!" as I leaned down, letting him put me into a playful headlock.

Abby glanced at Jenny and Mom, then asked, "Has Aaron's surprise gift arrived yet?" I looked around, knowing I hadn't unwrapped anything that would fit the bill.

"Excuse me? Surprise gift?" I asked, puzzled.

Jenny teased, "Well, not yet, Abby, but thanks for ruining the surprise. No need to worry, big brother—you'll know the gift when you see it." Now that everyone had arrived, it was time to open gifts.

I got Jenny's family tickets to the Taylor Swift concert coming to Cleveland next year. I knew Randy might have preferred classic or for him at times techno rock, but he couldn't help getting caught up in the excitement when he saw his daughters and wife talking about what they'd wear and whether they should stay in downtown Cleveland for the concert weekend.

Mom chimed in, "Where is my Taylor Swift ticket?" We all laughed, knowing she'd be game to join them if an extra ticket could be found. Then Mom added, "I'm kidding—I know those are hard tickets to get. I love the picture you got me," referring to the framed drawing Jenny and I had created for her. The picture featured Mom in various stages of life. It showed important moments of her as a little girl, her wedding picture with Dad, her curled up with a book by the bookshelf, her in her nurse's uniform, and pictured with all members of her family.

It was then time for Bobby and Ricky to open the customized championship belts I had gotten for them. They absolutely loved the gifts. The company had done a fantastic job, especially with Bobby's belt, which fit him perfectly despite most wrestling belts being too big for someone his size.

Abby then called out, "Okay, boys, let's give Aaron his gift."

I protested with a smile, "You guys didn't have to get me anything. Just being around you is gift enough."

"Stuff and nonsense," Abby replied teasingly.

Ricky handed Abby a flat, neatly wrapped package, about the same size as the framed art I'd gotten for Abby. As he handed the gift to me, I could tell it was a frame, and my curiosity began to grow about what was inside. "I think you should open the gift I got for you at the same time," I said, passing my package over to Abby.

When I opened her gift, I found the words "Holiday Headlock" at the top—cleverly designed, with the O in Holiday shaped like a Christmas ornament and the other O in Headlock resembling a Christmas wreath. The drawing depicted Abby and me in a wrestling ring: her, in a Santa hat, putting me in a headlock while my Santa hat tumbled off; Bobby, also wearing a Santa hat, playfully grabbing me by the leg; and Ricky dressed as a referee, seemingly counting the match.

I was in awe and finally managed, "I'm speechless."

Randy jumped in, "Fabulous Freddy Foxx, the best talker in wrestling, is speechless. We'd better warn Kennedy!"

Laughing along with everyone, I finally managed to say, "Abby...Bobby and Ricky, this is fantastic. I will treasure it always." Overwhelmed by the moment, I glanced over to see Abby with tears in her eyes as she looked at the drawing I'd gotten for her. Bobby and Ricky quickly moved to give her a big hug as she wiped away a tear.

"Mommy, are you okay?" Bobby asked.

"Oh, yes, Bobby. I'm just excited about what Aaron did for us," Abby answered.

"Aaron, I love this." She and the boys called everyone over to admire the drawing—a vibrant depiction of us in front of the downtown waterfalls with all the pageantry of our Deer Creek Falls Christmas on display.

It dawned on me that we had both visited Ryan Duffy's art studio on the same day. I wondered if the painting he had covered up when I walked in was the very piece Abby had him paint. Ryan's quick thinking had saved the surprise. I shared the story with everyone, and we all had a good laugh about it.

After a while, Abby checked her phone, excused herself, and Jenny immediately followed. I recognized the look. They were up to something mischievous, just like old times. Meanwhile, Bobby and Ricky carried their championship belts high as Mom and Randy admired the photos that Abby and I had swapped as gifts.

Then I heard it: "Happy Christmas, my brother Prescott." It was Robbie, doing his best Ian Hiland Scottish accent as he entered the room.

"Happy Christmas!" exclaimed Page as she walked in behind Jenny and Abby. I got up, and Robbie and I hugged like long-lost brothers.

I turned to Abby and Jenny. "This is the best surprise! You're here early!"

"Robbie got a hold of me about transportation and housing for the show," explained Abby, "and we instantly kicked off Project Robbie."

"Ah, a bunch of rubbish," Robbie said in his over-played Scottish accent. "I missed you, my brother, and I wanted an extra day to show Page my hometown."

I could see Ricky and Bobby watching us, clearly eager to meet *Rockin' Robbie*. I said to Robbie, "Hey, there are a couple of people I want you to meet."

Robbie's great with kids, and Abby's boys instantly took to him. I told Robbie about how Bobby had come up with the ideas for the dream match we'd be having with the Journey Boys while we played with his wrestling action figures. Bobby even mentioned his bit about having Vito wrestle Shady Shelby Peters.

"I'm glad I've got these guys in my corner," I said, intentionally using one of my patented Fabulous Freddy Foxx phrases.

Robbie pulled me out into our sunroom—though in Northeast Ohio, "sunroom" is a misnomer, so we had affectionately renamed it the Fun Room. Despite the chill,

Robbie and I slipped inside while everyone else continued the merriment.

"Hey, Aaron, I have to show you something," Robbie said, as he pulled out a beautiful, classic engagement ring from his winter jacket.

"Oh, my! Well done, Robbie," I exclaimed as I hugged him in congratulations. I was genuinely so excited for him.

"I'm going to leave soon, take Page down to the Falls, and ask her to marry me," he said.

"So happy for you, and Page will love the romantic setting," I replied.

Robbie went on excitedly, "I've known a few wrestlers who married fellow wrestlers and traveled together. They even got their own tour bus when they started having kids. Page and I love this business, and I want that life for us."

I was truly happy for Robbie. He had found his place in life, both professionally and personally. And Page? She was awesome.

Robbie and I returned to the front room where Mom, Moira, and Margo were back at the piano, joined by others singing, while Page chatted with Abby and Jenny. It wasn't long before Page hit it off with everyone, and little did she know that her night was about to get even better. I told Robbie he could use Mom's car, and he and Page headed out "to buy some ice"—a ruse to cover his plans to head downtown to the Falls.

It was hard for me not to tell everyone about what Robbie was up to, but the family bought the "ice" story whole. What they didn't know was that the basement's secondary refrigerator/ freezer was packed with ice. While Robbie was out, we all piled into Abby's mom's van and drove through our neighborhood, to view the yards where everyone had put out luminaries. This tradition had been going strong ever since Mom and some friends started it when she first moved in. Mom and Jenny always sent me photos when I was on the road. They lit up the neighborhood with soft, flickering lights.

As we pulled into the driveway, I noticed Mom's car was back, meaning Robbie and Page had already returned. They were sitting on the sofa together when we came in. Page jumped up and stuck her left hand out to us, squealing, "Look, look! It's the same one Robbie's grandpa gave to his grandma."

We gathered around offering congratulations and best wishes. Robbie showed us the photos from his phone of the two of them in front of the Falls just minutes earlier. I couldn't have been happier for them.

"Is Carter's Christmas Land open tomorrow?" Robbie asked.

I answered quickly, hoping to keep my secret engagement fantasy under wraps, "Yes, they're open every day except Christmas, and the display stays up until spring."

"Cool," Robbie said. "Page, I have to take you to see this. It's not just a tradition but something everyone should experience. It's not Christmas in Deer Creek Falls without a trip to Christmas Tree Lane."

This had truly been the best Christmas of my adult life, bar none. I had my family, Abby and the boys, and now Robbie and his future bride here, too. One more day until the big event!

Chapter 24

December 26 is Boxing Day in the UK and Canada. I used to make sure that Robbie and I integrated Boxing Day into our Hilanders gimmick, adding just the right amount of weird by confusing it with actual boxing. We would challenge anyone we wrestled on December 26 to a boxing match, sometimes even throw in the Marquess of Queensbury Rules… even though we didn't actually know what they were.

I had a lot of fun during my time as Ian and Prescott Hiland. The thought of reliving it tomorrow night at *Holiday Headlock* filled me with excitement. I hoped our match against the Journey Boys would live up to expectations. The words "Dream Match" and "epic" kept echoing through my mind. It was a lot to live up to, but with Robbie and the Journeys sharing the ring I knew we could do it.

Randy and Jenny were on shuttle duty crisscrossing to and from the airport, getting the talent in town and comfortable. Mom, Moira, Margo, Ricky, and Bobby were at the school setting up the Fan Fest. Abby and Arlo worked closely with the volunteers to arrange the chairs and merchandise tables, and stock the concession areas. I spent most of the day with Hank Hardway, shuttling him from one hotel to another where the wrestlers were staying so we could go over how tomorrow night would unfold. So far, everyone had made it, with the exception of the crew from Tanner's LA team, who were on their way.

Hank and I found ourselves in the wrestling training room waiting to go live on one of the most popular wrestling podcasts. Page and Robbie came in to surprise Hank. Hank was so excited to be reunited with Robbie, he pulled him aside to catch up. As a result, Hank was off screen when we finally went live. Having done my fair share of live television, I quickly improvised and used Robbie's arrival to my advantage. I introduced Hank Hardway as the trainer of champions and then introduced *Rockin' Robbie,* who would be reviving Ian Hiland for tomorrow night's match.

The segment went great, and it looked like everyone in the wrestling world was going to tune in for *Holiday Headlock.* Towards the end of the podcast, I introduced another special guest: the Wrestling Librarian, my friend and Robbie's new fiancé, Page Turner. Abby had just walked in while Page was conversing with a group of wrestling fans, so I called her over and, before she could object, I introduced her to the podcast world as the driving force behind the fundraiser. I also gathered Bobby and Ricky to introduce them as representatives of the school wrestling team and the students who would benefit from the sensory room.

The podcaster set up a fundraiser for our cause which was well on its way to raising $50,000. Once we wrapped up, everyone headed out to grab some much-needed rest before the big show the next day. Robbie and Page took the boys home so Abby and I could do a final check and walk-through. I had a feeling that Bobby would soon be showing off his wrestling matchmaking skills to Robbie once they got home.

After everyone had gone, Abby and I walked around the school, hand in hand, checking out the gym and Fan Fest areas.

Ralph—the Christmas tree lot guy—had arranged several Christmas trees along the entrance to the gym. Tanner's tech team had been in already, ensuring everything was set up for the livestream. Abby mentioned that the mayor had called, saying she'd never seen anything like this in her life. Every hotel room was full, all the restaurants were booked, and the mayor had even asked Abby to run for city council!

December 27th dawned early. We headed to the school to get the talent and vendors set up for the Fan Fest. These events take place almost every weekend all over the country, but wrestling fans, being the most loyal in sports, always packed them in. The wrestlers enjoyed them just as much as the fans, seeing it as a reunion of sorts. It brought together retired wrestlers, competitors from rival organizations, and new up-and-comers. While the corporate world might have called it a networking opportunity, I always saw it as a chance to reconnect with old friends, make new ones, and give back to the fans.

In response to the fans' ideas posted online, Robbie and I planned to work the first half of the Fan Fest as Ian and Prescott Hiland and then switch it up for the second half as *Rockin' Robbie* and Fabulous Freddy Foxx. Even the heels had lines from their most committed fans. The only one who wouldn't be part of the Fan Fest was Shady Shelby Peters. We deliberately left him out to build sky-high anticipation for his Foxx Denn appearance at the show and for his Main Event match against Vito Garramone.

Although we had similar plans for Vito, we couldn't keep him from joining the Fan Fest. Ever in character, Vito declared in his patented Italian accent, "We make-a the more moneys for the kidz."

Time flew by with so many people in attendance. Abby popped by a few times, clearly thrilled with how everything was coming together. Hank Hardway had the night's card fully worked out, and all the wrestlers were on board. The ring announcers and referees had arrived, and showtime was nearly here. I headed to the dressing room to put on my Fabulous Freddy Foxx outfit, wondering if this might be one of my last times in the ring. I still had the New Year's Eve show, but I couldn't help but wonder what the future held for me beyond that.

While the rest of the crew was getting ready, I met up with Abby, Hank, and Arlo ringside. The ring was being set up for a special edition of The Foxx Denn. We had planned that before I brought out Fast Frankie Folsom for his interview—as Kennedy had instructed—I wanted to take a moment: first, to thank all the volunteers; then, to introduce some of the students who would benefit from the funds raised; and finally, to have Arlo and Abby say a few words.

Abby wasn't too keen on being in the ring, but she understood it was important to thank the volunteers she had organized. With Bobby by her side, she turned to me and said, "On one condition…"

I asked, "What is that?"

She replied, "That Bobby and his friends get to help me thank everyone."

Bobby immediately piped up, "You mean in the wrestling ring? In that ring? That big, real one? I actually get to go inside it?"

I assured him, "Yes, buddy…that one right there. You, your mom, and your friends will get to step in and thank everyone for helping."

Bobby asked, "What about Ricky and the wrestling team? They helped a lot too."

Abby and I exchanged a surprised look. Once most kids hear they'll get to go into a real, life-sized pro wrestling ring, nothing else matters. Bobby, of course, thought right of his brother and his teammates.

"Of course, Bobby, Ricky and the whole team will be there too. We couldn't have done it without them," I reassured him as I glanced over at Ricky.

Ricky wiped his eyes quickly as he put an arm around Bobby, trying to play it cool, and in his best Macho Man Randy Savage voice he said, "Oooh, yeah brother, dig it."

Bobby yelled in response, "Macho Brother!" Clearly, it wasn't the first time Ricky had done his Macho Man impression.

Arlo told us that when he got on the microphone, he planned to thank Coach Miller. He mentioned that many of Coach's former students and wrestlers had reached out, and that they were going to bring Coach Miller to the ring. Former students and wrestlers would stand beside Coach and his wife in celebration, as the mayor was even set to present Coach with a Key to the City.

Abby reminded me that Robbie and I still had one more hype spot to do for a live podcast segment at the Fan Fest. I met up with Robbie in our old gym locker room, which was serving as the locker room for many of us wrestlers that night. It was kind of cool, feeling like I'd come full circle to the place where everything began for me.

We both donned our Ian and Prescott Hiland gear and, before heading over to the podcast, Robbie stopped me and said, "Aaron, this is awesome. What you're doing here is just incredible."

I replied, "Thanks, man. Everything really has come together. You and all the wrestlers are showing such incredible support. And Abby...we couldn't have done this without her. She's amazing."

Robbie grinned and said, "She is the one. I think we always knew she was."

I admitted, "I know, brother. No denying it. I just don't want to hurt her," I added as I thought about the decisions I had to make in the coming days.

"You'll do the right thing, and she'll understand no matter what. That's a lot on your plate," Robbie replied, adding with a laugh, "Do I move back to my hometown for love, or do I sign a multi-million-dollar contract? Sounds like a made-for-television Christmas rom-com."

I laughed at his comment. Even though Robbie was a better wrestling technician than I was, he never held it against me that my contracts had become more lucrative after Fabulous Freddy Foxx entered my life. Robbie is the epitome of a true friend, and, as we often call one another, brother.

As we walked over to podcast alley, the area where many wrestling podcasters gathered for the Fan Fest and *Holiday Headlock*, Robbie turned to me and said, "Big question for you, Freddy."

"Sure thing. What's up?"

His rock and roll hair was gleaming from the glitter hairspray he'd just applied, and he asked, "Will you be my best man?"

"How could I not? It would be one of the true honors of my life," I replied.

We hugged tightly, and in that moment, I reflected on how long our friendship had lasted and all the times we'd been there for each other. I added, "Your grandpa would be so proud of you, Robbie," knowing just how much that man had meant to him.

Dave and Denny—podcasters with a huge following that were about to give the event one last explosive boost—were eagerly waiting for us. Even though the show was already sold out, with Tanner sending his team out to livestream it, every extra viewer meant better advertising revenue to help the kids. Plus, both Robbie and I genuinely enjoyed these podcasts, often started up by the most dedicated wrestling fans in sports and entertainment. Dave and Denny asked about our hug just before we went live, and Robbie happily shared about his engagement to Page and that I was going to be his best man.

They then asked if they could mention the engagement during the show, and Robbie was perfectly fine with that. Being good guys, Dave and Denny wouldn't take a cheap shot. They did go down a bit of a wrestling rabbit hole, reminiscing about all of the wrestling marriage ceremonies that took place in the ring, and asked Robbie, "Will the marriage of wrestling's favorite rock star and librarian be televised? Will the wedding take place in the wrestling ring?"

I don't think Robbie had thought about such a scenario, but he was quick on his feet when he answered, "I think Page will have the final call on that."

Dave couldn't resist asking about my contract status. Knowing the audience was made up of wrestling fans, I kept my answer businesslike and diplomatic. "New York has been incredibly good to me. The fan base is off the charts and loyal to all of us wrestlers. It would be hard to leave, and hard to walk away from Robbie after all these years. On the other hand, as you can see, Stuart Tanner and his Los Angeles team really stepped up with wrestlers taking part and livestreaming the event. I haven't ruled out Miami either. Every place has something special to offer. There really is no bad choice."

Dave quipped, "And don't forget the money. Remember what The Million Dollar Man always said: 'Everyone has a price.'" I just shook my head and laughed along with them.

What I didn't know at that moment was that Abby was listening to the podcast. She'd been camped out in Arlo's office, keeping the business side of the show in line. Had I known, I might have slipped in a comment about possibly retiring or even moving back home. Looking back, I now understand why, despite everything seemingly coming together that night, Abby appeared distant later in the day.

And in the next few moments, the arrival of a very special person for *Holiday Headlock* didn't help the situation any.

Chapter 25

I later found out exactly what happened when Stuart Tanner arrived on scene.

I was in the thick of things when a sleek, black Lincoln Navigator pulled up outside. Abby saw the driver talking to a tall, well-built man in a dark blue Armani suit and wearing tan Oliver Cabell shoes. The man turned and walked toward the school's entrance. Abby didn't think this gentleman was just a fan.

Abby asked Arlo, "Do you know who this guy is? It's not time to open doors for the show yet. Is he a wrestler or something? He looks like what central casting would describe as a CEO."

Arlo looked up and replied, "I can't believe it. That's Stuart Tanner, the best marketer in America, always on Forbes' Richest Americans list every year…and the guy who sent some of his wrestlers and is livestreaming the event tonight."

Abby simply answered, "Oh, *that* Stuart Tanner."

Arlo later would tell me he took Tanner over to meet Abby, and though she was cordial, she knew he was one of those guys who might lead me back into the wrestling world and away from Deer Creek Falls.

"I cannot thank you enough for what you have done to support our efforts here," Abby said to Tanner. "Aaron told me what it has all meant to making this a success."

Then, with his typical charm, Tanner remarked, "Wait, you're Abby. Aaron told me about you. One of the times he called, you were about all he talked about. I had to remind him a few times we had business to discuss. You're quite the mom, I hear too. How are your boys?"

Abby paused—a bit shocked, probably, by both his attention to detail and that I'd spent so long discussing personal matters with a man who could make me a multi-millionaire. "Thanks, Mr. Tanner. You are too kind. I hope my boys, Bobby and Ricky, can meet you while you're here to thank you in person. They're also big fans of your wrestling federation."

"You are the one who's too kind. Teachers are my heroes! I can't wait to meet Bobby and Ricky. Do me one favor though, call me Stuart. Mr. Tanner is my dad."

Abby smiled and asked, "Will you be here for the show tonight?"

"I have to leave to catch a plane in Pittsburgh just around bell time."

"Well, I want to make sure my boys get to thank you while you're here," Abby added.

"I look forward to meeting them."

I later learned that Arlo had been in the outer office, using the intercom system trying to find me while this was going down. I'd left my cell phone back in my dressing room. Robbie and I had been catching up and thanking all the wrestlers who had come in. Vito Garramone was in one of the classrooms doubling as a dressing room. He was on his cell phone, alone in the room, and overheard an announcement over the intercom that none of us had caught.

When he came out and saw me, he boomed, "Did you all hear that? It was a message from the principal's office. Aaron, you got called to the principal's office!" Naturally, all the wrestlers joined in ribbing me.

I found a phone and pressed the button for Arlo's office, and Abby answered. I explained that we were tied up and hadn't heard the announcement that I was supposed to come to the office.

She then said coolly, "There's someone here to see you." There was something in her voice, an uncertainty, that I'd never heard before. Maybe she was nervous? I couldn't figure it out.

Later, of course, I realized that she'd asked Tanner about my future in the business. "Do you think Aaron will ever wrestle again after tonight?"

"Well, that's for him to decide, but I am going to give him millions of reasons to give it some serious thought," Tanner said, rubbing his fingers together in the universal gesture that invoked money.

I got to the high school wrestling room first and waited for Tanner and Arlo. As they walked in, I heard Arlo recounting stories about Coach Miller, the successful teams he'd built, the lives he'd touched, and his recent battles with serious health issues.

When Tanner and I finally connected, I extended my hand, only for him to bypass it and give me a warm, sincere hug. "Aaron McClellan. How are you, my friend? This is really something you've put together here. It's going to help so many kids. I just met Abby, by the way, the one you were telling me about."

I responded, "Mr. Tanner, the thanks go to you. The donation, the livestreaming, the team of wrestlers you sent—we can't thank you enough. And now you took the time to come here in person."

"Happy to be here. You were right. This is a lovely town, and the few stops we made while here confirmed that the people are just as you described them. And just think—I always thought you were from the dodgy part of Glasgow!" he joked.

That broke the ice and led us into a conversation about the highly anticipated match the Hilanders vs. the Journey Boys.

And speaking of the devil, Robbie walked in. He did a double-take when he saw Tanner.

"*Rockin' Robbie*, huge fan," Tanner greeted him.

"A pleasure, Mr. Tanner. It was great you sent your wrestlers, great meeting some and catching up with others. The match tonight between us and the Journey Boys is one for the ages. It couldn't have happened without you—and your tech team. They're top-notch. It's going to be a great night, and you're a big part of that."

Then, mid-conversation, Robbie stopped abruptly as he gazed up at the large lettering on the main wall of the wrestling room. "Sorry, but what is that?" he asked, pointing.

Tanner chimed in, "I was going to ask that too. Who is Richard Bartholemew Dobbins? I would have thought this room would be named after Coach Miller, the one you told me about."

Arlo explained, "Well, you're right. It really should be. But we had to raise private funds for this space, though, and the man who donated insisted on choosing the name."

Robbie pressed, "Richie Rich Dobbins named it after himself?"

Arlo sighed, "I know. It pains me every time I look up there."

Then Tanner said, "Well, boys, I have an idea. I came here today for several reasons. One was to see what you all have put together. *Holiday Headlock*—I really wish I'd thought of that name! I also wanted to make one more donation to help out while I'm here. Our company has gotten so much positive press for supporting what you're doing. Not that we did it for the press, of course, but we feel it's important to give a little more, anonymously. How about this? We make that donation for this room. You can return the donation to this Richard Dobbins character and explain that you want to restore the wrestling workout room's rightful name—Coach Miller."

I shook my head. Tanner continued to impress me. Not only did he go above and beyond without owing us anything, but he genuinely cared. He was turning out to be some type of Christmas angel. He added, "I'll write you a check for the donated amount plus $25,000. Please, keep it anonymous."

Arlo thanked him and then suggested, "How about we announce this when he's given the Key to the City tonight at the show? We've gathered many of Coach Miller's former students and athletes to honor him tonight. His illness forced his retirement, and tonight is our chance to thank him. Naming this room after him would be the icing on the cake."

Robbie then asked, "The big question is, who gets to tell Dobbins? You know, we're taking his name down and replacing it with Coach Miller's name." Despite being gone from Deer Creek Falls for so long, he hadn't forgotten how heroes and villains worked in a small town.

Arlo grinned, "Oh, I'll take care of telling Dobbins. Perhaps he'll grow a heart like the Grinch and let us keep the money to help the kids."

Then he added "Robbie, on second thought, how about you come with me to tell Dobbins? We can break the ice—remind him about you and my success back in high school—and then hit him with the news about the Coach Miller Wrestling Center. I'm sure his face will be priceless. He's actually here now."

I asked, "He is? Why so early? Doors haven't opened yet."

"Apparently, Ricky and Bobby asked him to have his business be a sponsor, and sponsors are setting up a little before the show."

"Got it. Let me know how it goes," I said to Robbie and Arlo as they set off.

Tanner and I talked about the show, and I shared some details of what was in store. He mentioned that he'd have to leave around the time we kicked things off and that he'd like to say hello to his team and meet some of the others before he left. He also confided that, with the donation for Coach Miller being announced anonymously, some might deduce he was the donor if he were present at the show. He truly wished to remain anonymous.

Then he brought up the upcoming decision I had to make. "Aaron, you know how much I think of you. I want you to understand—I didn't help with *Holiday Headlock* to win you over, and I hate to bring up your contract decision in the middle of all of this."

I understood completely; his actions had shown me that he wasn't trying to strong-arm me into signing. I also knew all too well that this was my one chance to get an official offer before the New Year's Eve show and before an offer from Kennedy could come through.

As Tanner continued speaking, I noticed Abby and the boys approaching through a mirror in the wrestling room. Tanner laid it out succinctly, "Your offer sheet is in this envelope. I'll get straight to the point: It's $2 million dollars per year, plus all your expenses. A five-year deal. Two-hundred-day contract with built-in five-day stints off. Of course, you'd do all Premium Live Events. We value you as both a wrestler and as a person, Aaron. We want you to join us. Think about it, weigh your options, and let me know if you have any questions."

I was at a loss for words. My first thought was that this offer would make me richer beyond my wildest dreams. It would set me and my family up financially for life. But I didn't give an immediate response, not wanting to speak in front of Abby and with Bobby running up to me, excitedly asking to be put in a "Holiday Headlock."

I managed to shake Tanner's hand, thank him, and tell him that I had "a lot to consider." I could tell he understood. He was the kind of man who saw the whole picture.

Afterward, Tanner talked with Bobby and Ricky. Bobby even asked, "Are there any wrestling action figures of you?"

"No, not of me," he answered.

And that was a shame, really—he had the height and build of a professional wrestler. I couldn't think of another man on the business side of pro wrestling whom I respected more. He had certainly won me over, though I wasn't sure if accepting the money and staying in wrestling was better than following my dream of teaching, coaching, and, most of all, having a family with Abby, Ricky, and Bobby.

Soon, Abby mentioned that she and the boys had to run along to ensure everything was running smoothly. Ricky told Bobby he could help the rest of the wrestling team get ready for the show.

"Mr. Tanner and I will walk out with you," I said. "He wants to check in with his team before he heads out."

"You're not staying for the show?" Ricky asked.

"Unfortunately, no. I have a business meeting tomorrow morning back home in California and some holiday events with my family. You all have done a great job with this *Holiday Headlock* event," Tanner replied.

Bobby proudly exclaimed, "I came up with the name!"

Tanner smiled and said, "It's the perfect name for a wrestling show during the holiday season. When you get older, you should come work for me. That's how I got my start, you know. I was in marketing, which is all about coming up with ideas like that."

Bobby beamed with pride as Ricky placed a hand on his shoulder and Tanner did the same.

I stood there quietly. With all the conversations still echoing in my mind, I found myself at a crossroads—torn between the lure of financial security that would allow me to support both myself and my family, and my deeper dream of teaching, coaching, and nurturing a family life with Abby, Ricky, and Bobby.

Which path would I choose? Which would bring me the happiness I'd been searching for?

Chapter 26

All of the wrestlers Tanner sent were genuinely happy to see him. Even Shady Shelby Peters, breaking from his usual heel character, stepped forward and made a heartfelt speech in the locker room about Tanner and his support of the event. At a charity show like this, it's customary to invite representatives of those being helped to thank the wrestlers before things get too chaotic.

I watched as Abby, Arlo, Bobby, Ricky, and a few other parents and students from the sensory room headed over to join the group of wrestlers. Abby was gracious as always and thanked everyone, although I could sense that she just wasn't herself. I was pretty sure she was thinking about all of the contract talk, but this wasn't the time to discuss it.

Ricky stepped up and shared how crucial the sensory room was for his little brother and others, emphasizing that none of this would have been possible without everyone coming together. Ricky continued to impress beyond his years, and I saw the wrestlers visibly moved by his words.

Soon it was time to get down to business. Hank Hardway gathered all the wrestlers to go over last-minute match details. Tanner's tech team reported that everything was running smoothly on their end, and Hank reminded everyone about the off-site interviews taking place in a classroom, turned into a green room for television production.

Soon after, Coach Miller arrived. Tanner was getting ready to leave when he heard the news and asked, "Hey, I've heard a lot about your inspirational wrestling coach here. Could I meet him?"

I wasn't sure if Coach Miller recognized who Stuart Tanner was, whether from the wrestling side or the business side, but Tanner had that ability to make anyone feel like they were the only person in the room. Hank Hardway joined Coach Miller, his lifelong friend, as I watched Tanner say his final goodbyes and head out just before the show was set to begin.

Before long, we were hearing ring announcer Phil Chaffee say, "Thirty minutes to showtime" and then, "Fifteen minutes to showtime." Nerves – good ones – gathered in my stomach, an entire flock of butterflies beating their wings as the event grew closer.

I headed over to check on Abby and see how everything was going. As we counted down to the ringing bell, I could hear Johnny and Mark playing rocking Christmas standards.

Even though I suspected the future was weighing on her, Abby was in good spirits, happy with the turnout and the success of the fundraiser for the sensory room. I wished I had time to explain Tanner's offer and that money wasn't everything. I managed to steal a kiss, which filled me with hope and extra energy, and I promised her I'd see her in the ring.

I joined Hank in the Gorilla Position, ready to conduct the orchestra that is a professional wrestling show. Coach Miller and his wife were seated in the front row, surrounded by adoring former students and athletes. Kids and families, who had long dreamed of making the sensory room a reality, sat in a section near the ring so they could come up and personally thank everyone.

Looking at the ring, I noticed it was decorated with The Foxx Denn backdrop, now accented with holiday influence—a live

Foxx Denn in my hometown, to be beamed across the world. I could never dream all of this would happen. When the ring announcer introduced me as Fabulous Freddy Foxx and called me up to "get things started," I realized this was yet another dream come true.

I glanced over to find Abby, and there she was, my dream girl, standing in my hometown, looking as beautiful as ever in her *Holiday Headlock* t-shirt. What more could I ask for?

I thanked everyone for coming out and supporting such a worthy cause. I made sure to acknowledge Stuart Tanner for his financial support of the show, for sending the wrestlers, and for livestreaming the event, even though I knew he'd rather stay out of the spotlight and his good deeds stay anonymous.

Then I called Abby up to the ring so she could thank all the volunteers and sponsors. Even though there was tension about the pending, potentially life-altering decision hanging over me, she seemed more relaxed and happier than before. I was lucky to get a hug as she joined me in the ring before I handed her the microphone.

As she thanked everyone, she also called up the students and parents on the sensory room committee and the high school wrestling team for all their help in getting everything ready for the day. She announced that we had raised enough so far for five sensory rooms to be built in district buildings, and the news was met with great cheers.

Bobby then stepped up and asked if he could say something. Abby looked at me and Ricky, and with our nod of support, she handed Bobby the microphone. "Hi. My name is Bobby. I want to thank everyone for coming and supporting me and my friends. I hope you enjoy *Holiday Headlock* tonight."

I nudged Ricky, asking, "Did you help your brother with that?"

Ricky just smiled as Bobby returned the microphone to Abby and then ran over to him, saying, "Did I do okay?"

Abby shared her thanks once more with the crowd, and soon they started chanting Bobby's name. She handed the microphone back over to the ring announcer, Phil Chaffee. Phil is a local city judge who dabbled in the regional independent wrestling scene and went to school with all of us at Deer Creek Falls.

Phil announced, "I would like to introduce Superintendent Arlo Ritchie for a special announcement. Thanks to Superintendent Ritchie for making all of this happen today. Let's hear it for Superintendent Ritchie," and the crowd cheered as Arlo took the microphone.

"On behalf of Deer Creek Falls Schools, I would like to thank everyone for supporting our kids and programs. None of us would be here without these kids, and we have the best right here in Deer Creek Falls," Arlo said. Then he invited the wrestling team back up to the ring, and the alumni who had come to support Coach Miller surrounded the ring as well.

Arlo handed off the microphone to Ricky, who said, "Thanks, everyone, for helping make tonight possible. Coach Miller and Mrs. Miller, can you come up to the ring?"

As Ricky invited the Millers up, the mayor joined them, and one of the alumni presented Mrs. Miller with a bouquet of flowers as well.

Ricky then gave the microphone to the mayor, who said, "As mayor of Deer Creek Falls, I want to thank you all for coming to our beautiful town. Christmas in Deer Creek Falls is something special, but I promise you, if you come back during the year, you'll find a town for all seasons. We have it all here, but our greatest asset is our people. I've lived here all my life, and no town has as much support and love as Deer Creek Falls. Tonight, I am proud to present the Deer Creek Falls Key to the City to one of those special people: Coach Miller."

The mayor spoke about Coach Miller's many accomplishments as a teacher, coach, and community pillar. Ever humble,

Coach Miller was moved to tears as the mayor presented him with the Key to the City. I noticed Hank Hardway slipping into the ring, being the first to congratulate his lifelong friend. He and Coach Miller were quite a pair of local legends.

Arlo took back the microphone and said, "Thanks, mayor, for this well-deserved honor for Coach Miller. As you can see—and hear—many of Coach's former students and athletes are here to honor him too. I join them in announcing that, thanks to a special anonymous donation, the Deer Creek Falls High School wrestling room will now be named The Coach Miller Wrestling Center."

The entire crowd erupted in cheers, all except for Richard Dobbins, who sat arms folded and looking grumpy. When offered his money back from his original donation, he actually did the unprecedented thing and took it back instead of letting the school use it to help students. A real "class act," as usual.

Coach Miller came forward to share a few words of gratitude with the crowd. Though he continued to lose weight and strength, that night he rose to the occasion. "Folks, I'm a pretty modest man, but this…" He looked around, and I could see tears in his eyes. "Well, I can't tell you how much I appreciate this honor."

The crowd cheered yet again, and I was bursting with pride and happiness about what we'd managed to accomplish in just a few short weeks.

After the wrestling team helped escort the Millers out of the ring, only the ring announcer and I were left, and then it was showtime.

Ring announcer Phil Chaffee turned the stage over to me as he introduced a very special edition of Foxx Denn with Fabulous Freddy Foxx. I immediately slipped into character. In real life, I definitely wasn't as extroverted as Fabulous Freddy Foxx. But I became known for being over-the-top with above-average wit and timing. It was a persona that helped me win over fans and set up many a storyline.

That was my charge during the opening segment with Fast Frankie Folsom. I was certain Kennedy would be watching to make sure I carried out his orders promoting Fast Frankie's match with Brent "Wrecking Ball" Haynie and integrating myself in the mix as Frankie's manager for the New Year's Eve show.

Fast Frankie and I used The Foxx Denn that night to bury the hatchet from our long-running feud. We talked about how, despite Fast Frankie's long career, he had never won a world title. During The Foxx Denn, he asked me to serve as his manager as we planned. To the shock of everyone, as Folsom is a heel, I agreed and shook his hand in a long, deliberated manner. The crowd, shocked at this new "alliance," went wild with the expected mix of boos and cheers as the fans took it all in.

It might have been even better had Kennedy arranged for Wrecking Ball to show up and challenge Fast Frankie, but Kennedy would never have helped that much. Ironically, thanks to Tanner's livestream, Kennedy's New Year's Eve show was bound to benefit from all this. I made sure to add my catchphrase to Folsom before we left the ring, telling him, "I will be in your corner."

As Fast Frankie Folsom and I exited the ring to my theme music—a high-octane take on Hendrix's "Foxy Lady" with a tinge of bagpipes in the style of the Dropkick Murphys and Ally the Piper—the pop from the crowd grew and exceeded all my expectations. A high school gym is much smaller than many arenas we perform in, but a hot crowd more than makes up for the size, and Deer Creek Falls brought it that night!

Phil Chaffee worked the crowd into a frenzy as he announced the entire card. Up first was the French Street Fight, featuring the Culinary Grappler Derek Cooke taking down Frenchman Jacques Juggernaut with his patented cookware-inspired finishing move, "The Mixer." It was an old-school airplane spin that, while not looking too bad at a glance, could actually make you quite dizzy.

Next up was the match billed as the Battle for Indy Supremacy. Hot Ricky Rahde and his manager Tremendous Travis Pruitt generated their usual heat, Rahde portraying a real beach bum character, while Tenacious Norman Thomas (The TNT Kid) put on a technical display, matching his opponent's moves in a 20-minute match.

In wrestling, time limits can sometimes really mean little, so we added that wrinkle tonight. Hot Ricky Rahde and the TNT Kid ended up wrestling to a time limit draw, and surprisingly, the crowd was fine with it—likely because both wrestlers were genuine pros, neither of whom deserved to lose. It was truly a technical wrestling clinic. All of this played out as Rahde's manager Tremendous Travis got caught about to hit the TNT Kid with Rahde's patented surf board and was ordered removed from the arena, much to the crowd's delight.

Hank Hardway then came out to referee the next match. This one featured the two nontraditional students, a little older than your typical wrestling hopefuls, who wanted to live out their dreams of training and getting in the ring. Hank told me these two had come a long way and that this was only their second match—and likely their last as they would cross this off of their bucket list. He put them in gear and set up a Christmas Chaos match for the night: the North Pole's Kris the Kringle versus the Mistletoe Mauler, hailing from what might be the most popular town for wrestlers, Parts Unknown. Even though it was only a seven-minute bout, they delivered an entertaining match for the crowd.

As is typical for an indie wrestling show, there was an intermission. This allowed everyone time to grab food, merchandise, and use the restroom. It also gave us time to get the ring ready for the second Foxx Denn of the night, building up to *Holiday Headlock*'s Main Event between Vito Garramone and Shady Shelby Peters. I spent some time with them in preparation, then quickly joined Robbie and Hank Hardway to go over things with Jason and Justin Journey.

Fast Frankie Folsom approached me to break the news that Kennedy had demanded that all the talent for the New Year's Eve Extravaganza show was to leave on a flight early the next morning. He said Kennedy wanted to ensure everyone arrived on time for the Extravaganza, as bad weather was expected. As I was frustrated about this news, I started to get the impression that Frankie was acting as Kennedy's lackey. Though disappointing and frustrating, I still felt for the guy as he has worked in the business a long time never have achieved the top spot or top money, and obviously has to follow the company line as Kennedy demands him. I was increasingly glad I had more and better options.

A headache started developing at my temples. That wasn't the news I wanted to hear. I didn't want to leave so soon. I was hoping to spend all day tomorrow with Abby. I glanced around, hoping to find her, but no luck. I knew she was behind the scenes, keeping everything running smoothly.

And I? Despite the news of having to depart earlier than planned, I was out front, where I loved to be, soaking in the energy and excitement and realizing how much I truly loved the pro wrestling world. It was a world of carefully curated stories told by athletes putting their bodies on the line night after night for the fans we love.

Chapter 27

Time flew by, and it was soon time for the night's second edition of The Foxx Denn. I came out, got the crowd pumped up, and introduced Vito Garramone. Vito emerged to his Italian-inspired music. Despite being a strong heel for so long, he commanded a loyal fan base that always cheered for him. He wouldn't break character, though he found subtle ways to acknowledge his fans.

I felt bad that Vito coming here ultimately is what cost him his job in New York. But he'd told me earlier that it was a long time coming, and not to worry.

During the interview, Vito started shooting a few jabs at Kennedy, even announcing he was done with the "New York outfit." Vito was shooting a bit. A shoot interview in the wrestling world was bringing some aspects of real life into the mix. Vito lamented that he had defeated everyone in his path in New York and now needed to seek new competition. It was the first time that even some of the most loyal fans heard that he was leaving Kennedy's wrestling organization.

Then came Shady Shelby Peters. Shady's about 15 years younger than Vito, roughly the same height, and with a similar build. Vito clearly sported full-blooded Italian roots. Shady, while American, looked to be an Irish strongman, one you'd want with you when things break loose in a pub. He came out to some dark-sounding instrumental mix of the intro to *The Walking Dead* and the *Halloween* movies. As the music built to a crescendo, he struck his signature pose on the ring apron.

The anticipation among the fans couldn't have been higher as these two top wrestlers faced off in what could only be described as a battle for the ages. This was an encounter meant for pay-per-view or Premium Live Events, yet here it was happening in the friendly confines of a high school gym. I was grateful that Tanner had come through with the livestream so that wrestling fans everywhere could witness this historic match.

The Foxx Denn went off as planned. "Folks, this is the first time these two titans will be matched against each other, competing for the World Championship in the Deer Creek Falls High School gym!" I said. I was as excited as the crowd to see these two square off!

I pushed Vito a bit, recounting all the others who had fallen to him during his lengthy title reign in New York, myself included. Unintentionally, our efforts were turning Vito into a babyface—a good guy. I wondered if this change would only be for *Holiday Headlock* or if his future was as a babyface.

Shady Shelby Peters, on the other hand, was the type of wrestler who could generate heat without uttering a word. His actions, facial expressions, and reputation had earned him the unofficial title of Most-Hated Wrestler. His famous "Shamu's dead" moment at Sea World had gone viral and remained one of the most-watched videos on social media.

We wrapped up The Foxx Denn segment with Shady and Vito posturing toe-to-toe until Vito turned and began to walk away. That's when Shady dropkicked Vito from behind, sparking a brouhaha. Several wrestlers rushed out to break up the commotion and escort the two to their respective locker rooms.

The next match was billed as a Grudge Match between Pittsburgh Steeler-supporting Turnpike Mac and Packer Backer Milwaukee Mike. Mike emerged wearing his cheesehead, and it was on.

He taunted those from Pittsburgh and said with a growl, "You know what? I'd rather drink this six-pack of Milwaukee's Best rather than wrestle someone from Pittsburgh like Turnpike Mac." Milwaukee Mike exited the ring and started to head back to the locker room, six pack in hand, when Turnpike Mac grabbed him to the crowd's delight and tossed him in the ring.

With Deer Creek Falls not far from the Pennsylvania border, many in the crowd waved their Steeler Terrible Towels in support of Turnpike Mac. Both competitors played up to the crowd, and Mac ultimately took down Milwaukee Mike with his finishing maneuver, The Hammer Down—the trucking term for driving quickly.

Next, the Teacher vs. Student match featured Dynamite Destiny and our very own Page Turner. Destiny had been Page's mentor from early in her career, advocating for her to get work in many regions, while Page returned the favor for Destiny back home in her native Puerto Rico, a wrestling hotbed.

Destiny and Page had clashed as often as any two wrestlers in recent memory, and their match was flawless—each move building on the last, leaving the crowd shifting their allegiance between them. Magnificent Melissa, who had been feuding with Page until her contract recently expired and she signed with Tanner, involved herself in the match when the referee was not looking. Since Page and Melissa's storyline in New York had never been resolved, the fans got a taste of what might happen if Melissa cost Page the match.

Fortunately for Page, she had secured the services of a manager for the night's action to guard against any shenanigans Dynamite Destiny might have in store. Page's longtime friend and independent wrestling legend "Stacy's Mom from the Suburbs" was in her corner and able to stop Magnificent Melissa from costing Page the match, and Page was victorious with her "Book Ends" finishing move.

I watched from a discreet spot where no one could see me, trying to stay out of the fans' direct view. Robbie joined me, and I finally caught sight of Abby. She was sitting with Bobby and Ricky, completely absorbed in Page's match. I couldn't help but tease her later for how she had almost jumped up, clearly ready to rush to the ring to help Page when Melissa interfered.

The next match was our reunion match. Robbie and I hadn't performed as Ian and Prescott Hiland for years, so we were excited to bring it home against the current Tag Team Champions of the World, the Journey Boys.

Being hometown boys, we decided to shake things up a bit and have the Journey Boys introduced first. The Journey Boys were the current Tag Team World Champions, and the champs would typically be introduced last, but they deferred to Robbie and I, or Ian and Prescott Hiland, for our hometown crowd. The Journey Boys, actual brothers with high-flying skills, entered to pop retro 1980's-style entrance music that had the crowd erupting. The loud live bagpipers inside a high school gym added to the return of the Hilanders when we came out, of course introduced from the dodgy part of Glasgow.

Although we hadn't worked with the Journey Boys before, our match turned out flawless. We exchanged moves back and forth; they used more high-flying, or *lucha libre*, maneuvers than I was accustomed to, but Robbie handled those masterfully. The technical wrestling we put on was at the highest level I'd ever seen, and while Robbie and I have had some great matches over the years, tonight's bout with the Journey Boys felt like one of our best ever. We made sure not to cheat the crowd with a convoluted finish. Eventually, I ended up getting pinned by Justin Journey while Jason and Robbie were mixing it up outside the ring.

The crowd cheered throughout the match and all the way back to our locker rooms. The Journey Boys came by our locker room to congratulate us on what everyone called an instant classic. Shortly thereafter, Abby came back to see me. She said that Ricky and Bobby had told her that our tag team match was the best ever. When the other wrestlers left to catch the Shady Shelby Peters vs. Vito Garramone Main Event, I stayed behind to talk with Abby.

"Listen," I began, "I know these last few days have been crazy."

She slipped her hand into mine. "It was all for the kids, Aaron. I wouldn't change a single thing." But still, a dark shadow crossed her face for a second.

I leaned over and kissed her, not caring who might see us. "Neither would I. I love you so much."

Her cheeks turned pink at my words, and then I joked that she should tell Bobby the match was just how he did the match in his room.

She playfully replied, "Tell him yourself," just as her boys entered the room.

They wanted to chat about all the matches. I asked them what their favorite match was, and they told me it was our match with the Journey Boys.

"So, what's your second favorite?" I asked.

They said they liked them all, though they kept calling the Hot Ricky Rahde vs. The TNT Kid match a barn burner. As we talked, we could hear the crowd reacting to the Shady/Vito Main Event. I walked over to the locker room entrance to watch. I told them they could go back to their seats, but I was glad the three of them stayed with me to watch the rest of the match.

In the end, Shady managed to keep his title as he and Vito battled it out, with Fast Frankie Folsom interfering at the end to cost Vito the match. Robbie, now in his *Rockin' Robbie* gear, came in to make the save for Vito and fight off Folsom's interference. It all felt like the beginning of a new feud. Now that Vito was basically a free agent, I knew I wasn't the only one thinking he might end up working in LA and go on a long run of matches with Shady Shelby Peters. I also hoped that Robbie could be put in the position of fighting the winner of Folsom and Wrecking Ball that was taking place in just a few days.

Later, Tanner's tech team told us that the number of people watching the livestream had far exceeded expectations.

"Aaron, the online donations surpassed all estimates," they said.

"I think we might be able to create a charity to help fund sensory rooms around the area," Abby added.

My head spun. I couldn't believe we'd found this level of success of Holiday Headlock. Abby was right – the crazy days had all been worth it. Hand in hand, we walked around thanking all the wrestlers, workers, and other talent who had contributed to making the event such a success.

Then my phone rang, and we both looked down. It was Kennedy calling directly. I told Abby I had to take the call.

Chapter 28

"Hi. This is Aaron," I said.

"Freddy, sounds like you had a heck of a show back in Ohio. I called Fast Frankie Folsom and he mentioned there was a lot of heat heading into his match at the New Year's show with Wrecking Ball. He also said you agreed to be his manager. The people will love it."

Before I could respond, he continued, "I need Frankie, you, Robbie, and Page at the Pittsburgh airport immediately. I'm flying you all to New York to go over everything for the show, and then we'll head to Cleveland. Make sure they all get to the airport on time," Kennedy said before hanging up.

As usual, he didn't let me get much of a word in, but I got his message loud and clear. This was it. My heart and my head warred with thoughts and desires. I wanted to keep wrestling. I wanted to make millions. And I wanted to stay here, too. I wanted to teach and coach and follow the high school dream I'd never let go. I wanted Abby. I wanted Bobby and Ricky in my life.

How could I have both? But I knew the answer already: I couldn't.

I went to find Frankie Folsom, and he told me he'd already informed everyone about when we had to leave. I spotted Ricky and Bobby near the wrestling ring and asked if they wanted to join in. We wrestled around in the ring, and even Abby joined in. I've made my living in this ring for many years, but I've never had this much fun. Robbie and Page came along too, and we even taught Abby how to do a sunset flip. Given her background in cheering and gymnastics, she picked it up naturally.

"I don't mean to break all of this up, but we have to head out," Robbie announced.

"Already? I thought we had all day tomorrow?" Abby questioned.

"We did, but Kennedy is calling everyone to New York before we head to Cleveland to tape the New Year's Eve show on December 30," Robbie explained.

"Sorry, Abby," I said. "We just found out, so we have to leave right away."

Abby looked disappointed. I hoped she understood. As we exited the ring, everyone started chatting about how quickly everything had come together. My mom, of course, was worried I hadn't packed my toothbrush, toothpaste, and all the other things moms worry about. I reassured her that I had my gear, a change of street clothes, and could grab any toiletries I needed on the road.

I did mention, half-jokingly, that I was a bit worried about Robbie. As he gave me a questioning look, I teased, "Think you have enough hair gel for the road?"

Then my heart flipped over as Abby approached me. "I'm sorry, Abby. I really thought we'd have all day tomorrow," I said.

She gave me a sad but understanding smile. "I get it. This, you, all of this has been so much fun and so rewarding. I'll never be able to thank you enough."

I took her hands in mind. "Abby, we did this together. I only wish I had told you how I felt when we were younger. There's no one I've cared about this much. Ever." I hoped she could sense the feelings I couldn't put into words.

She leaned in to kiss me just as Fast Frankie Folsom announced, "The van is here to take us to the airport." He gave me an apologetic look. "Sorry, but we better get going…you know how Kennedy is."

The wrestlers quickly said their goodbyes and gathered their gear, and Frankie added, "Freddy, you better be the first one in when we get there. I have a feeling Kennedy is going to make you an offer you can't refuse."

Standing there with Abby, I knew that was exactly the last thing she or I needed to hear. I leaned close one more time and gave her a quick kiss.

After that, I said my goodbyes to the boys and my family. Arlo came over, pulled me aside, and said, "Aaron, my man, I can't thank you enough. You know that teaching and coaching offer is still there for you. I understand the money they say you'll be offered might keep you in the ring longer, but we're here for you if you ever want to come back home."

"Thanks, Arlo. That means a lot," I replied. I glanced at Abby and the boys back in the ring as they were showing her some wrestling moves. Bobby even put her in a headlock, announcing, "Look everyone, it's a holiday headlock!"

A lump rose into my throat as I looked at Arlo and asked, "Will you look out for them?"

"Of course, Aaron. Always," he answered.

I told my mom and Jenny that I'd probably be back on New Year's Day. They assumed the show was taped on December 30 and aired on December 31, meaning I'd be home for New Year's Eve. But we weren't sure how post-production might affect that.

Randy jokingly asked, "You're working on New Year's Eve? Who do you think you are, Ryan Seacrest?" Randy was always good for a little comic relief to ease the tension. I explained that I'd be back on the first of the year, although I wasn't sure for how long or what direction my life would take.

I went up to Abby and the boys in the ring one last time. My family joined in too—Mom even got in the ring, all now in Santa hats—and we ended up taking lots of selfies. I didn't want it to end.

Mom asked, "Abby, do you and the boys want to come over on New Year's Eve and watch the wrestling show with us?"

Bobby yelled, "Can we, Mom? Can we?"

"Of course. Thanks for the invitation," Abby replied.

Then Bobby asked me, "Do I have to root for Fast Frankie Folsom if you're managing him? I kind of like Wrecking Ball better."

I smiled and said, "Bobby, you root for whoever you want. I know you're always in my corner." I said goodbye one more time and headed to the van.

"Sorry, man. I know you wanted some more time," Robbie said.

"Yeah." But time wasn't the only thing I wanted. I spent the entire ride to the airport talking about Abby and the boys.

The next morning, I Facetimed Abby and the boys from New York. I had a meeting soon at the hotel with the team for the New Year's show, but I managed to take a stroll around Manhattan before the meeting. I shared several sights with them as I walked, and as I headed back to the hotel, Abby and the boys showed me the plans for the sensory room. I admit, it brought me to tears.

I then headed into a conference room, a stark contrast to all of the holiday décor and merriment of the past few weeks. All this feels of a non-descript, button down, corporate meeting room. I was uncertain whether Kennedy would address my contract or if we'd sort things out during the New Year's Eve card. Instead, we ended up working with his head booker and producer. I didn't see Kennedy all day, and I couldn't help but wonder what his offer would be. If I stayed wrestling, it would feel odd not to be working for the Kennedy's New York promotion. I guess it's a loyalty thing.

Strangely, Kennedy never came to see any of us. I texted his assistant Pat, who assured me that Kennedy would see me on December 30 before the show. This wasn't like him; whether it was a house show or a Premium Live Event, he was always around.

Later, I caught up with Brent "Wrecking Ball" Haynie at the gym, the only place you'd typically find him. He thanked me for the spot on the Foxx Denn weeks ago and said that every show since, the fans had responded better and better to him. He also mentioned being sad about Vito and admitted he liked working with him. Good for Wrecking Ball. He was beginning to mature and understand that no wrestler does anything on his own… it all takes the right dance partner.

The next morning, we headed to Cleveland for pre-production, media events, and other publicity for the New Year's Eve show. Over lunch, I talked with Robbie and Page, and they agreed that Kennedy's absence was strange. Neither of them had seen or heard anything from him, which was odd. Robbie was excited that he would be in a match before the main event of the show, but he was disappointed that Kennedy wasn't there to approve the plan. He hoped this match would put him in line for a future title shot. Robbie and I had won tag team gold many times over, but he still hadn't achieved a singles title in his storied career.

Page told me about her upcoming match and that she was hoping to reclaim her status as the World Women's Champion. "Have you talked to Abby?" she asked.

"I did Facetime her and the boys when we were in New York City, but I haven't had a chance since. They told me…" Before I knew it, I'd been talking non-stop for a half-hour about Abby and the boys. Page and Robbie shared a knowing look.

For the first time in recent memory, Kennedy was nowhere to be found at the Premium Live Event arena. We were genuinely concerned. This was completely out of character for him. Despite the jerk he could be, I hoped he was alright. We gathered in the ring to discuss the evening's show, the order of matches and interview slots. I had a Foxx Denn segment with Fast Frankie Folsom, which Wrecking Ball was going to interrupt, as part of the build up to the Folsom and Wrecking Ball Main Event.

The show's head booker and producer seemed completely out of the loop regarding Kennedy's preferences and his whereabouts. I wasn't worried about the show going well. We were all a well-oiled machine by this time. Still, I couldn't shake the irritation of not having a contract offer from Kennedy.

He was still missing, and I was slated to start the show with The Foxx Denn, hyping the crowd for the main event. Cleveland wrestling crowds are always fiery, and I noticed many who had been at *Holiday Headlock,* being that Cleveland was so close by. I spotted several *Holiday Headlock* t-shirts in the audience, which was really cool.

After The Foxx Denn segment, I returned to the locker room and finally saw Kennedy. "Hey, is everything alright?" I asked.

"Why, yes. Sure. Why would you ask me that?" Kennedy said.

I hedged. Maybe I'd jumped to false conclusions? "I don't know. You normally don't leave us in the dark. You're always giving us a blow-by-blow analysis of our plans and matches. Here we are, on one of the biggest premium live events of the year, and we haven't heard from you," I pressed.

Kennedy looked like he'd seen a ghost. Without another word, he simply walked away without offering any explanation. I was in shock, and so was everyone else. This wasn't the Don Kennedy I knew. Even his bookers and producers appeared clueless.

Despite this, we continued with the show, and the crowd was electric. I helped the bookers with some of the matches in Kennedy's absence and the show came off incredibly well on television, and I was even happy about the role ahead as Fast Frankie Folsom's manager. It would be different as Kennedy wanted me to turn heel, interfering to help Frankie score an upset victory over the newest fan favorite, Brent "Wrecking Ball" Haynie and helping him win his first world singles title.

As the show unfolded, I received a phone call from Stuart Tanner. He asked if I had some time and said he wanted to see me. I told him that would be difficult since I was in the middle of the show in Cleveland.

"Any way we can get you up to the owner's box at the arena? We'll wrap up in time for you to be back for the Wrecking Ball/Fast Frankie Folsom match."

"Sure, I'll be there," I replied as I quickly processed that Stuart Tanner ended up in the arena during Kennedy's show.

Stuart Tanner opened the door and greeted me with a fist bump as I arrived. I was shocked to see that Vito was with him. I wondered if there had been a coup? Vito grinned at me on his way out, saying we would catch up later. Tanner and I began discussing something that would send shockwaves throughout the wrestling world.

"Aaron, I've purchased Kennedy's promotion," he said without preamble.

I stared at him. "Seriously? But how – and when –"

Tanner didn't share a lot of details, but it sounded like Kennedy hadn't managed his finances well over the years and was in a state of financial desperation. Tanner had caught wind of it, and now here we were.

"Vito had an inkling that things weren't going well with Kennedy's finances," Tanner explained. "He thought maybe cutting Vito out recently was one way to save cash. I had my team look at Kennedy's financials, and we could see something was clearly wrong. I even went to his offices to speak to him one-on-one. He was reluctant at first, but as we talked, I could tell he had no other choice. I didn't low-ball him, either. I did my best to set up a win-win for both sides."

I sat there in shock. I hadn't seen this coming, and I doubted anyone else had either. What did this mean for Robbie, for Vito, for Page—and for me? I still had the contract offer from Tanner, but I wasn't sure it was still valid. What happened once companies merged?

"Listen, can you keep this quiet?" Tanner asked. He assured me that no one currently under contract would lose their job.

"No one under contract…well, that's not me," I said, adding, "Mr. Tanner, I have your offer, but I never received any follow-up from Kennedy. How will this look?"

Tanner reached out and shook my hand. "We'll talk tonight after the show. But tell me what you want, Aaron. What can I do to keep you with us and still make you happy?"

Chapter 29

The fans were reacting great to the New Year's Eve Extravaganza live and I could not wait for the rest of the world to see it. Still, I couldn't help but think about what Tanner had said and ponder what would truly keep me in the wrestling business while still making me happy. I'd see him soon—he had told everyone that we'd quickly wrap up any post-production work and get everyone on the road home, with no one coming back until the week of January 5.

With uncertainty in my heart, I met up with him to talk about my future.

"You know I respect you greatly, Aaron," he began. "And I want you to tell me if the offer isn't enough."

I took a deep breath. I'd done a lot of thinking over the last few days. I knew where I belonged. "Mr. Tanner, the offer is very generous. More than I could've hoped for." I thought of Ricky on the wrestling mat, Bobby in the classroom, Abby in my arms, Deer Creek Falls in my heart. "I love this business," I went on, "but at this point in my life, I really feel like I belong in a school, teaching and coaching high school wrestling...and spending my days with the love of my life."

He gave me a look that told me he'd already guessed my decision. "I understand. But consider this..."

To my surprise, he added a twist: he wanted to offer me what they call a legends contract. Under the terms of this contract, I would make occasional appearances at shows, Fan Fests, or corporate events, and I'd serve as a consultant from home—occasionally training wrestlers in both physical techniques and microphone work. I did work just as hard throughout my career to be good both in the ring and on the microphone. I closely studied the best talkers in the business like CM Punk, The Rock, and Rowdy Roddy Piper and aspired to be that good.

I was stunned. Essentially, Tanner was offering me the opportunity to live in Deer Creek Falls, teach, coach, be with Abby and the boys, and have wrestling as my side hustle.

Feeling like I'd burst with excitement, I said, "Mr. Tanner, I'm all in on this. I'll need to secure a ring and a space for the training sessions, but I'm definitely interested in what you've laid out."

"Excellent, Aaron. I'll have this memorialized in writing and get a contract to you. Look for an email, but do me a favor—after you finish up tonight get on the road and go see your girl for New Year's Eve."

I shook his hand. "Thanks, Mr. Tanner. This is all a dream come true. You're a great man." I hesitated, then asked, "Would you be okay if I announce my retirement after tonight's match? I'm supposed to turn heel and help Folsom beat Wrecking Ball. I'm fine doing that, but I'd like to say some kind of goodbye to the fans as my time as a full-time wrestler comes to an end. I promise everyone I'll pop up now and then."

He smiled and said, "Aaron, you've earned the right to go out on your terms. Yes, please address the crowd after the match." With that, he called Vito back in as I headed down to manage what might be my very last time. I figured with Vito's standing with the wrestlers he would help Tanner explain all of this to the locker room after the show.

The match went off without a hitch, and I played my part well. The crowd was stunned when I got the attention of the referee so that Folsom could hit Wrecking Ball Haynie with the belt, knocking him out cold. Folsom quickly covered him for the three-count, securing his first-ever singles world championship.

I watched as a dazed Wrecking Ball made his way out of the ring to the locker rooms. Then Folsom grabbed a microphone amid a mix of boos and cheers, and after addressing the crowd, he thanked me. "I would never have been in this ring tonight without Fabulous Freddy Foxx. We've wrestled hundreds of times over the years, and I've learned so much. Thank you for being in my corner, Triple F." Those words, echoing the nickname we'd sparred over for years, meant a lot at this moment.

Folsom handed me the microphone, and I thanked him for his kind words while congratulating him on winning the title. I then turned to the audience and all those watching at home.

"Thanks, Frankie. I also want to acknowledge Wrecking Ball Brent Haynie. He fought a good fight and has a great future ahead of him." The crowd cheered, though likely a bit confused as Folsom and I just cost him an opportunity of being a world champion.

"I have been the luckiest wrestler in the world to be in the ring with so many talented wrestlers that have become my closest friends. I also want to acknowledge all of the wrestling fans watching here tonight and those watching in their homes, celebrating New Years Eve with us. Thank you for always being in my corner, and I hope you know I have always been in yours."

There were cheers but also the pause in the crowd of 'where is he going with this?'

"I want to thank everyone I have been fortunate to meet in this business. I also want to thank my friends and family for their love and support throughout the years. I may have missed some birthdays and holidays and been on the road during many important times in our lives, but please know I have always been thinking about you all and miss you."

A hushed silence of anticipation radiated from the crowd, "Tonight, I am announcing my retirement as a full-time wrestler." I heard a few gasps from the crowd before I added, "I'm so grateful to you all for letting me be part of your lives. While I might return to help out sometimes, Fabulous Freddy Foxx is officially retiring from full-time pro wrestling effective tonight."

The announcement shocked the crowd into silence. Although I had given Folsom a heads-up, he was still visibly shocked, as were Robbie and later Page, who were walking down the aisle toward the ring. Soon, as they approached, the crowd of 18,000 started chanting, "Thank you, Freddy! Thank you, Freddy!"

This past month had felt like a lifetime to me, and I couldn't imagine a better way to leave this business than with so many fans cheering my name and showing their gratitude. Despite it all, I was overjoyed at the thought of finally being home with Abby. Deer Creek Falls was where I belonged, where my heart is.

As Folsom had departed the ring to give me my moment with the fans, Robbie entered the ring and gave me a huge hug while the fans went wild. Then Page joined us, and both she and Robbie grabbed my hands and held them high, turning to face each side of the ring. Soon a locker room full of wrestlers entered the ring to celebrate with me, with Brent "Wrecking Ball" Haynie and Vito Garramone hoisting me on their shoulders. The best sendoff I could have ever imagined.

As Robbie, Page and I walked back to the locker rooms after the in-ring celebration, I said to them "Thank you both for always being there for me. Any chance you want to come back with me to Deer Creek Falls?"

They said they were headed to New York for a few days, and they both hugged me tightly. Robbie and Page, having experienced the joy of finding true love themselves, were genuinely happy for me.

"Good luck with Abby," Page said as we waved goodbye, and nerves filled my stomach. I hadn't talked to Abby about doing this tonight. I wondered what she'd say, how she'd feel?

I had some meetings with the production team the next day to work on post-production as well as helped get some of Tanner's people comfortable with Kennedy's bookers and producers. I wanted to see this merger work, as I had friends that would benefit from its being a success. Tanner asked me and Vito to help Kennedy's wrestlers through the process.

It was getting late as I finished up and headed to the Cleveland airport to rent a car to drive back to Deer Creek Falls. I didn't want to trouble Randy, Jenny, or Abby—I hoped to surprise them while they were watching the New Year's Eve show. For the first time ever, the show was scheduled to run from 8 p.m. to 11 p.m., giving wrestling fans their fill to end the year and allowing everyone to switch over to the Times Square New Year's Eve coverage right after.

It looked like I wouldn't arrive until between 10:30 and 10:45. I encountered some bad weather, just enough to force me to slow down on the Ohio Turnpike, something I rarely did. When I finally reached home and checked my phone, I saw a text from Robbie: the social media community was buzzing with rumors that Tanner had purchased the New York wrestling territory. Jenny had also texted, asking if it was true that Tanner had bought the federation and that I was about to sign a multi-million-dollar deal.

I didn't answer either of them. Instead, I pulled up to Mom's house and slipped in the back door. Quietly, I made my way into the living room, where my entire family was gathered to watch the show with Abby and the boys. I saw Jenny holding Abby's hand, clearly anticipating that the announcement they thought would likely be about me signing a new deal.

As a quick commercial ran, I decided to speak up, announcing, "You all need to watch the next segment very closely."

They all turned in surprise.

"Aaron!" said my Mom.

I was enveloped in hugs and inundated with greetings and questions. "Happy New Year's Eve!" "You're here!" "Welcome home!" "What did they offer you?" "What happened to Kennedy and the sale?" I told them all I would answer all the questions I could soon, but they really needed to watch the next segment very closely.

Abby just gave me a funny look when I insisted they all pay close attention to what was coming next on the New Year's Eve Wrestling Extravaganza. I walked over to my mom just as my segment was coming back on and gave her a kiss on the forehead. Then I took Abby's hand, and said, "It's all going to be okay. I promise you."

Before long, I watched with my loved ones as they showed me announcing my retirement as a full-time wrestler, shocking the room into silence once again. The boys stared at me. Randy held up both palms in a gesture of what the heck?

But it was Abby's reaction I cared most about. "What does that mean, Aaron?" she whispered.

I grabbed her hand, and together we slipped into the kitchen. "It means that I want to be here. I'm returning to live in Deer Creek Falls, seeking a teaching and coaching position, and—most importantly—I want to be a constant presence in your life, and Bobby and Ricky, if you'll have me."

Tears rose to her eyes. "Really?"

"Of course, really. I love you, Abby, you and the boys too. I choose all of you. Pro wrestling used to be my life. Now it's you, and Bobby and Ricky."

With that, she kissed me like never before. Her hands went to my face, drawing me close, and I felt like I'd come home for the first time in my adult life. *This* was what mattered, and *this* was where I wanted to be.

When we went back to the living room, I saw Robbie and Page on television, hoisting my hands in the air for the cheering crowd, while my mom sat crying in her chair. I explained to everyone that I wouldn't be on the road anymore; instead, I'd be teaching and coaching—and hopefully, my mom wouldn't mind if I moved in with her for a while.

Suddenly, my mom grabbed one of my hands and one of Abby's, stood up, and hoisted them aloft just as we had done in the ring. Margo snapped a quick photo, and I still use it as my phone's screensaver to this day. That was the moment I knew I'd found my forever.

When my mom let go, Abby and I shared another kiss under a mistletoe, while everyone around us cheered. The holidays had never felt so sweet. I felt like a world champion.

Epilogue
One Year Later

ooking back on last Christmas, it would be hard to beat, but this one may have done it. Mom is still with us and doing well. I've been living with and helping her all year. I've also been teaching and coaching the wrestling team since the beginning of the school year, thanks to Arlo helping me follow my dreams. Bobby is one of my students and is doing great both academically and socially. Ricky won the High School Wrestling State Championships.

Abby and I took Ricky, and Bobby of course, to sixteen colleges to visit to help him make a decision on where he wanted to go. We were proud of him as he wanted to check out their accounting programs as much as he wanted to check out their wrestling programs. For his high school graduation party, we even put together a poster in the style of a bracket tournament showing all sixteen colleges we visited and how he decided, it was a crowd-pleaser. In the end he selected Kent State University and got a full scholarship too. Abby, and I, were so proud of him. I was equally happy the four of us got to spend so much time together checking out the colleges as it brought us even closer as a family.

Rockin' Robbie was mired in a nearly year-long feud with Shady Shelby Peters, finally winning his first world title by pinning Peters at an October Premium Live Event! I was thrilled for him and made sure I was at the match to celebrate with him and Page.

Last year we threw *Holiday Headlock,* and this year Robbie and Page are getting married on Christmas Eve in Deer Creek Falls. We were about week away from the big day and Abby, me, Bobby, Ricky, mom, Jenny, Randy, Margo, Moira, and Abby's mom all headed out shopping. The only one not going was Dasher who I am sure made himself comfortable on the oversized, giant pillow he got last year, his inaugural McClellan family Christmas.

We had not only Christmas gifts on the list but gifts for Robbie and Page for their upcoming nuptials. We also planned a stop for Carter's Christmas Land to take in this year's display.

Little did Abby know I had a surprise in store for her. We walked by all of the tree displays and I saw it, the Snowman Christmas Tree. When we approached it, I got down on one knee.

"Abby, my love, would you do me the honor?"

For a moment, she stared at me, seemingly taking it all in.

"Please," I went on. "Will you marry me, Abby?"

Her hesitation lasted just long enough that my family caught up to us. Then Abby said, "Yes. Yes. Oh, Aaron… absolutely, yes."

Before I could get up to give her a proper kiss, Randy said to me jokingly, "Hey, kid, get up off the floor. You're holding up the line."

I just laughed, happier than I'd ever been.

Abby and I kissed to seal the deal, while I slipped the engagement ring I'd bought onto one finger. It glittered in the Christmas lights, throwing sparkles of white in every direction. Bobby and Ricky gave me congratulatory fist bumps and our entire clan became one big group hug.

A line of people formed behind us, but, rather than yell at us about holding up the line, they clapped and celebrated our engagement.

"Hey, man, did you see that?"

"Is that Freddy Foxx?"

"I think it's Coach Aaron."

"Did he finally pop the question to Abby? It's about time!"

I looked around, smiling and holding my bride-to-be close. That's Deer Creek Falls, where people make you feel like you're wrapped up in a great big hug, never having to go through life alone.

The End

Acknowledgments

Thanks to my wife for not only helping with the editing of this book but for introducing me to the world of made-for-television Christmas movies. We have not missed a Hallmark Christmas movie in years, and their movies and many others like them inspired this book. When I said to her, "They have never made a holiday rom com with a wrestler as the main character," she said back to me, "there may be a reason for that." It was then I set out to write *Holiday Headlock*.

I want to thank my daughter for being an inspiration for everything I do and giving me the advice to "Da, write what you know." I want to thank my lovely hometown of Warren, Ohio and all who live in the Warren/Youngstown area for being the inspiration for Deer Creek Falls.

I huge thanks to all of the professional wrestlers who put their bodies on the line every night to entertain fans of all ages. Thanks to all of my fellow fans of pro wrestling for being one of the most loyal fan bases in sports and such a friendly community to belong to.

Thanks also goes out to both the writing community and holiday rom com community. I had no idea there were so many supportive authors that continually encourage fellow writers to follow the dream of completing your book and getting it out to the world of readers. Equally supportive and informative are the many holiday rom com sites on social media and in the podcast world. I likely would not have finished Holiday Headlock without the knowledge and passion for the genre they have all shared.

I also want to want to thank those who helped edit and support the writing and make up of *Holiday Headlock*, making it better and making it a reality: editorial cartoonist Rick Muccio, a good friend to all who took a vision for the book cover and made it come to life (book cover artwork/illustrator), Christopher Fowler (illustrator), Thomas Symalla (editor), Allison Miller (editor) and Sharon Rawlette (book designer/consultant) who helped me get the book to the finish line in more ways than one.

Lastly, and as they say certainly not least, to all of my friends and family. I truly cherish your friendship. You inspire me and have given me so many stories and laughs during my life. You all have likely listened to too many wrestling and holiday rom com stories from me and all should be rewarded championship belts just for that. You gave me feedback and support not only while writing this book but in life. I am the luckiest person in the world to know and love all of you.

About the Author

Terry Armstrong is a proud dad to Moira and husband to Kim, as well as an avid viewer of holiday romantic comedies and a life-long fan of professional wrestling. When not checking out the local music scene with friends and family in his beloved northeast Ohio, he is probably somewhere enjoying one of the five "Bs": Baseball, Books, Broadway, Bodyslams and Bruce (Springsteen)!

Terry has served much of his professional life as an educator and was lucky to have the greatest students a teacher could ever ask for. He currently serves as a School Treasurer. *Holiday Headlock* is his first work of fiction. Terry co-authored *Aerosmith to ZZ Top: A Dad and Daughter's Rock and Roll Journey* with his daughter Moira, sharing their love of music and attending live concerts.

*Stay in touch with Holiday Headlock
and author Terry Armstrong*

Email: holidayheadlock@gmail.com

Facebook: Search for "Holiday Headlock"

Twitter/X: @headlockbook